On the Magdale... ...ng up to a ringing phone in the middle of the night ranks just below sharing a bed with my sister Susannah. The next step down is to have someone shake you out of a sound sleep.

"Miss Yoder!"

I opened my eyes, only to find myself gazing into the terrified eyes of Jonathan Hostetler.

"Jonathan! What on earth are you doing?"

"*Me?*" he croaked.

I released Jonathan's neck and scooted back under the covers. I may have been sleeping in two long-sleeved, ankle-length flannel nightgowns, but the nightgowns were a provocative pink.

"Jonathan, what's wrong? Is it Mose? Is your father worse?"

"Papa's feeling better. A little bit. But my Rachel—*ach,* that can wait. There's an Englishman in your barn, Miss Yoder. I think the man is dead."

"*Dead?*"

Jonathan nodded victoriously, his grim news finally delivered. "*Yah,* dead. Maybe very dead."

EAT, DRINK, AND BE WARY

A PENNSYLVANIA DUTCH MYSTERY WITH RECIPES

Tamar Myers

A SIGNET BOOK

SIGNET
Published by the Penguin Group
Penguin Putnam Inc., 375 Hudson Street,
New York, New York 10014, U.S.A.
Penguin Books Ltd, 27 Wrights Lane,
London W8 5TZ, England
Penguin Books Australia Ltd, Ringwood,
Victoria, Australia
Penguin Books Canada Ltd, 10 Alcorn Avenue,
Toronto, Ontario, Canada M4V 3B2
Penguin Books (N.Z.) Ltd, 182–190 Wairau Road,
Auckland 10, New Zealand

Penguin Books Ltd, Registered Offices:
Harmondsworth, Middlesex, England

First published by Signet, an imprint of Dutton NAL,
a member of Penguin Putnam Inc.

First Printing, September, 1998
10 9 8 7 6 5 4 3 2 1

REGISTERED TRADEMARK—MARCA REGISTRADA

Printed in the United States of America

PUBLISHER'S NOTE
This is a work of fiction. Names, characters, places, and incidents either are
the product of the author's imagination or are used fictitiously, and any resem-
blance to actual persons, living or dead, events, or locales is entirely
coincidental.

For Marsha Bassel Holowinko

One

I was an adulteress. An inadvertent adulteress, to be sure, but an adulteress nonetheless. This is not an excuse for the tragic events that were about to unfold here at the PennDutch Inn, it is merely an explanation for my muddled state of mind. A clearheaded Magdalena would have put her big foot down the second Freni Hostetler came to me with her outrageous request. But even under normal circumstances, that's easier said than done.

Freni smiled pleasantly, a warning sign if there ever was one. "It's only a little cooking contest."

"How little?"

"Five contestants is all."

"And you're one of them?"

"Ach!" Freni beamed with pride and stroked the blue ribbon she wore pinned securely to her ample bust.

"*Hochmut,*" I said in Pennsylvania Dutch. It means pride. It is one of the few dialect words I know, but one I am not likely to ever forget. Mama used it on me all the time. It is, perhaps, the worst epithet one can ascribe to someone of Amish or Mennonite persuasion.

Freni Hostetler colored. "It isn't prideful to use the talents God gave you, Magdalena."

I will confess to enjoying the woman's discomfort.

The short, stout woman is both my best friend and my employee. I have known her my entire life, although I will confess to being uncertain of her age. Freni is one of the few women I know who actually pads her age, in a misguided attempt to gain more respect. I suspect that Freni is pushing seventy, although she would have you believe that she's a half-dozen years older. At any rate, ever since Mama and Papa died an untimely death in a tunnel, squished between a milk tanker and semitrailer hauling state-of-the-art running shoes, Freni has functioned as a substitute parent. Nevertheless, the woman drives me crazy.

"Your slow-baked bread pudding is very good, Freni. I'm sure it deserved to win first place at the Pennsylvania State Fair. But isn't wearing the ribbon going a little too far?"

Freni is Amish, you see. She is required to adhere to a strict dress code—a plain, long-sleeved dress of modest length, topped by an apron. Her head must be covered at all times by a prayer cap. Even buttons are considered too worldly for her sect.

I, however, am a Mennonite. My religious denomination has close spiritual and historic ties with the Amish. There are many varieties of both sects, so it is hard to make comparisons. In general, we Mennonites are more liberal than the Amish, but far more conservative than your average Protestant. My dresses have buttons, a few even short sleeves. Although some women in my church wear slacks at home, I choose not to. If the good Lord wanted me to wear pants, he would have given me hips upon which to hang them.

"The State of Pennsylvania awarded me this ribbon," Freni said. "It is my civic duty to wear it."

"Does the bishop know?"

"Ach, you're jealous," Freni said, and made an awkward attempt to cover the ribbon with her small, plump hand.

"Me?" Perhaps I was—but just a little. I don't have any discernible talents. Sarcasm is not a sanctioned skill, after all.

"We were never legally married," I wailed. "Since he was already married, our marriage license was totally meaningless."

"Totally?"

"As worthless as last year's corn husks, I'm afraid."

"You don't mean?" She waggled her scant eyebrows.

I hung my head. "Go ahead and say it. I'm a trollop, a tramp, a—"

"Harlot?"

I drew myself up to my full five feet ten inches. "I most certainly am not that! I paid all the bills, remember? Aaron was as broke as a teenager on vacation."

Freni nodded. "The man didn't have a penny to his name. So, you aren't a harlot. But you're still an adulteress, aren't you?"

"Inadvertent! There is a big difference between a deliberate adulteress and someone like me. Not that most folks seem to care. I'm branded, you know. I waited forty-six years to give myself to the right man, and see what happens?"

"Yah, but look on the bright side, Magdalena. At least now you know what all the fuss is about."

"You mean sex?"

"Ach! So direct!"

"But that's what you mean, right?"

"Yah. So now you know?" Freni pretended to be examining her fingernails, but I knew she was intently interested in my answer.

I blushed, remembering my wedding night. The male anatomy proves that the Good Lord has a sense of humor.

"Yes, I know what it's all about, and it's a wonder the human race doesn't just die out."

Freni nodded solemnly. "It is a wonder."

Her unexpected sympathy made me feel suddenly charitable. "So when is this little cooking contest of yours?"

"November."

That was three months away. There would be plenty of time to back out if I changed my mind.

"Fine. So what is it you're really after, the use of my kitchen for a couple of hours?"

"Yah."

I sensed a "but." "Okay, I get it. You want me to be the judge, right?"

She fidgeted, shifting from one short, broad foot to the other. "They have their own judges."

"Who is *they?*"

Freni reached deep into a pocket of her navy blue dress and extracted a color brochure. I snatched it from her.

"It's all in there," she said.

I scanned the glossy pages. "East Coast Delicacies? I've never heard of that company before."

"They make gourmet foods." She pronounced the word so that it rhymed with sour pet.

"*Goor-may,*" I said, although it didn't really matter how she said it, Freni knows as much about gourmet cooking as I do about writing mysteries. Although she is the cook at my very popular inn, the dear woman is gastronomically challenged. For her, there are two food groups: meat and other. The latter is a broad category centered around starches—usually potatoes, but often noodles. Fruits and vegetables are relative terms. For instance, Freni considers cheese a fruit, because she frequently serves it with apple pie. Butter, which she dollops liberally atop any cooked vegetable, becomes by extension a vegetable.

"That means fancy food, Magdalena."

"I know what it means, dear."

"Read about the prize, Magdalena."

I read, not believing my eyes. "A hundred thousand dollars?"

"Yah. And I'm going to win."

"Wait a minute. It says here that contestants are by invitation only. Who invited you?"

"A very nice young man named Mr. Anderson. He's the one who gave me that." She tried to snatch the brochure out of my hand, but at five feet two, she was no match for me.

"Freni, this sounds like a scam."

Brown beady eyes blinked. Freni is not well versed in the ways of the world.

"It means that someone is trying to take advantage of you financially."

"Ach, don't be ridiculous, Magdalena."

I scanned the rest of the brochure. Except for the preposterous prize, money wasn't mentioned.

"Freni, did this nice Mr. Anderson ask for money?"

"No!"

"Well, there's got to be a catch somewhere."

Freni was fit to be tied. "You should be ashamed of yourself, Magdalena," she said, waggling a finger at me. "Just because I'm old doesn't mean I'm stupid. Mr. Anderson was one of the judges at the state fair. When he tasted my bread pudding, he said it was the best thing ever to pass his lips."

I hoped humble pie was half as tasty. "Well, in that case, I'm terribly sorry. You're absolutely right. I should have trusted your instincts."

"Apology accepted," Freni said graciously.

I handed the brochure back. "Sure, you can use my

kitchen for the contest. Just make sure they clean up after themselves, and that it doesn't interfere with serving our guests."

"There won't be any guests, Magdalena."

I jiggled a pinkie in my left ear, just to make sure it was functioning properly. Ever since Miss Enz, my fourth-grade teach, clapped me up the side of the head with a chalkboard eraser, that ear has been unreliable.

"What did you say?"

Freni cleared her throat. "I'm afraid you're going to have to cancel your regular guests, Magdalena. I promised Mr. Anderson that the contestants, and some of the judges, could stay here. The sponsors will pay your normal rates, of course."

"Over my dead body!" I screamed, and then immediately regretted it.

Those four words invariably mean deep trouble for me.

Two

I took a couple of deep cleansing breaths. Maharishi Lophat Yoggurt stayed at my inn once, and although he swiped one of my best sheets, he taught me some wonderful breathing techniques.

"The PennDutch is booked solid for the next three years," I said calmly.

It was the truth. I have, in some ways, been a very fortunate woman. My parents' untimely death left me with a dairy farm and a younger sister for whom to care. I am still caring for Susannah, but I sold all the cows but two, and turned the farm into a full-board inn. As luck would have it, one of my first guests was a travel writer for the *New York Times,* and she declared my establishment "quaint, but chic." It has been easy street for me ever since.

The first hordes of overwashed and heavily scented visitors were East Coast yuppies. Washington bureaucrats began beating a hot trail to my door soon after. The last great influx has been from Hollywood. Confidentially, they are the easiest to dupe.

I offer a special package I call A.L.P.O. (Amish Lifestyle Plan Option), whereby guests may clean their own rooms and do their own laundry by paying extra for the privilege. I explain to them just how lucky they are to be honorary Amish for a week, and without having to give up *all* of their many vices (I will not allow drinking or smoking!). If that doesn't work, I tell them that housekeeping will be the "in thing" for the new millennium, and don't they want to express their individuality by getting a jump on the rest of the country? That invariably clinches it for the celluloid crowd. There is nothing quite like the prospect of being an individual to start a stampede down from the Hills.

"Now this is a broom, and that is a mop," I'll say, and with every "ooh" and "ah" and look of wide-eyed wonder, my bank account grows. But please don't get me wrong. I give most of my profits away to charity, because as a Mennonite woman, my needs are very simple. A decent meal, a good book, a pair of comfortable shoes (dare I add a bra that fits?)—a body requires little else in the way of earthly pleasures. Still, I couldn't just back out of my obligations to the glitzy-ditzy bunch, now could I?

Freni seemed to think so. She tried her usual litany of guilt trips, stopping just short of recounting a long and arduous labor. Although she is not my mother, I fully expect to hear that one someday.

"Freni, Freni, Freni," I said, shaking my head. Perhaps I was grinning as well.

"Don't you Freni me, Magdalena. When your friends found out you were an adulteress and dropped you like a hot potato, who stood up for you?"

That was a low blow. It wasn't entirely true, either—my real friends never dropped me. Sure, a few folks at Beechy Grove Mennonite Church gave me the fish eye, but only until Reverend Schrock reminded them that the church needed a new organ, and that yours truly was the most likely person to donate one. It was true, however, that whenever tongues wagged—at least within earshot—Freni readily silenced them. If a tongue is indeed sharper than a two-edged sword, Freni wields a mouth full of scalpels.

"All right," I said, worn down to a mere nub. "I'll make some calls and see what I can do. But Bill and Hillary are going to be mighty disappointed. This is the second time I've had to cancel out on them. Who knew Dole was going to lose?"

Freni smiled happily. "So it's settled then?"

I pretended to glare. "Just as soon as I make the calls. But tell me, Freni, what is a—uh—elderly Amish woman, who lives with her son and daughter-in-law, going to do with one hundred thousand dollars?"

"Ach, Magdalena, some things are personal!"

"I haven't made those calls yet, dear. Besides Bill and Hillary—and of course their usual entourage—I have a rock star booked."

"Pat Boone?" The woman knows nothing about music, but she and Pat enjoy praying together.

"Not Pat. Someone of indeterminate age and gender called Roach Clip. I heard he—or was it she—flashed the audience at Madison Square Garden last week. Even after the flashing, folks weren't quite sure."

Unlike me, the poor woman is clueless when it comes to modern-day lingo. "What does this flashing mean, Magdalena?"

"To take off your clothes in public."

Freni froze.

"But, like you said, you have been very supportive of me in my time of need, so I really do owe you. If you'll just tell me—"

"Ach! All right, already!" She turned away and mumbled something that an elephant with a hearing aid would have had trouble deciphering.

"I can't hear you, dear."

"I said, 'It's for Barbara.' "

"Barbara? Your daughter-in-law?"

"Yah."

"But you don't even like her, Freni. In fact, you despise the woman."

"Ach, that's not true. The Bible tells us to love our enemies, and I do my best, Magdalena. Think of this money as love."

Perhaps I snorted. "She's not your enemy. Her only crime is that she married your son."

She glanced at me and hung her head. "I thought maybe if I gave her the money she would go home."

"But she is—"

"I mean back to Kansas."

I furiously jiggled both ears. "You're trying to buy off your daughter-in-law? You want to *pay* her to leave your son?"

She looked up. "Ach! You always had such a harsh way with words, Magdalena. If the money makes her happy, what's the harm?"

"And what about your son, Jonathan? If Barbara leaves him, it will break his heart. They've been married twenty years, and he still adores her."

She looked stricken, as I suppose only a mother can look. But it was a fleeting look, an emotional flash, if you will.

"Okay," I said, satisfied. "I'll make the calls."

Freni remained rooted to her spot. A stout, but very short oak.

"Yes?" I asked, with admirable patience.

"There's one more thing, Magdalena."

"Oh, I get it. You have to pay a huge fee to enter this contest, and you want to borrow a bundle."

"Ach, a bundle!"

I didn't bother to find out what she presumed. "Money. You want a loan, right?"

She shook her head vigorously. "It doesn't cost a

thing . . . except, well, the guests will be arriving on a Sunday."

"*This* Sunday?"

"Ach, no, in November, like I said."

"So?" Guests often arrived on Sunday, but *after* church.

"They're coming from all over, Magdalena, and they're providing their own transportation. Mr. Anderson said they could arrive anytime."

I thought about that while Freni beat a nervous staccato on the floor with one of her brogans. Doing business on a Sunday morning was a sin, pure and simple, but this wasn't strictly business. Sure, some money would be changing hands, but that could all be done later. Besides, it was a contest to see who was the most talented cook, and doesn't the Bible say we should use the talents the good Lord has given us?

November came right on schedule that year, and I really had to scramble to get the inn ready for Freni's contest. It wasn't just a simple matter of letting a few people use my stove for a day. This was a much bigger deal than either Freni or the brochure let on. The winner of the East Coast Delicacies Cook-off, as it was now being called, would not only receive one hundred thousand dollars, but their winning recipe would be marketed by the company up and down the East Coast. To do this successfully required attention from the media. Neither Freni nor Mr. Anderson, with whom I had had several conversations by now, bothered to mention that last detail.

It is no secret that I loathe the press. I truly strive to live up to the Christian ideal, but some of those folks who claim to have ink in their veins have pulp for brains. Dealing with celebrities as I do, I know whereof I speak. You wouldn't believe some of the things they've said about me.

Well, maybe you might. So, just for the record, I am not pregnant with Michael Jackson's baby, nor am I Michael Jackson. I have never had an affair with Ellen Degeneres, nor am I ever likely to. I have never weighed over a thousand pounds. I was not discovered, as a child, clinging to the breast of an albino gorilla in Tanzania. I never, to my knowledge, gave birth to Cabbage Boy, and I am not Bill Gates's mother.

Perhaps now you'll understand why I was not exceptionally warm to the press when they began to trickle into Hernia. But I most assuredly did not chase them off my property with a pitchfork. Been there and done that, as the young folks say, but that's a different story. This time I used a good old-fashioned push broom.

My point is, I was not in an especially merry mood when the old green Buick rolled up my long gravel driveway. And, in my defense, the dented car looked just like the one driven by Derrick Simms from the *National Intruder,* and it was six-thirty in the morning, for crying out loud. Even though we are a farm community, and therefore early risers, none of us would dream of visiting our neighbor until after morning chores, and guests who can afford my prices wouldn't be caught dead in a vehicle that ugly. But the leech-licking vermin who prey on the rich and famous drive the most hideous cars imaginable, and they never even go to bed. That may sound like a harsh judgment coming from a good Mennonite woman, but a fact is a fact.

It wasn't Derrick, however, but a woman—a co-worker no doubt—who emerged from the battered Buick. Not that it mattered though, because I am just as capable of giving a woman a piece of my mind as

I am a man. Although, frankly, I prefer sharing my mind with the needier sex.

"This is private property," I yelled, brandishing my trusty broom. Since I was still in my bathrobe and slippers I was reluctant to leave the porch. Besides, the porch's height gives me a certain tactical advantage.

The woman, who was bundled in a brightly colored blanket coat, stepped slowly from her car and regarded me calmly.

I waved the broom menacingly. "Get back in that rattletrap, sister, and keep driving."

"Is this the PennDutch Inn?" she called. It was a stupid question because there is a discreet sign at the end of the drive.

"No comment!"

She had the nerve to advance. "I'm looking for the PennDutch Inn."

"Keep looking."

"But the sign says—"

"If you saw the sign, why did you ask?"

The woman continued to approach. "I'm here for the cooking contest. But there's only one other car here. It's not what I expected."

My heart pounded. "Are you one of the judges?"

"Me?" She laughed, and reaching into a shabby brown purse with a leather fringe, extracted an official-looking invitation. "No, I'm one of the contestants. Alma Cornwater, but just call me Alma."

She was within spitting distance now (not that I would, mind you), and I studied her closely. For starters, I figured her to be about my age. She was much shorter than I, approaching even the petite range, but she was a good fifteen pounds overweight. Her broad face was all but obscured by oversized glasses with thick lenses. She wore her thick dark hair, which was streaked with gray, pulled back in a bun. Faded blue jeans peeked from beneath the long blanket coat. From what little I could see of her, she was either very tanned or—to put it frankly—of an ethnic persuasion uncommon in Hernia. Simply put, she was not lily white.

I was delighted. "Magdalena Yoder," I said, extending my hand. "I'm the owner of the PennDutch. I wasn't expecting the contestants to arrive until much later."

Alma nodded. "I drove up, but I wasn't sure how long it would take."

"Where did you drive from?" I asked politely.

"Cherokee, North Carolina."

"You drove all night?"

She shrugged. "I didn't have any choice, really. I didn't get off work until almost seven last night."

"You poor dear."

"Oh, it wasn't that bad. I napped for a few minutes at the roadside rests."

"I have a nice soft bed waiting for you, dear. And since you're the first to arrive, you can have your choice."

"That would be great, thanks." She glanced around. "Actually, I'm sort of on an adrenaline high. There wouldn't be anyplace around here to get a bite to eat, would there?"

We talked over stacks of Freni's pancakes and homemade cocoa. The latter had full-size marshmallows floating in it, not those itty-bitty good-for-nothing things the mixes provide. You can rest assured the maple syrup was pure, and the butter real.

"I live on the reservation," Alma said.

"How interesting," I said.

Freni looked at me. "What reservation are we talking about?" Her knowledge of the world is pretty much limited to a day's drive in a buggy.

"Cherokee Reservation," Alma said between bites. "I'm a Native American."

"So am I," Freni said.

Alma did a quick appraisal. "Which tribe?"

Freni shrugged.

Alma smiled. "Then how can you say you're a Native American?"

"Because I was born here," Freni said.

"That doesn't make you a Native American."

Freni frowned. "Why not? I have to be a native from somewhere, and I was born in America."

"Where are your people from?"

Freni pointed to the window with her fork. "See those woods? On the other side of the woods."

Alma shook her head. "Not your parents, your *people*. Where did your ancestors come from?"

Freni pointed again. "There. Just like I said. My grandparents were born there, and so were their parents, all the way back to 1738."

"Ah," said Alma, "but before 1738?"

"Switzerland," Freni mumbled.

"Switzerland!" Alma said triumphantly. "So you're Swiss."

"No, I'm American. Native. American born and bred."

"But not *Native*!"

"Just as native as you. Your people came from somewhere originally too."

"Yes, but thousands of years ago," Alma said, "not hundreds."

"Ach," Freni said, "it's all relative."

"I'm afraid she's not politically correct," I explained to Alma.

Freni's fork found my elbow. "Tell her about the Indians, Magdalena."

I swallowed. "Well . . ."

"Magdalena and I are cousins," Freni said, and looked to me for confirmation.

"Not first cousins," I hastened to say, "but cousins of a sort. Our family trees are so intertwined, they form an impenetrable thicket. Anyway, three of our ancestors were captured by the Delaware Indians in 1750, and the two youngest, just boys, were formally adopted into the tribe."

Freni poked me again. "Go on."

"When they were released years later, they had forgotten their mother tongue and spoke only Delaware. In fact, they kept in touch with their adopted families until the day they died."

Alma smiled and turned to Freni. "Ah, so then you're Delaware."

"Yah?"

She nodded. "You're my sister."

Freni beamed. From that moment on, Alma could do no wrong in Freni's eyes.

I will admit that I was beginning to like Alma, as well. But experience—especially my recent experience with you-know-who—had taught me never to trust someone further than you could throw them. Like I said, Alma was on the chunky side.

Three

I had just come downstairs from showing Alma to her room when my sister Susannah floated through the front door, trailing enough filmy fabric to clothe a small third world country. That is only a slight exaggeration. My baby sister eschews ready-made clothes, choosing instead to drape herself in yards of material straight off the bolt. While my tongue is still tainted from tattling, allow me to state that Susannah started wearing mascara about ten years ago, and while she adds to the clumps on a daily basis, I am not sure she has ever removed as much as a single layer. She claims to get fan mail from Tammy Faye.

Please understand that I love my baby sister dearly, but it is impossible to accurately describe her without sounding unkind. The three most benign words I can think of are: slatternly, slovenly, and slothful. Even Mama and Papa recognized her shortcomings, and when they died they left the farm in my name. It is to remain solely in my name until Susannah proves that she can behave as a responsible adult. My name is still the only one on the deed.

"Where is he?" she demanded.

"Where is who?" I gave her a quick, careful hug. My sister is even scrawnier than I. She compensates for her lack of discernible bosoms by carrying her dog, Shnookums, around in her bra. I kid you not. It gets worse—this pint-size pooch is eighty percent mouth, and twenty percent sphincter muscle. Hugging Susannah can have disastrous results.

She pushed my loving arms away. "Come on, Mags, I see his car out there!"

Needless to say, I felt hurt by her greeting. After all, I hadn't seen my sister for almost three months. Susannah is given to frequent, but brief love affairs that have been taking her increasingly far afield. This is to be expected, I suppose, since she has a penchant for dating truckers. Never mind that she is supposedly engaged to our local police chief.

Of course Susannah wasn't always like this. Like me, she was raised to be a good Christian, a nice conservative Mennonite girl. But shortly after our parents' death, Susannah did the unthinkable and married out of the faith. A Presbyterian, no less! In no time at all, she was wearing shorts and painting her fingernails. Then she started listening to rock and roll. After that it was booze, cigarettes, and finally a divorce. By the time the ink dried on that document, her apple had not only rolled from the tree, it was out of the orchard entirely.

"Whose car are you talking about, dear?" I asked pleasantly.

Susannah rolled her eyes. "Don't play dumb, Mags. Roach Clip, who else?"

"Roach Clip?" I asked, stalling. Perhaps I had forgotten to tell her that Mr. Clip's stay—well, at least Susannah thought Roach was a he—had been rescheduled for some time after the millennium.

"That's his car, Mags! Everyone knows Roach Clip drives a beat-up old green Buick. It's part of what makes him so funky."

"I'm sorry, dear, but I had to cancel the Clip."

"You what!" she shrieked.

"Freni's in a cooking contest. I had to clear the inn for the other contestants."

I have never seen my sister so mad. She ranted and raved, while the mangy mutt in her bra bayed. Poor Alma didn't stand a chance of sleeping.

Who knows how long the tantrum would have lasted, had not Mr. Anderson appeared at the door. He was not, as Freni described him, a young man—he was probably a few years older than I—but he was an uncommonly comely fellow. Imagine, if you will, Tom Cruise with gray sideburns and a mustache.

"Who is that hunk?" Susannah didn't even bother to whisper.

I pressed my finger to my lips. "He's the contest organizer, and one of the judges," I whispered.

"You've been holding out on me, Mags."

"Susannah, you're an engaged woman now, remember?"

My sister rolled her eyes again. One of these days they're going to stick in that position, and she's going to have to learn to part her hair in back.

"Melvin pisses me off," she said. "I'm thinking of calling off the whole damn thing."

First, allow me to assure you that I do not countenance vulgarity in my home. I would have sharply rebuked Susannah, had not my heart been skipping with joy. Melvin Stoltzfus, the aforementioned police chief, is my nemesis. The good Lord put him on this earth for the sole purpose of reminding me of Adam and Eve's sin. Woman's punishment is the pain of child-bearing, but since I will forever remain as barren as the Mojave Desert, God gave me Melvin.

The man is as bright as a two-watt bulb. He once sent a gallon of ice cream to his favorite aunt in Scranton—by U.P.S. His mother would have you believe that he wasn't always this stupid, that it really began when he tried, unsuccessfully, to milk that bull. She claims it was the kick in the head that did it.

But I am a tolerant person, and can overlook gross ineptitude, if it isn't accompanied by arrogance. Unfortunately, Police Chief Melvin Stoltzfus is a graduate of the Paris School of Humility. He delights in throwing his meager weight around, and once even had the audacity to accuse me of murder. I would do just about anything—even play matchmaker—to knock Melvin out of the picture.

I thought fast. "I understand Mr. Anderson is single."

That may have been a mistake. If given a choice, she prefers the challenge of married men.

"Oh."

"And he does look like Tom Cruise."

"Give me a break."

"Well, he is a vice president of a major corporation."

"So?"

"He's probably well-to-do."

Her eyes lit up like a pair of flares, and she flounced off to flirt with her next victim. Melvin, with his policeman's salary, was out of luck.

Moments later a distinguished-looking gentleman, carrying a matched set of luggage, strode into the office. Close on his heels was a tidy woman dressed in a tweed skirt suit and black pumps. Her mousy brown hair was cut in a neat bob, and she wore a moderate—might I say tasteful—amount of makeup.

"Gordon Dolby," he said, and handed me the prerequisite invitation. "I'm here for the East Coast Delicacies cooking contest."

I took the paper and checked it against my list. His name was there all right. G. Dolby, but there was nothing on the invitation, or my list, about his wife.

It was precisely at that point that my "vexometer," as Susannah refers to my temper, began to rise.

"I'm Magdalena Yoder, your proprietress."

"Ah, a learned woman," he said and glanced at his wife.

I smiled pleasantly and asked them to each sign the guest register. Much to my irritation he signed both their names.

"I'm giving you room number one," I said curtly.

"And my daughter?" he asked.

I peered around the pair. There didn't seem to be a child with them. Mr. Anderson was going to get an earful for withholding such crucial information. It's not that I'm anti-children, you see, but it's just that I've never been terribly fond of the little brats.

The woman I'd pegged as Mrs. Dolby stepped forward. "I'm the daughter, you see. My name is Gladys Dolby." She seemed more resigned than embarrassed.

That revelation vexed me even more. My inn has eight guest rooms, one of which Susannah uses during her intermittent stays. There were to be four contestants, besides Freni, and three judges. If father and daughter desired separate accommodations, Susannah was going to have to bunk with me. I would sooner have the inn crawling with urchins.

I pretended to scan the ledger. "Hmm. I don't suppose—I mean, would one room be all right?"

"Certainly not!" he barked.

Gladys looked away.

"I'm putting you in number eight, dear," I said. As long as I was going to be inconvenienced, I may as well do someone else a favor.

After that, the inn began to fill up rapidly. Unfortunately, my mood did not improve. I have an aversion to snobs, present company excluded, and can smell them a mile away. Especially when they are wearing expensive French perfume.

"Ms. Kimberly McManus Holt," the woman said. "Boston, Massachusetts."

"Magdalena Yoder, Hernia, Pennsylvania. How may I help you?"

"I'm afraid you don't understand," she said, peering up at me along a perfectly sculpted nose. "I am *the* Kimberly McManus Holt."

"I am *the* Magdalena Yoder," I said, peering down the length of my considerable proboscis. Actually there are five Magdalena Yoders, that I know of, in Bedford County, but I am perhaps the most notorious.

Ms. Holt clucked in annoyance. "I'm the star of *Cooking With Kimberly.*"

She dropped the familiar admission slip on the counter, as if it were something disgusting. "I've been invited to participate in the East Coast Delicacies cooking contest."

I gave her the quick once-over. If that woman was a serious cook, then I was Leona Helmsley's twin sister. Ms. Holt looked to be in her late thirties, a very put-together woman in a pearl gray suit, matching shoes, purse, gloves, and a faux fur coat. She even wore a coordinated hat, although it was one shade darker. The hat, incidentally, matched her eye color exactly. Not one auburn hair appeared to be out of place, and the handful of freckles on her pale face were sprinkled artfully across the perfect little nose. It was a toss-up as to which could make me gag faster, a four-inch stack of tongue depressors or Ms. Holt.

"Welcome to the PennDutch Inn," I said. "Magdalena Yoder, proprietress, at your service." Forced cheer is a skill that can be learned, and I was an "A" student.

"So, this is the place," she said, wrinkling the perfect nose, which in turn made the freckles dance.

"And isn't it charming, dear?"

"You do have me down for a nonsmoking room, don't you?"

"That's the only kind I have." From time to time, Susannah risks my ire and lights up, but few guests have had the nerve. I handed her a key. "Room number three, top of the stairs on the left."

"I can't be fooled, you know." Fat chance. With all that perfume she was wearing, I could have kept a pair of breeding skunks in the room and her nose would have been none the wiser.

She glanced around. "Well, I guess I'll go on up and check it out. As soon as the bellhop returns, I have a million things that need bringing in."

I scooted playfully around the counter. "At your service, madame."

"I beg your pardon?"

"That's me, the bellhop. I get to wear many hats."

"Oh, really?"

"Of course none of them are as nice as your hat. That's the most realistic fur I've ever seen."

"The hat is genuine fox," she said crisply.

"So the coat must be five or six foxes then. Maybe even a whole den."

Ms. Holt was not amused.

The gentleman from South Carolina was more my style. His smile preceded him into the lobby, and his clothes were off the rack. Wal-Mart, possibly, or maybe even JC Penney.

"Welcome to the PennDutch Inn," I said warmly.

"My name is Magdalena Yoder, and I'm the pro-prietress."

He extended a large black hand. "Pleased to meet you, ma'am. My name is Arthur Strump. But you can call me Art." He had a heavy southern accent, which I found rather pleasing, although it made his name sound like "ought." I took him to be in his late twenties.

"Are you here for the cooking contest, Mr. Strump?"

"Yes, ma'am." He reached into the pocket of his plaid flannel shirt, and finding it empty, patted it a few times. When nothing magically appeared, he turned, and that's when I first saw the little girl.

"You told me to stick it in my purse," she said, and handed him the paper.

I stared at her. She didn't look anything like her father. She was as white as cottage cheese, and he as dark as a pan of brownies. From a genetic standpoint, it seemed more likely that it would be the other way around. But since I know very little about these things—my ancestral pools are about as varied as freshwater lakes in the Mojave—I prudently kept my mouth shut.

Now, I am not one to judge, but black tights and a baggy black sweater do not an outfit make. Where was the bottom to the ensemble? No skirt, no slacks, the poor child didn't even have a coat to keep her warm, although she did have boots—the kind my daddy used to wear when he mucked the barn. And rings! That child wore them everywhere. I'm no babe in the woods, catering to celebrities like I do, and I've seen some bizarre cases of body piercing, but she had more punctures than an inner tube in a cactus patch. It was a wonder the girl didn't just ooze away through all those unnatural apertures.

Arthur put the invitation on the counter. "This is Carlie," he said.

I smiled. "Hi, Carlie," I said sweetly. Between you and me, however, I was seething. Mr. Anderson was going to get an earful, or was the culprit Freni? I had specifically instructed my kinswoman to make it crystal clear to the E.C.D. folks that children were not welcome at my establishment. That was a nonnegotiable condition for holding the contest at the PennDutch.

Carlie, who was chewing on a wad of gum about the size of the planet Pluto said nothing.

"She's kind of shy," Art said, and fondly rumpled Carlie's bleached spikes.

"How old is your little girl?" I asked pleasantly.

"I'm eighteen, and I ain't his little girl."

I swallowed. I have a sixth sense for trouble, thanks to Susannah.

"Well then, whose little girl are you?"

"That ain't none of your business." She grabbed Art's left arm. "This here is my boyfriend."

I grabbed the counter for support. Nine generations of Yoders turning over in their graves produce a palpable seismic activity.

"Oh, no, you don't, not in this house," I said through clenched teeth.

The ball of gum found a parking place in her cheek. "What's the matter, you prejudiced or something?"

"She really is eighteen," Art said quickly. "Carlie, show the lady your driver's license."

The child rummaged in her purse for an eternity. The license, if it existed, was far more evasive than the invitation.

"Just like I thought," I said quietly.

"Aha!" The girl had abandoned her pocketbook and was feeling around the waistband of her tights.

Her sweater, in case you were wondering, was hiked shamelessly, the hem tucked beneath her chin.

"Carlie!" At least Art had the decency to be appalled.

I did him one better and looked away. When one is as easily offended as I am, there is no point in courting cardiac arrest. You'd be surprised what these peepers have been privy to in my capacity as proprietress.

"Here it is," she cried triumphantly and thrust the plastic-covered document at me.

I took it gingerly. It was her in the picture, all right, and she was eighteen. She was also the only person I'd ever met who looked better on her license than in person. I made a mental note to consider immigration to South Carolina.

"Congratulations," I said, "but it doesn't change a thing. I am a God-fearing woman, and I won't have any hanky-panky under my roof."

Carlie looked to Art for clarification. "She has the same house rule as my folks," he said.

She lobbed the gum ball from cheek pouch to the other. "Oh, that. Man, this really reeks, Artie. You told me this was going to be a fun trip."

Art shifted from one foot to another. He looked at everyone around the room except directly at me.

"Maybe she'll let us have two rooms," he said to no one in particular.

"No can do," I said. "I'm booked as solid as a concrete wall. And there aren't any other motels in Hernia, but Bedford's just up the road. Want me to make a few calls?"

Carlie turned to Art. "Now what am I supposed to do?" She whispered in a voice loud enough to wake the dead two counties over. "I didn't bring any money, you know."

Call me a softy. Call me a saint. At the very least, give me credit for being a decent human being.

"Well, I guess I can fix up a place for you to sleep somewhere," I said. "But no funny business, or it's out on your ear." I looked from her to him. "That goes for both of you."

"Cool."

Art reached for his wallet. "How much will this cost?"

"That depends. Do you know how to do dishes, dear?"

"Yeah." The gum changed sides.

"Dust and vacuum?"

"Yeah." The gum ball picked up speed.

"Then it's on the house," I said. "Well, in a matter of speaking. It's actually under the house. You'll be sleeping in the basement."

The gum ball beat a furious tattoo, distending her cheeks with each blow, but she wisely made no protest.

My last two guests arrived in tandem as well, although they were not a couple. That much I could tell just by looking out the window when the two rental cars pulled into my parking lot. When the occupants emerged, they greeted each other like total strangers. At least there would be no more moral dilemmas to deal with that day.

Marge Benedict, food critic for *American Appetite* magazine, was, much to my surprise, one of the skinniest women I had ever seen. It was a shame really, because otherwise she might have been very beautiful, what with her large brown eyes and long, shiny brown-black hair. But just between you and me, the woman might do well to consider a life of crime; surely no prison cell in the world had bars that closely spaced.

That said, she was neatly dressed in a winter-white pantsuit, and adorned with a tasteful amount of simple gold jewelry.

George Mitchell, CEO of E.C.D., entered carrying both their bags. He was a dapper, older gent, in a navy pinstripe suit and brown wing tip shoes. His golf course tan was the perfect foil for his silver hair and mustache. His eyes, which were periwinkle blue, seemed to twinkle in constant amusement. In short, he was exactly the sort of man I wished my grandfathers had been—a thought that immediately caused me an appropriate amount of guilt.

My inbred hand shook their well-bred hands as I welcomed them to my humble establishment. They accepted their room assignments without complaint, and Mr. Mitchell, big shot though he was, gallantly offered to carry the bags upstairs. Of course I allowed him the honor, and he heroically struggled up my impossibly steep stairs. That was all rather silly, since I do have an elevator now, but there is simply no explaining machismo. Especially in men of a certain age.

I breathed a tremendous sigh of relief. Freni's cooking contest was in competent hands. Since I am a religious woman, I have no time for superstitious nonsense, but I was just about to knock on wood to cover my bases when Marge Benedict wheeled and returned to the front desk.

"How well do you know that man?' she whispered.

"What?"

"Mr. Mitchell," she mouthed.

"I know who you mean, dear, but I just met him. You were standing right there."

"He has an extremely negative aura."

"Aura, shmora. I don't believe in that stuff."

"Just the same, something terrible is going to happen this week, and that man is the reason."

Perhaps I rolled my eyes.
"I can feel it in my bones," she said.
I bit my tongue.
She wheeled again and floated off to the elevator.

Four

Put the blame directly on my broad, but bony shoulders. In retrospect, it was stupid of me to assign seats at dinner that night. But that's what I'm used to. At the appointed dinner hour my guests congregate in the parlor, and then I graciously seat them around the table my great-grandfather, Jacob "The Strong" Yoder, made for his wife and their sixteen children. Unless they are special favorites of mine, I seat folks in order of their arrival. Don't act so surprised. Of course I play favorites with the seating arrangement, but isn't that one of the "perks"—as Susannah is fond of saying—of being an innkeeper?

My place is at the head of the table, and Susannah generally sits at the foot. Fortunately, our taste in guests seldom coincides, so there is very little sibling rivalry in that department. Since I wanted to encourage Susannah's interest in the comely Mr. Anderson, I placed him at her right. I will admit to being mildly interested in the dapper Mr. Mitchell, negative aura and all, so I put him up by me. Those two assignments made, I decided to put the haughty Ms. Hold on Susannah's left, and taking mercy on the somewhat delicate Gladys, I separated her from her overbearing father and seated her opposite Mr. Mitchell. Where the others sat is, frankly, immaterial.

No doubt you will find me strict and unyielding, but

I firmly believe in a set dinner hour. The PennDutch Inn is not a restaurant with a fast-order cook on standby. Freni works hard to produce edible, if not attractive meals, and the least my guests can do is eat the food when it is at its peak. No special provisions are made for latecomers. When I ring my little brass gong at half past six, the savvy diner will be present and accounted for.

That first evening, neither Susannah nor the comely Mr. Anderson appeared. Perhaps, given Susannah's history, I should have assumed that they were up to something wicked—the horizontal mambo, as Susannah so crudely puts it—but I am a God-fearing woman, and I preferred to think they were in Bedford having a burger someplace and chatting about the meaning of life.

Ms. Holt was the last to enter the parlor—she was five minutes late—and therefore the last to be escorted into the dining room. She was actually quite pleasant to me until she saw the spot I had reserved for her.

"Well," she huffed, "this smacks of favoritism to me."

"Excuse me?" I was still adjusting to the fact that she had dressed for dinner. I mean *dressed*. She had made her entrance to the parlor in a black, floor-length gown, with a full taffeta skirt and a long-sleeved velvet bodice. Her pearl necklace and earrings were real, I'm quite sure. Of course far more oysters had had to die than did foxes. The woman was a walking monument to animal mortality.

Mr. Mitchell had already been seated, and she nodded in his direction. "Why do I have to sit at the opposite end of the table? I have my own television show in Boston, you know."

"I know," I said calmly, "and I've heard good things about it."

"Oh?" I could feel her backing down. And since I'd already sinned by skipping church, I decided to placate her further with a little white lie.

"My sister Susannah is a big fan of yours. She watches your show all the time." It seemed a safe fib at the moment, because Susannah had yet to swirl on the scene. The odds were that my sister was still in bed anyway. Ever since marrying that Presbyterian, Susannah has made it a habit of rising with the moon, not the sun.

"Really?"

"Oh, yes," I gushed, and needlessly, I might add, "she thinks you're better than Julia Child."

"Really!" The frozen face of Kimberly McManus Holt began to thaw.

I smiled. In for a penny, in for a pound.

"In fact, she's the president of the Bedford County Kimberly McManus Holt fan club."

"Well, in that case . . ." Ms. Kimberly McManus Holt was beaming like a jack-o'-lantern with two candles inside.

I gulped. As usual, I had gone too far. Through the ball of my left foot I could feel the vibrations as Mama began turning slowly over in her grave. But of course it was too late to retract my lie. A word laid is a word played, Freni often says—never mind that the woman is metaphorically challenged. At any rate, Ms. Holt seemed sufficiently mollified, so it was time for the festivities to begin. I took my seat and gently rang the little brass bell, shaped like a southern belle, that I keep to the left of my plate.

A few seconds later Freni practically waltzed into the room carrying a huge platter of pork chops stuffed with mushroom puree.

"Voilà!" Freni said. It is the only French word she knows, and she pronounces the first syllable to rhyme with "boy."

"Mrs. Hostetler invented this dish," I said proudly. Since it wasn't myself who was being recognized, I was permitted to brag.

Everyone oohed and ahed appropriately. The loudest ooher and aher, incidentally, was the handsome Mr. Mitchell. At any rate, we oohed at every course until Freni brought in and served the desert. It was, I'm ashamed to say, her famous bread pudding.

With Mr. Anderson absent, Freni might have gotten away with her stunt had not the downtrodden Gladys blabbed. "Isn't this one of the dishes that someone is cooking in the contest?" she asked.

Forks and spoons froze in midair.

After more time than it took my bigamist pseudo-husband to you-know-what, I found my voice. "What a coincidence!" I sang out merrily.

"Wait a minute," Art said in his charming Charlestonian voice, "isn't your cook one of the contestants?"

"Ach!" Freni squawked, and fled to the kitchen.

The contest itself was to last five days, with each of the contestants getting a full day, or three tries—whichever came first—to re-create the best example they could of the dish that had made them famous. The contestants had yet to be assigned their particular days, and Freni, bless her heart, was itching to get her turn over with.

I glanced at Mr. Mitchell, who merely smiled and shrugged.

"Well, yes, as a matter of fact, she is," I said, "but I'm sure this isn't *exactly* like the bread pudding she's going to make for the contest." That was technically true. Freni doesn't measure with spoons or cups, and she uses the "pinch of this" and "handful of that"

method of cooking. In the event she won, East Coast
Delicacies was going to be hard-pressed to transpose
her instructions into a written recipe.

"Yah, it is so," I heard Freni mutter through the
kitchen door. Since my end of the table is the farthest
from the kitchen, and I had neglected to swab my ears
that morning, I'm sure the rest of the group heard her
as well.

Gladys glanced at her father, and then down at her
dessert plate. "Then it isn't fair."

More muttering from the kitchen. This time it was
unintelligible.

I swallowed a spoonful of the delicious pudding.
"How isn't it fair, dear?"

Art leaned forward and addressed me. "With all
due respect, ma'am, it's a form of brainwashing."

"What?"

"The judges—" he made a point of nodding at each
of them—"now have this taste in their mouths, and
the contest hasn't even officially begun. Subcon-
sciously it might affect them when they taste it again
under contest conditions."

"Why that's ridiculous," I said, not unkindly. "From
what I understand, Mr. Anderson had already tasted
all your dishes in preliminary contests."

"Yes, but not in a social situation such as this, and
not twice in the same week."

"That's my point exactly," Gladys said, without
looking up.

"It isn't cool to be unfair," Carlie said. It was a
remarkable achievement, since the child had her
mouth full of both bread pudding *and* the wad of gum,
which she had refused to discard at the beginning of
the meal. Well, to be truthful, she had made a lame
attempt at parking it on her plate, which of course I
could not allow.

I glared at the impudent girl. "How does this relate to you, my dear?"

"Well, maybe it doesn't but fair is fair."

"She's right," Ms. Holt said, and I could hear her words icing over. If only Susannah had shown up to distract her.

"And not only that," the audacious urchin said, egged on by Ms. Holt's approval, "but your cook shouldn't be serving the judges anything else she cooks until it's her turn in the contest. And y'all know what else? She should only be allowed two tries on her day."

I snorted. "That's ridiculous."

"That makes sense to me." Ms. Holt dabbed at the corners of her mouth with just the tip of her linen napkin.

"Me too," Gladys mumbled.

"Count me in," Art said, and gave his gal pal a big smile.

I looked to Alma for support, but she was conscientiously studying a framed quilt on the wall opposite her. It was time to appeal to the powers that were.

With the comely Mr. Anderson absent, I had no choice then but to take it straight to the top. Surely the CEO of the E.C.D. could talk some sense into his mutinous mob. I turned to my right.

"Mr. Mitchell?"

His blue eyes twinkled. "Maybe we should take a vote, Miss Yoder."

There was a clatter from the kitchen, and more buzz than you get from a hive in a clover patch.

I tapped my water glass with my bread knife. "Order!" I called. "Order!"

Everyone turned my way, including Mr. Mitchell.

"This is *my* inn," I said. "I get to decide who cooks for me, and who doesn't."

At that the kitchen door flew open, and Freni, face flushed and arms flailing, flounced into the room.

"You can't fire me, Magdalena. I quit!"

My stomach churned. Freni has quit her job as cook more times than the Democrats have raised taxes, and twice as many times as the Republicans have been caught raiding the cookie jar. She means it when she says those two awful words, and invariably I have to do something as demeaning as stand on my head in a snowdrift just to get her to recant.

"See what you've done?" I wailed to the group. "Now who's going to cook for us?"

Freni threw her shoulders back. "Yah, who is going to cook?"

Several pairs of eyes fixed on me.

"No way, Jose," I said. "I couldn't cook if my life depended on it."

Freni nodded vigorously. "Magdalena can't boil water, without burning it."

Marge Benedict, who had heretofore remained silent, actually raised a bony hand before speaking.

"Miss Yoder, perhaps we judges could take turns."

The twinkle left Mr. Mitchell's eyes faster than you-know-who fell asleep after you-know-what. He stood up.

"Well, I see no reason why Mrs. Hostetler shouldn't continue to perform her regular duties here at the inn, provided she doesn't serve us any more of this delicious bread pudding."

Freni smiled smugly, her mission accomplished.

There were, of course, some muttered protests, but they went either unheard or ignored.

Monday was supposed to be a settling-in day for the contestants. Theoretically they were supposed to familiarize themselves with the kitchen and check the supplies of ingredients they had brought with them. It was expected that many ingredients had to be purchased fresh, and a sort of field trip into nearby Bedford had been planned for after lunch.

Hernia, you see, has a population of only fifteen hundred and thirty-two, and that includes the two New York retirees who moved here last summer. Yoder's Corner Market on Main and Elm is our only local source of food. Sam Yoder—and yes, he is a cousin—relies heavily on the American canning industry, and fresh produce is as foreign to his coolers as Japanese squid. The last time I shopped at Sam's, I saw a head of lettuce that had been there for three months. I know, because I gouged it with my thumbnail the day it came in, just to see how fast it would be bought. Sam once hung on to a cauliflower for six months before taking it home to his wife.

At any rate, I was to be the official tour guide on the field trip. At the appointed hour I was ready and willing to do my part, dressed for the trip into the big city (Bedford has 3,743 residents, after all) when the hounds of hell were released on my peaceful inn. Armageddon had come to Hernia. I have never heard such a ruckus in my life. The clatter of swords against shields and anguished cries was deafening.

That final battle between good and evil was being fought in my kitchen, and I rushed to catch a glimpse. I am a believer after all, and have no fear of death or what comes after. Although, confidentially, I am not very fond of pain and would prefer to die in my sleep.

Just as I reached the kitchen door, it flew open, narrowly missing my prominent proboscis.

"Hallelujah!" I cried, quite prepared to meet my Maker.

Unfortunately, it was not my Maker I was seeing face-to-face. To the contrary, I had to look down considerably to see that face, and when I did my heart sank. No matter what those liberal theologians say, the face of God does not resemble Freni Hostetler.

"It's only you!" I wailed, when I could catch my breath.

Freni took a step forward and the door swung shut, hitting her ample derriere. The short, but somewhat unbalanced woman took an unintentional step forward.

"Des macht mich bees!"

"You're mad? I was headed for my mansion in the sky, until you came barreling through that door."

"Gut Himmel, Magdalena! Make sense for a change."

"Me? What on earth is going on in there? I thought it was the end of the world."

"Ach, it's only a little disagreement. It will pass."

My hair would have stood on end had I not been wearing it in a rather tight bun.

"A disagreement with who?"

"Ach, that English woman who wears dead animals."

The Amish refer to outsiders as English, regardless of their ethnic or national origin. Even we Mennonites, who are closely allied with the Amish, are sometimes referred to in this way.

I stormed into the kitchen. Pots and pans were strewn everywhere. Drawers of ladles, spoons, and the kitchen implements had been dumped on the floor. It was the culinary equivalent of Susannah's bedroom. Standing there in the middle of it all, looking cool as a cucumber on ice, was Ms. Kimberly McManus Holt.

"Goodness gracious me!" I railed. My faith forbids me to swear, or I might have said a few choice words I've heard my sister use—words that she learned from that Presbyterian ex-husband, of course.

Ms. Holt actually smiled. She was wearing a leopard

print pantsuit with what looked like a real fur collar. She looked disgustingly elegant.

"Your cook has quite a temper," she said.

I counted to ten, prayed, and bit my tongue. And then just to be on the safe side, I said the alphabet backward.

"Freni is a pacifist," I lisped. "Both Amish and Mennonites have a four-hundred-year tradition of turning the other cheek. I'm sure she wouldn't have lost her temper unless she was thoroughly provoked."

"I only asked her for a little more shelf space. Quite honestly, I was very polite about it. Suddenly she just lost control and—" she turned slowly in a semicircle, gesturing at the shambles that had been my kitchen— "there you have it."

"Well, I'm sure—"

I felt a sharp poke in the back of my ribs. "Ask her about the list," Freni hissed.

"The list?"

"Oh, that!" The leopard lady reached into a spotted pocket and withdrew a small notebook. "I was just inquiring about the whereabouts of some basic kitchen equipment. You know, electric can opener, Cuisinart, metric scale, that kind of thing."

Freni flapped furiously. "When I told her we didn't have those things, Magdalena, she said this was the most primitive kitchen she had ever seen. She said she'd seen more sophisticated kitchens on a safari."

My dander rose, despite the strictures of my bun. "*Primitive*? You called my kitchen primitive? I'll have you know, Ms. Holt, that—"

The door to the kitchen slammed open and Susannah swirled onto the scene. "Oh, Mags, I can't believe it! It's just awful!"

"Not now, dear," I said through clenched teeth. "I'm in the middle of something important."

"But, Mags—"

"Unless," I hissed, "it's a matter of life and death, your business can wait until later."

"But it is a matter of life and death," Susannah cried. "Mr. Anderson is dead!"

Five

Freni Hostetler's Prize-Winning Slow-Baked Bread Pudding

✦

1 loaf (lb.) day-old bread, crust removed,
  and broken into pieces
½ lb. seedless raisins
1 cup brown sugar
3 cups whole milk
1 teaspoon ground cinnamon
½ teaspoon ground nutmeg
1 teaspoon vanilla extract
½ teaspoon salt
Butter to grease pan or dish

Preheat oven to 325 degrees (slow oven). Generously grease two-quart glass dish or 9-inch by 13-inch pan. Mix bread pieces with raisins in pan or dish. Pat lightly to compact. Sprinkle brown sugar, cinnamon, and nutmeg over bread. Whisk together milk, salt, and vanilla and pour evenly over mixture. Set pan or baking dish in a roaster containing hot water. The water should come within a half inch of the top of the bread pudding pan. Put roaster in oven. Bake for two hours, gently turning pudding over several times as milk rises to the top and crust forms. Best served warm with fresh cream or milk. Also good with whipped cream or caramel syrup topping.

Serves 8.

Warning: the smell of this baking might drive you crazy with hunger!

Six

I cringed. "Dead?"

As much as I hate to admit it, there have been previous deaths at my inn. Ancestors have died here, of course—the most recent being Grandmother Yoder, whose ghost I have seen from time to time. Alas, there have been other deaths as well. One or two have even been officially classified as murders.

But lest you panic and cancel your reservations, allow me to assure you that death is *everywhere* on this planet. It's just that now it tends to be concentrated in hospitals and on the streets, but there was a time, not too long distant, when folks at home dropped like flies. And I'm not talking about just the Black Plague, either. My point is that an occasional demise adds a certain psychic patina to an establishment, and should be celebrated. Too many deaths, however, can be problematic.

"Yes, dead," Susannah wailed.

"Ach, here we go again," Freni said, throwing up her stubby arms.

"Maybe it's murder," Ms. Holt said.

I ignored her. "Susannah, are you sure?"

"Positive!"

My sister has been known to dramatize at times. "Start at the beginning, dear," I said kindly.

"I knocked on his door and it just swung open.

Then I saw him, lying on the floor, as dead as a doornail."

"That's a cliché, dear. Now tell me, what makes you think he's dead? Did you take his pulse?"

She recoiled in horror. "Are you crazy? *Me,* touch a dead man?"

"Well—"

"He's white as a sheet, Mags, and I don't think he's breathing."

That sounded just like Jimmy Kurtz, one of the few boys I dated in high school. To my knowledge, he was still ostensibly alive. But Mr. Anderson was a paying customer, and an important executive. I wasn't about to take my chances with a lawsuit.

Perhaps I sounded calm to you, but my heart was pounding like a madman on a xylophone. Even the soles of my feet were quivering.

"Freni, you call 911 in Bedford. Susannah, you sit down and catch your breath. And you," I said to Ms. Holt, "clean up this mess in the kitchen."

"Why, I never!" she said, but she did.

Mr. Anderson was the color of boiled rice. I am relieved to report that he was indeed still breathing— Susannah tends to exaggerate, as I said—since I have never been too fond of mouth-to-mouth resuscitation. It was me who was having trouble breathing. My newly installed elevator is not as reliable as I had hoped, and I can no longer take my impossibly steep stairs two at a time without it showing.

At any rate, although Mr. Anderson had a pulse, he was only semiconscious, and incapable of communicating beyond the occasional unsolicited moan. But Bedford 911 was on the ball, and Mr. Anderson was whisked away to the hospital in less time than it takes to bake an angel food cake. In the meantime, all my guests were milling about, like ants when you've brushed away the crumbs—that is, all my guests except for the twinkling Mr. Mitchell. He and his rental car were missing.

I grabbed my car keys. "Freni, I'm driving into Bedford Memorial to see what's what. While I'm gone, you're in charge."

"Ach!" she squawked, but then smiled slyly. "What I say goes then?"

"You're the man," I said, borrowing one of my sister's favorite phrases.

Freni beamed. A wise guest would have followed Mr. Mitchell's example and made herself as scarce as diamonds on an Amish woman's wrist.

"What about me?" Susannah whined.

"Well, dear, Freni is the cook, and there's lunch to make, and—"

"I don't mean that. Can't I come with you to the hospital?"

I gave her one of my sterner looks. "All right, you can come, but not the pooch."

"Ah, Mags—"

My sternest look shut her up, and she stomped off to divest herself of the minuscule mangy mutt.

"And wipe off some of that makeup!" I called kindly to her retreating back. "The folks at the hospital will think Barnum and Bailey had a crackup on the turnpike."

Perhaps I should have frisked Susannah, but the last time I did that, I ended up with teeth marks that didn't heal for a week. I am proud to say, however, that my baby sister has done a lot of growing up in recent years. True, it has been a slow process, and her emotions are bonsai replications of the real thing, but she has come a long way since our parents' tragic deaths.

At any rate, when my sister rejoined me, she was wearing an outfit that actually had seams. And although she was still sporting decades-old mascara, there were isolated patches on her cheeks where the skin showed. Just for the record, she was as pale as Mr. Anderson.

"Can I drive?" she asked.

I was tempted to say "yes," but I have a brand-new BMW, and not only does Susannah have a lead foot, she has rubber wrists.

"*Please,* Mags. I'll take it real easy, I promise. I'll hardly even take my eyes off the road."

"Not today, dear. I have too much on my mind."

"Then *when*?"

"When you stop smoking, dear."

Our parents died when Susannah was twenty-two, and supposedly raised, but that doesn't mean it was too late for me to feel guilty about the way she has turned out. I am a Mennonite, after all. In the guilt department we outshine the Baptists, eclipse the Catholics, and jump past the Jews.

Frankly, I feel more guilt in association with Susannah's smoking habit than I do about the fact that my baby sister has slept with more men than Mata Hari. At least *that* is a natural instinct. But for her to spend money for the privilege of asphalting her lungs . . . on the other hand, I suppose it really is none of my business, as long as she doesn't smoke in my inn or my car.

"But I *have* stopped smoking," she said.

"You didn't!"

Her head shook like the paint mixer at Home Depot. "I quit two days ago. Cold turkey. Here, smell." She leaned forward and blessed me with a blast of her breath. She had indeed quit smoking. Flossing and brushing as well.

"Congratulations!" I cried. Two days isn't even long enough to defrost a turkey, but I didn't want to discourage the girl.

"Then you'll let me drive?"

I sighed deeply. "All right, but slow down when you enter a curve, and no talking on my cell phone."

"Aw, geez."

"And no giving yourself a pedicure on that straight stretch of Route 96. Remember what happened the last time you did that?"

"That's because I had a hard time getting the cap off the polish bottle. This time I'll have the cap already loose."

"Not by the hair of my chinny-chin-chin," I said, and then immediately regretted it. A woman my age should know better than to draw attention to her flaws.

"You're no fun, Mags, you know that?"

I dangled the keys in front of her painted peepers. "Time's awasting, dear, what's it going to be? Diligent driver, or puerile passenger?"

"Man, you're mean," Susannah snarled and snatched the keys.

Susannah and my Beemer each made it to Bedford Memorial in one piece. I, however, had to spend several minutes gathering my wits. I'm still not sure I found all the pieces. I certainly was in no shape to run into the infamous Melvin Stoltzfus in the front lobby.

"Yoder!" he yelled the second we walked in the door. "I have to have a talk with you."

I cringed as heads turned. After all, there are more Yoders in Bedford County than Burt Reynolds has hair plugs, and half the room had turned to look our way. Much to my surprise, Susannah cringed as well. If I had been in possession of those missing wits, I would have suggested that we make a run for it. Praying mantises are not known for their speed.

Okay. There, I said it. As a woman of faith I am supposed to have a charitable tongue, but in all charity I cannot accurately describe my nemesis cousin without likening him to that bulbous-eyed insect. Bald, with a huge head on a rope-thin neck, his picture adorns page 52 of *Pritchard's Encyclopedia of Helpful Garden Insects*. Unfortunately, the man is anything but helpful. If this brief description is a sin, then so be it.

"Yoder," he shouted again as he closed in on us, his victims, "it's about time you showed up."

"You see," Susannah hissed, "I told you to let me drive faster."

I ignored her. They say the best defense is a good offense, and I can be quite offensive if need be.

"What on earth are you doing here, Melvin? Wouldn't the vet give you your rabies shot?"

"Very funny, Yoder. I'm here to visit Mama who, you very well know, is having her bunions removed. I was just about to leave when that ambulance came in from Hernia. From your place, it seems."

"So?" It was a defensive response, but the wrong one. I tried again. "Is he . . . ?"

"He's not dead, if that's what you mean."

"That's a relief," I said carelessly.

The praying mantis took a menacing step closer. "I want you to tell me everything, Yoder."

"Tell you *what*?"

"That man—" he consulted a notebook—"Mr. James Anderson, what have you been feeding him?"

"Me?" I trilled.

"I just spoke to Dr. Rosenkrantz. He says it looked like a case of food poisoning."

"Don't try pinning it on me, buster. I haven't cooked a thing in five years."

That was nearly true. While in a romance-induced haze, I cooked one meal for my pseudo-husband, Aaron. The gas it gave us could have powered a hot-air balloon around the world. Instead it merely dampened Aaron's ardor, and set world records of a different sort.

"Well, then, that cook of yours—"

"That cook happens to be your first cousin once removed, Freni Hostetler. You've known her since you were a pupa, for crying out loud."

"You know what I mean, Yoder. When the man was brought in, he was obviously at death's door, and this isn't the first time Freni's cooking has done someone in."

That was an outrageous lie. The only food-related death at my inn was caused by a vengeful guest, and had nothing whatsoever to do with Freni.

I looked slowly around the room, glaring at each eavesdropper in turn. "That's slander, Melvin, and you know it. You take that back, or I'm going straight to your mama and telling her what you did in the seventh grade."

Melvin's left eye locked on me, his right swiveled in Susannah's direction. "You wouldn't dare."

"Oh, wouldn't I?" The truth is, I had nothing to tell—nothing new, at any rate—but Melvin had been a real stinker as a kid. There were undoubtedly more secrets in his past than there were in the Clinton White House.

"Okay, so maybe Freni didn't intentionally poison Mr. Anderson, but he ate something that nearly put him in a coma. We'll find out just what that is when the lab tests come back."

"I might know the answer to that now," Susannah said.

"You do, Sugar Dumpling?"

"Yeah, Lamb Pie, but you might get mad."

Melvin's left focused on his precious pastry. "No, I won't, Sugar Dumpling."

"You sure, Lamb Pie?"

I wanted to retch. I never called Aaron Pooky Bear in public. Terms of endearment, like hand-holding and osculation, are strictly private things.

"Positive, Sugar—"

"Out with it," I snapped. "You're making me hungry, and the hospital cafeteria doesn't open for another hour."

"Well," Susannah said, glancing nervously at me, "it wasn't really a date, you see. He just asked me to show him around, so we went for a ride."

"Who are you talking about?" Lamb Pie asked.

"Mr. Anderson, of course."

"You went out on a date with someone *else*? I mean, someone here in Hernia?"

Funny, but Melvin either doesn't stop to think what his Sugar Dumpling might be up to during her protracted absences, or else it's only local dates with other men to which he objects.

"I said it wasn't a date, Lamb Pie. We just drove up to Stucky Ridge to see the sunset. And then we took in a movie."

Melvin's crustaceous countenance crumbled. I hate to admit it, but I didn't blame the poor guy. Stucky Ridge may be the highest point around, but it is notorious as Hernia's *parking* spot, and by that I don't mean it's a good place to leave an unattended car. Things go on up there that would make the Whore of Babylon blush.

"Stucky Ridge?"

"Don't be silly, Lamb Pie, we didn't *do* anything."

It was time to hurry things along, and maybe cut off a tiff at the pass.

"I still don't see what any of this has to do with Freni."

Susannah turned gratefully to me. "Well, we missed dinner, see. And the popcorn at the movie was stale, so by the time we got back, we were starved."

"You must be on time, to dine," I said, quoting a sign I keep posted in the dining room. "It serves you right."

"Yeah, but it wasn't Jimmy's fault he didn't know the rules."

"*Jimmy*?" Melvin croaked.

Susannah tapped a long, narrow foot. "Well, nobody calls him James except his business associates. So, do you want to hear the rest of the story or not?"

"Hit it, Paul!" I brayed.

"So, anyway, when we got back I suggested we raid the fridge." She looked at me long enough to roll her eyes. "I know, I know, it's supposed to be off limits to anyone but you and Freni."

"Then you deserved to eat what you did. What was it, something in an unmarked jar? Because if it was, it may be older than some of your boyfriends—present company excluded. You know how Freni is about throwing things out."

Her foot tapped faster. When it starts to blur, stand back.

"It was bread pudding," she said.

Seven

"**B**read pudding? Why, that Freni! She told me it was all gone!"

"There was a whole pan of it. Still warm from the oven. Jimmy ate almost half."

"Whipped cream?"

"No, no whipped cream. But Jimmy didn't seem to mind."

"You, of course, did."

"You know how I feel about bread pudding." She made a face that required more elasticity than a spandex bathing suit. "But the tuna casserole was delicious."

"Blue and white Pyrex dish?"

She nodded.

"That wasn't tuna casserole, dear. Freni's son, John, has been working on a new starter mash for the piglets he's weaning. That's ground corn and sow's milk. He made too much in that batch, and asked if I could keep some of the stuff at the inn overnight."

Susannah turned green around the gills, staggered, and sat heavily on a molded plastic chair.

Melvin was unmoved. "Jimmy? You've been seeing this Jimmy?"

My sister took a deep cleansing breath. Actually she took several. Weaning mash is a hard thing to purge from one's system.

"You don't own me, Lamb Pie. It's not like we're married yet."

"We're engaged, aren't we, Sugar Dumpling?"

"I don't have a ring yet."

She had a good point. I know this is going to sound shallow, but never commit your body or your soul to a man unless you get a sizable rock first. Then make sure you take that rock to a competent jeweler A.S.A.P. Aaron bought the ring he gave me for $12.99 in a Philadelphia novelty shop. Had I known how much he valued me at the time, I would have been saved a lot of heartache.

"You're damn right I don't own you, you two-bit tramp," Melvin snarled. "What's more, I don't want to marry you. The engagement is off."

To his credit, Melvin had shown commendable restraint. Perhaps it was all the Yoders in the waiting room—the Good Lord knows we can be intimidating—but without another word, not even another snarl of derision, Melvin Stoltzfus turned and walked through the automatic doors of Bedford County Memorial Hospital. As the doors whooshed shut behind him, Susannah burst into tears.

I plunked my weary body down beside my sobbing sister. "Don't worry, dear, your Lamb Chop will be back."

"That's Lamb Pie!" she wailed.

In a rare gesture of tenderness, I clasped her bony chest to mine. "Whatever you say, dear. My point is—"

My point, however, was drowned out by an ear-piercing squeal. I released Susannah just in time. A second later a black ball of fur burst from her blouse and streaked across the room.

"It's a rat!" somebody shouted.

Before I could react, half the folks in the room were

standing on their chairs. A few folks were standing in
their wheelchairs.

"Shnookums!" Susannah screamed and took off
after the miserable mutt, who was now headed past
the reception desk and down Bedford Memorial's
main hall.

I joined her in pursuit of her pitiful pooch. Much
to my surprise, it was actually rather fun. Chasing the
hound from hell down a hospital hall is certainly more
entertaining than listening to some famous guest yam-
mering about his or her latest tax shelter, or examining
Cher's backside for cellulite (although, confidentially,
this one was a close tie).

Of course there were one or two crotchety souls
who were not amused by our antics. If pressed, I
would accuse Nurse Dudley of being the most difficult.
The surly woman has been a fixture at Bedford Memorial since Florence Nightingale died—gave or take
a few decades. She has, and I say this with all Christian charity, a heart of stone. I have seen sides of beef
at the locker plant handled with more sensitivity than
Nurse Dudley handles her patients.

What's more, Nurse Dudley is curiously obsessed
with cleansing the colons of the victims assigned to
her ward. In all fairness, she's very good at what she
does. I was in the hospital once for reasons totally
unrelated to my digestive tract and, quite against my
will, Nurse Dudley gave me a thorough house-
cleaning—so to speak. I left Bedford County Memorial as hollow as a piece of macaroni. We all have our
callings, but leave it to an anal-retentive woman to
devote her life to giving enemas.

"This is a hospital!" Nurse Dudley roared as we
ducked past her in mad pursuit of Shnookums.

"We know!" I shouted over my shoulder.

By then, Susannah's bundle of joy had rounded the

corner and was headed down another corridor. We might have caught the dinky dog had not Dr. Rosenkrantz rounded that very corner and blocked our way. And I mean that literally.

Dr. Rosenkrantz is an enormous man with a matching ego. While he prefers to see himself as God, I see him as the sun. There are always an intern or two, and a handful of orderlies, caught in Dr. Rosenkrantz's orbit, and that day was no exception.

The bad news is that Susannah ran smack into young Dr. Balu Nagpur, an intern, toppling the rather slight man. The worse news is that it was Dr. Rosenkrantz's prodigious paunch upon which I came to rest. Dr. Nagpur, who was not in any way hurt, had the grace to laugh it off. Dr. Rosenkrantz, who claimed a cracked coccyx, was not amused.

I tried to help him to his feet, but it took a pair of orbiting orderlies to do the job.

"Are you all right?" I asked kindly.

That's when Dr. Rosenkrantz accused me of breaking his bottom. He also said a few things I cannot repeat and which, until my pseudo-marriage with Aaron, I never would have thought possible.

"Why, I never, in all my born days! You, sir, have a mouth like a hog wallow." I said it to his back as he limped away, supported by several satellites.

"He is being irritable because he is being in pain," Dr. Nagpur said gently.

"But that is no way to talk to a lady!"

Nurse Dudley had the temerity to grab me by the arm. "You're not a lady. You're a menace. I want you and your sister out of here this minute!"

"Get your filthy hands off me," I snarled, "or it will be more than your backside that needs mending."

The earth shook as twenty generations of pacifists turned over in their graves.

Nurse Dudley released her grip. "Out!" she shrieked. "Get out this minute!"

"But we can't leave until we find my baby," Susannah wailed.

The kindly Dr. Nagpur put his hands together in a gesture of peace. "You are losing a baby in this hospital?"

"It's not a baby," Nurse Dudley panted, her rage escalating, "it's a monkey."

Dr. Nagpur's eyes widened. "You are owning a pet monkey? Oh, how delightful! In India we are having many monkeys."

"He's not a monkey," Susannah shrieked, "he's a dog."

Nurse Dudley recoiled in horror. "A dog! That's even worse than a monkey!"

"He's a seeing-eye dog," I said quickly. "A very little seeing-eye dog, to be sure, but she's had him ever since she was a child."

Nurse Dudley pounced on Susannah. "I've seen you before, and you're not blind."

"It comes and goes," Susannah said without missing a beat.

I gave Dr. Nagpur a discreet, but guiding kick. He grunted, and then nodded solemnly.

"Ah, it is true. This *intermittent ocular interruptus* is indeed a rare disease, but we are seeing more and more of it among white women over forty."

"I'm thirty-three," my ungrateful sister whined.

"Thirty-five, dear."

"And she claims to have had it since she was a child," Nurse Dudley huffed.

"Ah, that is true, and you both are being correct. It is particularly prevalent among women in their thirties, but we are seeing more of it in the women over forty, because there are more women in this category these days. Of course some women are not knowing they have this disease, but this is a very lucky woman who has been knowing it since she is a child." He paused and scratched his head. "Am I making myself clear?"

"As clear as Freni's ham and bean soup," I said, and patted his arm gratefully. I faced Nurse Dudley. "The law says she is permitted to take her seeing-eye dog into public places, and this is a public hospital."

"Seeing-eye dog, my ass," Nurse Dudley hissed, but she made no attempt to stop us from searching further.

We found Shnookums whimpering in a hamper. Mother and child enjoyed a warm reunion, and then we hightailed it back to the inn. We returned not a minute too soon.

The first thing I noticed was that the mysterious Mr. Mitchell had returned. Both he and his rental car were in the driveway. The next thing I noticed is that, wherever he'd been, he'd left the twinkle behind.

"Ms. Yoder! Where the devil were you?"

Susannah breezed on past us.

"Me? Where were *you*?"

"I drove into Bedford to get in some jogging. You don't have a gym."

Nor would I ever have one. Folks who need to exercise are not doing a full day's work.

"Did you consider milking the cows and sweeping the barn?" I asked, a bit miffed.

"No, but—"

"Or feeding the chickens and gathering eggs?"

"Chickens?"

"And even though I sold most of the farm after Papa died, there's still three and a half acres of pasture you could have jogged in. There was no need to go all the way into Bedford."

For some reason the twinkle returned. "You actually milk your own cows?"

"Not me, Freni's husband, Mose, does the milking. You're welcome to help him anytime you want. He does it twice a day. About six-thirty in the morning, and five in the afternoon."

"I just might do that. But now I'd like to ask you some questions, if you don't mind?"

"About cows?"

His eyes danced. "No, they're about my employee, James Anderson. I understand that he was rushed to the hospital this morning."

I needed to go inside. A cold November wind was whipping around my stocking-clad legs. Just for the record I do not wear pants. Amish women always wear skirts, and even though I am a Mennonite, and somewhat more liberal, I refuse to wear trousers of any kind. You can blame it on Mama.

There was a time when I dearly wanted a pair of pale pink pedal pushers, but Mama said no. Pants were men's clothes, she said, and cross-dressing was a sin. Then, less than ten years later, when Susannah wanted to wear blue jeans, not only did Mama change her mind, she changed her clothes. But that figures—Susannah had Mama wrapped around her little finger from the day she was born.

At any rate, I'll never forget the day that Beechy Grove Mennonite Church held their annual covered-dish dinner up on Stucky Ridge. Mama and Susannah showed up in pants, and pranced around that picnic like a pathetic pair of pagans. You could be sure tongues wagged. When Mama cut her braids and started wearing lipstick, Amish and Mennonite tongues were a blur. I don't mind telling you, the faster tongues wagged, the happier I became. Finally, it was Mama and Susannah who were committing some of the sins in our family, not just me.

Mama never came right out and said it, but I know it irked her that I never joined the pants parade. I'm sure it irks her still. And while my resistance to trousers may be partly out of spite, I do not, as Aaron insisted, have a lot of issues I need to work through.

But perhaps I've digressed enough. My point is, it was too cold to continue even a short conversation on the front porch.

"Come on inside. I could use a cup of hot chocolate about now."

"With marshmallows?"

"Big ones. Not those microscopic ones that melt too soon."

"Ah, a woman after my own heart."

He followed me in, and after getting our cocoa, we settled ourselves into the most comfortable chairs in the parlor. When I inherited this place all of the furniture was wood. Hard, gleaming, much-polished wood. My forbears looked down their long noses at relaxation. Idle hands were the work of the devil, and busybodies did not need to be pampered with padding. Frankly I'm surprised that given her revolution, Mama hadn't started on a softening binge. Undoubtedly she would have in time. Susannah couldn't stand straight if you taped her to a railway tie.

"Now, tell me about Jim."

"There's not much to tell. My sister found him on the floor of his room, passed out. We called 911, and had him taken to the hospital. The doctor thinks it's food poisoning."

"I see."

I swallowed too quickly, burning the back of my throat. "But it wasn't anything he ate here, of course. You knew he was out most of last night, didn't you?"

"With your sister, I take it."

"How did you know that?"

"Jim has an eye for women, and your sister is very attractive."

"She *is*?" Just between you and me, Susannah is the plainer of us. What I mean is, if you stood the two of us side by side—without all that makeup and gunk—and spotted me a few points for age, I'd be the more attractive sister. At least that's what Aaron said when we were courting. Then again, the man didn't tell me he had a wife stashed up in Minnesota.

He nodded, but didn't seem inclined to elaborate.

It was just as well. I had some important business to broach, and flattery and money do not mix. Contrary to popular opinion, the Bible does not label money the root of all evil. It says that the *love* of money is the root of all evil. I, for one, do not love money; I merely enjoy its benefits. To put it simply, money has been good to me.

Flattery, on the other hand, got me into a bogus marriage that made me the laughingstock of the county. It almost cost me membership in my church. And Lord only knows how many times it's gotten Susannah to do the horizontal hokeypokey, as she so crudely puts it.

"Well," I said, after a decent interval, "I suppose you'll be canceling the contest. That's understandable, of course, but I'm not going to be able to give you a full refund. In fact, I can't even give you a prorated refund, because you'll be leaving me with empty rooms for the rest of the week. You see, I had to cancel some very important guests to squeeze you in. But—" I spread my hands magnanimously—"how does fifty percent sound?"

He shook his head.

"Look buster, I had Bill and Hillary coming, not to mention Roach Clip."

"*The* Roach Clip?"

"You've heard of him?"

"My secretary loves his music—to use the term loosely," he said. "And you don't need to bother with a refund, because I'm not going to cancel."

My mouth opened wide enough to catch a golf ball. I willed it into speaking position.

"You're *not* going to cancel? But you only have three judges, and one of them is in the hospital, maybe dying, and—"

"Jim will be fine." He patted a cell phone in his suit pocket. "I talked to his doctor just before you drove up. A nice Dr. Gilderstein, I believe."

"That's Dr. Rosenkrantz," I snapped.

"Anyway, you were right. It is a case of food poisoning. But a fairly mild one at that. Jim passed out because he was dehydrated. He'd been throwing up all night."

That explained all the flushing I'd heard. I had all the plumbing updated when I turned the family home into an inn, but there's just so much you can do with two-hundred-year-old walls.

"It's a good thing I have my own well," I said. "Those motels in Bedford would charge you extra for all that water."

He chuckled. "The good news is that the paramedics hooked him up to an IV right away, and by the time I called, Jim was coming around."

"So he's going to judge, after all?"

He chuckled again. "Not hardly. I don't think he'll be able to look at solid food for a day or two, and our schedule has us judging the first entry tomorrow."

"Two judges is an interesting concept," I said kindly.

"Oh, there will be three of us, if my hunch is right."

"If you don't mind my asking, who's the third?"

He laughed outright. "You are, Miss Yoder."

Eight

"**M**e?" His blue eyes danced the tarantella. "That is, if you'll agree. And I'm pretty sure you will."

"And just what makes you so sure?"

He slapped his knee, an unseemly thing for the top executive of a large company to do. "You're a pistol," he said, between laughs.

I felt my eyebrows arch involuntarily. "I beg your pardon?"

"A real live wire. You've got sass. I like that in a person."

"I do not have sass," I said hotly. "I'm just a mild-mannered woman with an attitude."

"You see what I mean? Anyway, you'd make a great judge. You've got exactly what it takes."

I stood up. "Mr. Mitchell, I don't have time to sit here and play games. Not if you want me schlepping your guests into town on a field trip."

"*Schlepping?*"

"Babs says that—she's a frequent guest here. It means—"

"I know what it means. Now give me one good reason why you couldn't be a judge."

"Because one of your contestants is my cook. She also happens to be my cousin. Not to mention my closest friend."

He put his well-manicured hands together, fingertip to fingertip, forming a tent. "And you don't think you're capable of making an impartial decision?"

I stared at him. What a silly question. I am the fairest person I know. At the risk of sounding vain, King Solomon and I are soul siblings. Unfortunately, impartiality does not seem to be valued highly in today's world. I've played hostess to a few presidents since the inn opened, and the fact that none of them has offered me an appointment to the Supreme Court baffles me.

"Well, could you?" he asked.

"Does a cow have four teats?"

The fingertips did a nervous dance. He was obviously a city boy.

I made it easy. "Do politicians lie?"

"Excellent! Welcome aboard, Miss Yoder. One more thing—would you be so kind as to not tell anyone about this, until I make an official announcement?"

"Cross my heart and hope to die, stick a needle in my eye. And you may call me Magdalena, if you wish." I know, that was very generous on my part, but after all, we were now colleagues of a sort.

"Then you may call me George." He winked. "And if you're really good—Georgie Boy."

I recoiled in horror, and justifiably so. Aaron Daniel Miller, my pseudo-ex-husband, used to refer to a significant portion of himself as Danny Boy. There was no way on God's good earth that I was ever going to get that well acquainted with George Mitchell.

"That was a joke," he said quickly.

Perhaps I'd misunderstood. "My sister calls me Mags," I said charitably.

"If you don't mind, I prefer Magdalena. *Mag-da-len-a.* What a beautiful name. It just seems to roll off the tongue."

I could feel myself blush. It's possible I even twittered.

"It suits you well," he said.

I twittered some more, and might not have come to my senses in time, had it not been for Freni.

"Ach, there you are!" she said, bustling into the room. "Where—" She stopped, eying our mugs with the telltale rings of cocoa. "So it was you who made a mess of my kitchen!"

"Mr. Mitchell and I were cold, Freni. Besides. You weren't anywhere around."

"I was out gathering eggs, Magdalena. They don't gather themselves, you know."

I gave her a placating smile. "Pull up a chair and join us, dear."

"Ach!" She threw up her hands. Freni won't sit still until well after she's dead. Work is what the Good Lord expects of us, and my cousin is not about to let Him down.

"Say, Freni, what's this I hear about two pans of bread pudding? When we asked for seconds last night, you said there wasn't any left."

Freni turned the color of pickled egg. "I do not lie, Magdalena Portulacca Yoder!"

"I wasn't suggesting that you did." I winked at Mr. Mitchell. "Maybe you just forgot that you made that extra pan."

"That pan was for Mose, if you must know. Bread pudding is his favorite, and I don't have time to make it anymore, thanks to all the work you have me do around here."

I ignored her implication that I am a slave driver. "But Susannah said she found it in the fridge in the middle of the night."

Freni's color deepened. "Ach, so I forgot to take it home! Is that a sin?"

"Absolutely not, and you have my deepest apologies." I tried to sound sincere.

Freni stood rooted to the ground, like a stout, black stump. While I was wracking my brain for something more soothing, but that I would be willing to say, it occurred to me that I might be on the wrong track.

"Is there something specific you wanted to talk to me about dear?"

"Yah. You were supposed to take this bunch of English shopping in Bedford, yah?"

So that was it! "Yes, but—"

"They were going to eat lunch there too, yah?"

"That was the plan, but—"

"Look at your watch, Magdalena."

I glanced at my five-dollar Wal-Mart special. "Ach!" I squawked. "It's almost noon."

Freni nodded with satisfaction. "And I have nothing in the house except Mexican pancakes. I was going to go shopping myself, remember?"

"Mexican pancakes?" George asked. "Sounds interesting."

"She means flour tortillas," I said. "Willie Nelson was here last week and had a hankering for some Tex-Mex." Mama would be amazed at how savvy I have become since she died, despite my skirts.

"You have chicken?"

"Ach, you don't gather eggs from cows," Freni said, clearly annoyed. The English haven't a clue, as far as she's concerned.

"I mean, chicken meat. Like in the freezer."

"Plenty," I said, wondering where this was headed.

"How about cheddar cheese and sour cream?"

"Two cows, with four teats each," I reminded him.

"Salsa?"

"Yes—homemade—but we call it tomato relish."

"Black beans?"

"Ach!" Freni clapped her hands. "Terrible things. But Willy liked them so much, I bought two extra cans."

George jumped to his feet. "Then it's settled. My wife Marilyn created a terrific dish with not much more than that. With your permission Mrs. Hostetler—Miss Yoder—I'd like to make lunch."

Freni frowned.

"I promise not to make a mess, and of course I'll wash the dishes."

"Ach, a man after my own heart," Freni said, and practically dragged George off to the kitchen.

I may have a negative quality or two, but laziness is not among them. First Grandma Yoder, and then Mama, saw to it that my hands were always busy. I will be the first to admit that I have no special talents, but I can clean house with the best of them, sew, garden, and even kill and pluck a chicken. Why is it then that I feel guilty every time I sit down—unless it's to eat, or go to the bathroom? Even then I can never totally relax. I generally gulp down my food, and I refuse to keep a *Reader's Digest* on the john. A quick entry, and a quick exit, has been the story of my life. And confidentially, my pseudo-marriage to Aaron didn't change a thing.

Is it a sin to put one's feet up on a hassock, close one's eyes, and daydream just a *little*? I would like to think not, but I nearly jumped out of my skin when Marge Benedict walked into the parlor and interrupted my reverie.

"I was praying," I said. Then I really did pray, asking forgiveness for my lie.

"Pardon me," she said, and patiently waited until I was quite through.

I opened my eyes wide, as an all-clear sign.

"Do you have a fax machine, Miss Yoder?" It was more of a statement than a question.

The first time I was asked that question I recoiled in horror. "The only safe fax is no fax," I blurted, much to the confusion of my guest. Thank heavens I am more sophisticated now.

"Actually, I don't," I said, and barely blushed.

I know that astounds people, almost as much as the fact that I do not own a computer. These are not religious restrictions, mind you, just manifestations of my technologically challenged condition.

"You're kidding—I mean, where can I go to find a fax machine?"

"There are a couple of places in Bedford, I think. This afternoon when we go into town, I'll help you find one."

She sucked on her bottom lip. "That'll have to do, I guess."

I motioned to the chair vacated by George. As long as we both sat and made conversation, I didn't need to feel guilty.

"Thanks."

"So, you're a magazine editor," I said.

"Food critic," she corrected me. "Do you read *American Appetite* magazine?"

"Ah, the one with the meaty articles," I said. Lies by implication are off-white at worst. This one was ecru.

"Yes, that's the one. I travel constantly, trying to keep up with the food trends." She sighed. "People think it's a cushy job, but it definitely has its downside."

"Like what?" I wondered aloud.

"You have a very nice place here," she said, waving a hand as thin as a talon, "and, confidentially, Mrs. Hostetler is a passable cook, but this is more the ex-

ception than the rule. I've eaten in dives that the
roaches gave up on."

"But you must find something satisfying about your
work—don't you?"

It was a question that was beginning to nag at me.
While I enjoyed presiding as proprietress over a pros-
perous pension, there is a lot of stress in my line of
work. Quite frankly, there are times when there simply is not enough room under this roof for my ego
and those of the rich and famous. As Robin Leach
once said to me—never mind, that was confidential.
At any rate, in recent months, especially since the un-
raveling of my mock marriage, I have entertained the
idea of becoming a missionary. There is an eccentric
lady at church whose parents were missionaries in the
Belgian Congo, now just the Congo, and she has been
encouraging me to go there and work in the refugee
camps. She thinks I'd be a natural, due to my organi-
zational skills and take-charge attitude. Of course such
a drastic step is unthinkable until Susannah finally flies
the nest for good. But by then, I'll probably be or-
ganizing wheelchair races at the Bedford County Mennonite Home for the Aged.

Marge Benedict leaned forward. Her chair was near
the parlor window, and although the November sun
was hitting her back, I couldn't see a shadow.

"I used to love my job—before *he* took over."

I leaned forward. "Who's he?"

She glanced at the parlor doors. The one on her
left opens into the lobby. From where I was sitting, I
could see that the lobby—really just a small vesti-
bule—was empty. The other door, over my right
shoulder, was problematic. It opened onto the back
hall that, I hate to admit, is fairly dark and narrow.
Susannah claims it is a perfect place for lurkers.

"Mr. Mitchell," she whispered.

"George Mitchell?"

She held a finger to her lips. No fairy-tale witch would ever eat her.

"I was on the road for six years before I worked myself up to management. Three years as assistant editor, and two years as editor. I was supposed to be presiding editor when Agnes Harkgrew retired, but he had other ideas."

"What does *he* have to do with it?" I whispered. In all fairness, my whispers have been likened to a drill sergeant on a bullhorn.

Her large brown eyes seemed to be searching the darkness behind me. "*He* owns *American Appetite* magazine, that's what. East Coast Delicacies bought us out last year. Agnes Harkgrew retired early and I—well, I didn't get her job. In fact, I got demoted."

"Back to square one," I said sympathetically.

"Well, not exactly square one. I used to do straight reporting—run-of-the-mill reviews, that sort of thing. Now I get to judge contests, and write inspiring articles on food trends. Of course this is all really just publicity for East Coast Delicacies."

Both Freni and Susannah think I'm bitter, but you could sweeten Marge Benedict by sprinkling her with lemon juice.

"Why don't you just quit?"

"Food review is a specialized niche, you know. It's not like I run a motel."

"Well!"

"I'm sorry," she said. "I meant a B and B."

"This isn't a B and B," I may have snapped. "This is an inn with atmosphere."

And as far as I was concerned—due to the atmosphere—our conversation was over.

*   *   *

There is no rest for the wicked, Mama always said. If that maxim applies only to the wicked, then I make Saddam Hussein look like a Goody Two-shoes. No sooner had I closed my eyes again than the doorbell rang. One of these days I'm going to drive into Pittsburgh and select a doorbell with a pleasant chime—perhaps the opening bar from "The Sound of Music." My current bell squeals like a terrified pig. Ned Beatty once said it gave him goose bumps.

When I saw that it was Lodema Schrock standing there, her pocketbook clutched in front of her in both gloved hands, I almost didn't open the door. But I am ever the optimist, and the woman did owe me five dollars she'd borrowed from me at a church bazaar the year before.

"Yes?' I said guardedly.

"Well, aren't you going to invite me in?"

I thought about it. Lodema is a pillar of Beechy Grove Mennonite Church. She is president of Mennonite Ladies' Sewing Circle, leader of the Wednesday Women's Bible Study, church organist, Sunday school teacher to the senior high class, adviser to the Mennonite Youth Group, *plus* she's married to the pastor.

None of this has stopped Lodema from being the town's biggest gossip. To make matters worse, she has a razor-sharp tongue, which she wields like a scythe in a wheat field, and unfortunately I was experiencing a bumper crop that year.

"Invite you in?" I echoed, stalling for time. "Well, you see, we're just about to eat lunch."

"I haven't eaten my lunch yet."

"You haven't? Oh, well, then I won't be keeping you." I started to close the door.

Lodema has disgustingly small feet, and she's remarkably quick with them. She also wears sensible shoes that can hold up to a good slamming.

"Magdalena, I need to talk to you, and I need to talk to you *now.*"

I wracked my brain for sins past, present, and future. In all honesty, all I could come up with was the fact that I had skipped church the day before and pawned my Sunday school class—the junior high—off on Annie Blough. Although Annie is a sweet person, she has the intelligence of a hitching post, and half the personality. Whenever she substitutes for me, the kids tend to get out of hand. The last time I was absent the girls locked themselves in the bathroom and smoked a cigarette, and the boys stuffed X-rated pictures in the tract box.

"Annie promised she'd stay on top of things!" I wailed.

"Your Sunday school class is only part of it, Magdalena."

I prayed for wisdom and patience. There's nothing quite as frightening as a pacifist pastor's wife on the warpath.

"Make it quick, dear. Like I said, it's almost lunch."

I made no move to let her in, and if I was letting enough warm air out of my house to turn the front yard into a tropical jungle, so be it. Lodema has made no secret of the fact that she thinks the PennDutch should be renamed The Den of Iniquity. Of course that doesn't stop her from gawking at my celebrity guests whenever she gets the chance.

"If I catch my death of cold out here, at least *I'm* going to heaven," she said.

"Bon voyage, dear."

"What? Magdalena, I suppose you think that's one of your funny worldly jokes?"

I tugged harder on the door. Even the best shoes have their limits.

"Well, it wasn't funny, you know that? In fact, that's why I'm here."

"My salvation is assured," I said. I know that's not a popular position with some folks, but I firmly believe that.

She fumbled with her purse, extracted a clump of tissues, and dabbed at her reddening nose. "I'm not talking about your salvation per se. That's between you and the Lord. I'm talking about how you flaunt your worldly ways in front of the rest of us. The stumbling blocks you set in our paths, so to speak."

"That's not a stumbling block at the front of the driveway," I snapped. "That's a concrete urn, and if you've hit that again—"

"Your adultery!" she barked. "That's what I'm talking about! Your sin of lying with a married man, and then not having the decency and humility to confess it publicly."

I was stunned. Public confession of sin was an old Mennonite custom, but one that had been largely ignored in a church as progressive as Beechy Grove Mennonite Church. But even then, whenever it occurred, it was always voluntary, and always involved sin. *Sin,* not stupidity. And more likely than not, the sin confessed was invariably one that had been directed against the entire congregation.

"Is that what Reverend Schrock says?"

"The reverend"—Lodema never calls her husband by his first name—"is a very busy man right now. Margaret Kauffman is dying of cancer, and Reuben Gindlesperger was almost decapitated when his combine overturned. Of course, you'd know all that if you came to church."

"I only missed one Sunday!" I took a deep breath of freezing air. "So, the reverend didn't say that, did he? Then you have no right to put words in his mouth.

And not that it's your business, Lodema, but I *didn't know* Aaron was married. Where's the sin in that?"

She honked into the wad of tissues. "A sin is a sin. The Bible says—"

" 'Judge not, lest ye be judged,' " I said. I made it a point of looking her squarely in the eyes.

"Very well," Lodema said, shoving the wad of soggy tissues back into her purse, "try and hide behind Scriptures, but it isn't going to work. We've already taken a vote."

"A vote? And who is we? You and the Lord?"

She gasped. "Now you can add sacrilege to your list of sins! For your information, the *we* I was referring to was the membership of the Mennonite Ladies' Sewing Circle."

It was my turn to gasp. "You didn't! Did you?"

She nodded smugly. "Unfortunately it wasn't unanimous, but nevertheless, a majority of us voted to revoke your membership."

"*Ach, du lieber!*" I said, reverting to the Pennsylvania Dutch of my ancestors.

"You brought this on yourself, Magdalena. Fortunately Annie Blough has agreed to take over your Sunday school class on a permanent basis."

"*What?*"

She sniffed. "You can't possibly expect to continue on as a teacher, given your morals."

"My morals are not contagious!" I wailed. "Besides, I didn't intentionally do anything wrong."

"Of course we had to leave you in the Wednesday Women's Bible Study Group—how else will you learn right from wrong?"

"How generous of you!" I flung the door open all the way, inadvertently knocking Lodema Schrock to the porch. When I saw that she wasn't hurt, I slammed the door shut and locked it.

I know, a better Christian would have helped her up, and maybe even made her a cup of tea. But the Church is a hospital for sinners, not a country club for saints, and I had a whole lot of healing still to do.

"Beware the wages of sin!" Lodema screamed, pointing a gloved finger at the peephole in my door. " 'The wages of sin are death!' "

A sensible woman would have gone straight to bed and stayed there for the remainder of the week. Enough said.

Nine

George Mitchell was a first-rate cook. His Marilyn Mitchell's Tortilla Cake Surprise was a hit. Even Freni grudgingly admitted to liking it. In fact, I found her in the pantry after lunch, scribbling what she remembered of the recipe on the inside of a brown paper bag. No doubt future generations of Amish will eat this tasty dish and believe it to be part of their cultural heritage.

At any rate, our noonday meal should have been a delightful experience for everyone. I am, after all, more lax at lunch than I am at breakfast or dinner. This particular occasion, for instance, I went so far as to permit free seating. Bear in mind that my dining-room table is extraordinarily long—thanks to my ancestor's lusty loins and fertile wife—so there is invariably a lot of empty space. This is never a problem when I seat folks, because I spread them thin, like a single pat of butter on a double order of toast.

Imagine my dismay when everyone but Alma Cornwater and Gordon Dolby squeezed together at Susannah's end of the table. If Gordon hadn't seated himself at my immediate right, and Alma at my left, I might have been deeply wounded. I shower every day, and change my clothes almost as frequently, so hygiene couldn't have been the problem. I did a quick sniff test just to be sure. Everything seemed to be okay.

I smiled benevolently at my two loyal companions and then, just to punish the others, said the longest grace that table has witnessed since Grandma Yoder, bless her senile heart, said the Lord's Prayer twenty-three times in succession.

"So tell me, Mr. Dolby," I said, after grace had been said and the food passed around, "are you a native of Baltimore?" That wasn't a lucky guess, mind you. I take the time to read the addresses recorded in my guest book.

"Baltimore, born and bred," he said. "Birthplace of 'The Star-Spangled Banner.' "

"Is that so? What do you do for a living?"

"I'm retired," he said, and helped himself to a double portion of the entree.

"Oh? Retired from what, dear?"

He glanced at his daughter, Gladys. "Let's just say, I've served my country."

I turned to my left, where Alma Cornwater sat, her glasses about to slide off her nose, her thick hair straying from its bun.

"Miss Cornwater," I said pleasantly, "what do you do when you're not competing in a cooking contest?" I already knew that woman was a Cherokee Indian, but that isn't an occupation.

She pushed her glasses back into place with a pudgy brown finger. "I'm a mother."

"Oh." I don't mind telling you that I was disappointed. Some of my most unpretentious guests have been my most interesting. Who knew that Nevada Barr was a park ranger who once flung a tranquilized wolf over her back?

But Alma wasn't done. "Now that Jimmy, my youngest, is in school, I plan to look for a job."

"How many children do you have?"

"Eight." She sounded defensive.

"I just have the one," Gordon said, nodding at Gladys.

"And I have none," I said lightly. "At least none that I know of."

Nobody even smiled. When a man tells that joke, however, folks think it's a hoot.

"Being a parent is never an easy task," Gordon said. Again he nodded in his daughter's direction. Fortunately she was sitting at the far end of the table and engrossed in a conversation with Marge Benedict. I couldn't imagine the mild-mannered Gladys giving her father an ounce of trouble. Clearly the man had no perspective.

"Being a big sister is no picnic, I can tell you that," I said and stared down the table at Susannah's empty place. Lunch is a meal she never eats, falling as it does in the middle of her sleeping schedule.

"In fact," I said, "look up at the ceiling."

They looked up. Mercifully, no one else did.

"See those footprints up there?"

Alma nodded. "Women's size eleven, double A. You don't see that very often."

I gaped like a gulping guppy.

"My daddy was a traveling shoe salesman. We used to play with his stock."

"I see. Well, those are my sister's. And that's a ten-foot ceiling. Lord only knows how they got up there. Now look closer."

Alma nodded again. "A man's ten right beside hers. Faint, but definitely there."

"Kids," Gordon said.

"She wasn't a kid when that was made," I said, and stabbed at my salad. "Those were made last week. Susannah is thirty-five years old."

"My Gladys is thirty-five."

"I bet she doesn't leave her footprints on the ceiling."

"There are other ways to rebel."

Rebel? Do thirty-five-year-olds rebel? Perhaps Gladys was a rebel, but that is not a word I'd used to describe my sister. Any woman who has been married and divorced, and served more men than McDonald's, is not rebelling, she's indulging. Yes, I know, that makes me a codependent, because I allow her to use the inn as a home base, and I give her money from time to time. But what choice do I have?

"Only one of my kids ever gave me trouble," Alma said.

She had a matter-of-fact way of speaking that didn't invite questions. I questioned, nonetheless. She didn't have to answer, if she didn't want.

"What kind of trouble, dear?"

Alma looked down at her plate. "That was before Ed died. Ed was my husband. He was always hard on the kids. Made them act out, like they say. Anyway, Gary took a car that didn't belong to him."

"You mean, he stole it."

"Yes, but he was only fourteen. The slate was wiped clean when he turned eighteen."

I patted her arm. "That's nothing, dear. My sister's slate is white with chalk dust."

She sighed. "Okay, so maybe that's not all he did. But holding up that gas station was his girlfriend's idea. And Tiffany's the one who shot the clerk."

I will confess to an intermittent mean streak. "So, Mr. Dolby, can your daughter top that?"

"What can be worse than a daughter deserting her father?"

A father deserting his daughter, I said to myself. I still have not forgiven Papa for dying in that tunnel, squished between a milk tanker and a load of Adidas shoes. Neither has Susannah. Sometimes, however, I think my sister is more upset that the shoes weren't Nike than that Papa perished.

Alma reached for the ranch, full-fat salad dressing. "In what way has your daughter deserted you?" she asked.

Gordon Dolby stiffened. "Well, uh—"

"Go ahead, dear," I said with a smile of encouragement. "Mrs. Cornwater and I are both parents—so to speak. We will certainly understand."

Alma nodded, her glasses held snugly in place with an index finger.

"She wants to move out," he said, his voice barely a whisper.

"Please pass the ranch," someone at the other end of the table called in a loud voice.

"Will the farm do?" someone else said.

There was the expected twittering that, I'm proud to say, I ignored. The fact that I tossed the bottle down to the other end of the table was only partly due to the distance it had to travel.

"Is that really so bad?" I asked Gordon Dolby. Susannah has moved out several times, and each time I danced for joy. Believe me, that's saying a lot for a woman whose religion not only frowns on dancing, but forbids performing the sex act in a standing position, lest it lead to dancing.

"She's all that I have," he said to his plate.

Alma stabbed at her salad. "Where does she want to go?"

"Albuquerque."

"New Mexico?" I asked stupidly.

"That's the place. She's never been farther away from home than Washington, D.C., and now suddenly she wants to move to a foreign country. I don't suppose you could talk her out of it?"

"New Mexico is a state, dear," I said kindly. You'd be surprised how many people, even well-educated folks—i.e. my guests—are unsure on that score. Of course there is no excuse for such ignorance. I learned all forty-eight state capitals, and so can they. But, in their defense, naming a state after a neighboring country is a little confusing. And why, for crying out loud, are there two Dakotas? Why not, in the spirit of New Mexico, rename North Dakota and call it New Canada?

"Just the same," Gordon Dolby said, "a daughter's place is in the home. She's never been married, you know, and her mother's been dead since she was three. We're all each other has."

"Maybe she wants more," I said.

Alma nodded.

Somewhere in my youth or childhood, I must have done one thing really rotten. That might help to explain why Art Strump was laid up at the inn with a migraine headache, and I was traipsing up and down the narrow aisles of Pat's I.G.A. with the child Carlie glommed to my side. Well—maybe not literally, but close enough. I let her push the buggy (what we call shopping carts up this way) while I walked a few respectable, but wary paces ahead. The last thing I needed was to have the buggy sever the tendon to my heel.

"Do you have a last name?" I asked pleasantly.

"Davis. I'm supposed to be some kinda relation to Jefferson Davis."

"*The* Jefferson Davis? President of the Confederate States of America?"

She looked at me in surprise. "You know that kind of stuff?"

"I paid attention in school, dear."

"School! What a waste."

We were supposed to be looking for cooking sherry, something which made me extremely uncomfortable. We Mennonites do not drink alcoholic beverages of any kind. Even our communion drink is grape juice, sipped from thimble-size glasses. I know, the Bible says that Jesus turned the water into wine, but it doesn't mean he *didn't* go one step further and turn the wine into vinegar.

I studied the shelf of flavored oils and cooking sherries. The sherries were, by necessity, watered down. Thank heavens one can't buy full-strength drinking spirits in Pennsylvania supermarkets. One has to go to a state-run store for that. Still, there was the distinct possibility that generations of teetotaling ancestors would simultaneously turn over in their graves, sending the bottles of diluted sherry crashing down on us.

"Are you sure we can't use Welch's?"

She blew an enormous bubble, and then deftly popped it, without splattering any of it on her lips, like Susannah usually does.

"You don't know anything about cooking, do you?" she asked. "The alcohol burns off. It's only the flavor that's left."

"Then grape juice will do just fine," I said.

"Art said it has to be *dry*."

"Dry, shmy!" I lunged for the offending bottle, grabbed it between a thumb and forefinger, and practically flung it into the buggy. When nothing untoward happened, I breathed a huge sigh of relief.

Carlie laughed. "You're funny, ya know? But I wouldn'ta minded so much having a mama like you. Your daughter's lucky."

"I don't have a daughter, dear."

"Yes, you do. That tall, skinny woman, who looks

kinda like you, only she wears bedsheets instead of clothes.''

"Susannah? She's my sister, you little . . ." I bit my tongue. Carlie, at least, was young enough to be my daughter, and what kind of a mother replacement would I be if I resorted to four-letter words? No, I would save *brat* for the next time Susannah really made my angry.

"No kidding? She's your *sister*? Geez, she must be a lot older than I thought."

"Perhaps I'm a lot younger."

"Hunh?"

"Never mind. What else is on the list?" Although we were buying some of the nonperishables, this was basically a reconnaissance trip. The order in which the contestants would cook had yet to be established.

"Monkfish."

"You're pretty funny yourself, dear. Now tell me what it really says. I have better things to do than to risk the backs of my heels while I listen to stand-up comedy."

"You didn't have to come, ya know? I coulda done this by myself."

I turned. "You mean it really says that?"

She thrust the paper at me. It had been folded and refolded so many times that the ink had worn off the creases. It was more a case of connect the dots than actually reading the words. It may well have been monkfish, or money dish, or even monkey kiss.

"He says if you can't get that, then get red snapper."

"What size can does it say?"

Carlie snorted. "You really crack me up!"

I decided to take that as a compliment and headed toward the seafood section. There are stores in Pittsburgh with veritable glaciers piled high with marine produce, but Pat's I.G.A. does not even pretend to compete with those. In recent years, however, Pat has made a conscientious effort to cater to the tastes of urban refugees to Bedford from The Big Apple, The Crazy Orange, and points in between.

The man means well, but he is still in need of a little tutelage. The one live lobster Pat obtained, he kept in his son's freshwater guppy aquarium, where it promptly turned slime green and died. The next day Pat offered complimentary lobster salad on saltine crackers to his customers. I am happy to report that everyone survived.

"You seem to know something about cooking," I said. I truly meant it as a compliment.

"Yeah? Well, I learned it from Art. I wouldn't be nowhere, if it weren't for him."

"You mentioned your mother before. What about *her*?"

"What about her?"

"What I mean is, what do your parents think about—"

"Me living with a black man?"

"With any man," I said. "You're only eighteen. And you two aren't married, are you?"

"Who says I'm sleeping with Art?"

I stopped, and was nearly crippled by the buggy. Okay, so my cries of pain drew a small crowd, but I wasn't trying to attract attention, no matter what Pat claims. I most certainly did not intend to knock over a stack of canned peas taller than the Tower of Babel, and I refuse to pay for the dented cans. Grocery store owners who do not want to have merchandise rolling every which way but Sunday should not set up displays in the aisles. Who knows when the next Carlie is going to come along.

"Do you know what the Bible says about fornication, dear?"

Normally I would not take the liberty of speaking like that to a guest, but she was a mere child, and had expressed a preference for me over her birth mother.

"Ha! Just shows you how much you know. It ain't none of your business, but Art is gay!"

"Oh."

"So I suppose now you're going to preach to me about what the Bible has to say about that."

I told her everything Jesus had to say on the subject, which was nothing.

Ten

Marilyn Mitchell's
Tortilla Cake Surprise

◆

1 package 8-inch flour tortillas
1 15½ oz. can black beans
¾ cup chopped onion
¾ cup red and yellow pepper, chopped
¾ lb. sharp cheddar cheese, shredded
8 chicken tenderloins
taco seasoning to taste
2 16 oz. jars salsa
sour cream

Cook black beans, onions, peppers, and taco seasoning (to taste) in an uncovered sauce pan until most of the liquid has evaporated. Meanwhile, sprinkle chicken tenders with taco seasoning and sauté in a little oil until lightly brown and cooked through. To assemble the cake place one flour tortilla on a greased pie plate and spread with half of the bean mixture. Sprinkle with cheese. Place another tortilla on top and arrange four chicken tenders on it. Sprinkle with salsa. Repeat the process. Place one last tortilla on top and sprinkle with salsa and remaining cheese. Bake for 20 minutes at 350 degrees. Serve with extra salsa and sour cream.

Serves 8 *English,* or 4 Amish-Mennonites.

Eleven

Art was feeling better when we returned. In fact, he and Freni were have a tête-à-tête over tea when I walked in. I daresay they looked guilty, almost like they'd been enjoying themselves. Freni jumped up and immediately began directing the putting away of perishables. General Schwarzkopf would have been proud of her, the way she marshaled the troops, although I know from personal experience that the general is a far gentler person than my cousin.

Much to my astonishment, no one seemed to mind Freni's barked orders, or chiding clucks, when her instructions weren't followed exactly. By and large, our foray into town had been successful, and there was a festive, anticipatory feeling in the air. The contest was going to begin the next day, and by the end of the week, some lucky soul was going to walk away with one hundred thousand dollars.

I watched wide-eyed from the sidelines as Ms. Holt and Alma Cornwater shared a shelf of my ancient, and already crowded, refrigerator. They reminded me of little girls playing house. One of them even giggled.

It was too much to take when Freni *volunteered* to cart a load of seldom used pots and utensils down to the cellar so that my guests could have more room to set up their shiny, high-tech equipment. If I believed the kind of stories Derrick Simms prints in the *Na-*

tional Intruder, I would have concluded an alien had taken over Freni's body. On the off chance that Derrick and his ilk were on to something, I nabbed Freni when she emerged from the cellar and steered her through the kitchen and into the hallway. Then I closed the kitchen door on the shocking display of merriment.

"Okay, dear, what gives?"

Freni's faded blue eyes registered genuine confusion.

"Why are you being so nice, Freni? You'd rather dance naked at a barn raising than share your kitchen."

"Ach," Freni said, blushing, "how you talk!"

"Well, something's going on, dear. When Mose dropped you off this morning, you were as cranky as a cow that hadn't been milked all day."

Mose is Freni's husband of fifty years. After Papa died, Mose took over the farm chores, and even after I sold Papa's herd of dairy cows, Mose continued to work for me as a handyman. But even though, like Freni, Mose is a distant cousin, he is made from less sturdy stock, and has been plagued with a litany of minor illnesses. None of them have been life threatening, nor particularly costly, but they have prompted him into semiretirement. Now I only get to see him at milking time, or when he drops Freni off each morning and picks her up in the evenings with his horse and buggy.

Freni rubbed futilely at a jam spot on an otherwise immaculate apron. "*Some* people don't give me any reason to be cranky."

"You mean Art?"

"Ach, what a nice man that one is."

I was pleased to hear her say that. Freni, and I too for that matter, seldom get to meet members of other minority groups. When we do, they fall under the rich and famous category, which is not a barometer of anything resembling normal. One extremely rich and famous guest, who represents at least three minority groups in one person, was irate when I insisted that his pet llama be lodged in the barn along with my two remaining cows rather than share his bedroom.

"I'm glad you like Art," I said. I decided to show off. "I suppose he told you that the child is not his girlfriend."

"Yah."

"He did?"

"Yah. The man is a saint." As a deeply religious woman, Freni does not use that word loosely.

"So you don't disapprove?" Freni is not a Bible beater, but she does take it all literally. I couldn't imagine her not objecting to Art's sexual orientation.

"What's to disapprove of? He takes in runaway children—not little ones of course—whose parents won't take them back, and helps them get on their feet. He calls it Operation Lazarus, because many of these children would be dead if they didn't have someplace to go. If you ask me, Magdalena, the president should give him a medal."

"But he's just a cook!" I wailed. Frankly, Freni's beatification of Art made me jealous. I had been teaching Sunday school for eight years—let me assure you, Mennonite children are no angels—yet Freni had never suggested that I get a medal.

"He's a cook with a golden heart," Freni said. "Do you know what he wants to do with the prize money?"

"Erect a statue of himself?"

"For shame, Magdalena! That man wants to buy his own restaurant, so he can support a shelter for runaways like that sweet, innocent child he brought with him. I have half a mind to drop out of the contest, to make it easier for him to win."

I jiggled a pinkie in each ear to make sure they were working properly. "Then half a mind is all you have! *Sweet innocent* child, indeed! That girl has more holes in her head than a mosquito net, and her clothes barely cover the essentials. You are an Amish woman, for crying out loud—you're not supposed to approve of immodesty."

"And you're not supposed to judge, Magdalena."

"Fine! Have it your way. Worship Art Strump for all I care. But if he wins the contest, you'll be stuck with a daughter-in-law you can't stand."

Freni blanched. "Ach! Bite your tongue."

"Just last week you said she was as stubborn as a team of mules."

"Yah, but—"

"And barren as the Gobi Desert."

"The Sahara."

"Which, I believe, is even more barren than the Gobi. You're never going to have any cute grand-babies to cuddle, if Barbara stays in the picture."

"Ach, but divorce is wrong, Magdalena. Even if I win, and Barbara takes the money, my John can never remarry."

I knew it was wrong to egg her on, but I couldn't help myself. "So, which would you rather have, a barren Barbara right under your nose, or a barren Barbara two thousand miles away in Kansas?"

"Get behind me, Satan," Freni moaned, but I knew she was back in the contest.

The phone in my bedroom rang and I sprinted to get it. It is a private line, and I give the number out to only a select few. I happened to be expecting a very important call.

"Babs?" I asked breathlessly.

"Yeah, right, Yoder. Like you ever get a call from her."

"Melvin?"

"In the flesh," he said, "but since this is official police business, I suggest you call me Officer Stoltzfus. No, make that Chief Stoltzfus."

"In your dreams, dear."

He said a few words his Mennonite mama would not have approved of, and then got down to business.

"How long is that bunch staying at your place?"

"Through Saturday. Why?"

"Just what sort of bunch are they?"

"They're circus performers," I said, without missing a beat. "Acrobats from Taiwan."

"No kidding? Mr. Anderson too?"

"Cut to the chase, Melvin."

"I just got a call from Dr. Rosenkrantz."

"And?"

"I was right, Mr. Anderson did have food poisoning."

"I know, dear, and it was a very mild case. His real problem was dehydration."

"Who told you?"

"We have our sources. Did the doctor tell you what caused the poisoning?"

Melvin, assuming as usual, fell right into my trap. "All right, so it was probably the burgers he and Susannah had at Desperate Joe's."

"So it wasn't Freni's bread pudding?" I said, gloating.

"Speaking of Susannah, is she there?"

"Was it?" I demanded.

"Okay, so maybe I jumped the gun a little. Is she there?"

"Actually, I haven't seen her since lunch. Can I give her a message?"

"What's the real story about your sister and this Mr. Anderson?"

"There is no story, dear. She was just showing him around the area, like she said."

"But up on Stucky Ridge?"

"You know Susannah—she's a free spirit. You also know that she is, for some inexplicable reason, deeply in love with you."

"Are you certain?"

"To the extent that it makes me nauseated."

He said nothing for a full minute. During this time I could hear his antennae click against the receiver. Okay, so it may have been his fingernails, but you can't prove that it was.

Finally he sighed. "She likes to flirt a lot, doesn't she?"

"That's who she is."

"But you're not like that. Don't get me wrong, Yoder, but you're so sensible, and she—well, like you said—is a free spirit. It doesn't seem possible that the two of you could be sisters."

"Thank you," I said. I meant it. "I remember the day Susannah was born—we're sisters all right. But there are eleven years between us. It may as well be the Grand Canyon. Unless there's a major earthquake—and I'm speaking metaphorically—that gap is never going to close. Still, where there's life, there's hope."

"There has never been a major earthquake in Bedford County," Melvin said sarcastically, "so don't hold your breath."

"I said I was speaking metaphorically, you nincompoop!"

"That's chief!"

"Chief nincompoop!" I slammed the receiver down. Then—and I'll never know why—I burst into tears.

Allow me to assure you that I wasn't always a cry-baby. As a little girl, I practically never cried. As a young woman, my eyes were dry as cotton balls. Even when Mama and Papa died, I only cried once, and that was at the cemetery. Tears are useful only for getting dirt out of one's eyes, or so I used to think. But more and more lately, I find my eyes welling up, and after those rare occasions when I don't fight back the tears, I actually feel better.

I was feeling fine by supper. A little soap and warm water, and I was almost as good as new. I would have been totally squared away if Susannah had shown up.

"Does your sister have a job?"

I turned and smiled pleasantly at Ms. Kimberly McManus Holt, who was sitting at my left. She was wearing a beige cashmere sweater dress and a discreet amount of gold jewelry. While I eschew snobs, and wasn't particularly fond of Ms. Holt, I am honest enough to admit that I much preferred her attire at my table than the jeans and denim jacket Alma Cornwater was wearing.

"My sister is self-employed," I said. It isn't a lie. Susannah's job, as far as I'm concerned, is to stay out of my hair as much as possible.

"Oh?" Mr. Holt arched her perfectly plucked brows. "Is she an artist?"

I don't know why people have to assume that Susannah is an artist just because she dresses like a curtain rod. So much for assumptions. Susannah couldn't draw water from an overflowing well, much less a straight line. Yes, I know, one doesn't need to have technical skills to succeed as an artist these days, but talent should count for something.

This may surprise you, but I am actually quite good with both a sketch pad and an easel. Miss Enz, my fourth-grade teacher, said I had the potential to be a professional artist. Mama, my fourth-grade parent, said that professional artists, like actors, were talent scouts for the Devil. Mama never once hung my school paintings on the refrigerator, although when Susannah came along, our kitchen was turned into the Louvre.

"My sister is an entertainer," I said barely able to keep the rancor out of my voice.

Miss Holt's nose wrinkled, puckering a few of the faint freckles. "What *sort* of entertainer?"

Before I could answer, George Mitchell tapped on his water glass. All eyes, including Ms. Holt's, turned to him.

"Ladies, gentleman—may I have your attention? You are all aware that Mr. James Anderson, vice president in charge of acquisitions at East Coast Delicacies, and contest judge, was hospitalized this morning due to a mild case of food poisoning—"

"Which he did *not* get here!" I interjected.

George Mitchell smiled. "Yes, apparently you folks would do well to avoid Desperate Joe's over in Bedford, unless you're really serious about losing weight."

Sycophants that they were, everyone chuckled, including the rail-thin Marge Benedict.

"I'm glad to report, however, that Mr. Anderson is doing fine. The doctor says he can probably be released sometime tomorrow. But I don't think he's going to be up to judging a food contest any time soon."

More laughter, this time nervous.

George Mitchell held up a shushing hand. "Not to fear, though, because I have found a capable replacement."

There was a brief, excited buzz. I smiled, waiting for my moment of glory.

"Miss Yoder here"—George Mitchell nodded at

me—"has graciously agreed to take Mr. Anderson's place."

There was a shocked silence, followed by several gasps.

"That's not fair!"

I turned and looked at Kimberly McManus Holt. Now she was shaking like the paint mixer at Home Depot.

Twelve

"It wasn't my idea, dear. Mr. Mitchell asked me to fill in."

"Miss Yoder's right. I take full responsibility for the idea, and I think it's a fine one."

"But Mrs. Hostetler is her aunt, or something," Ms. Holt said through clenched teeth.

"She's my cousin, dear. Actually, she's my mother's double first cousin, once removed, and my father's second cousin twice removed, or is it the other way around? Anyway, we Amish and Mennonites have such tangled bloodlines that I am, in fact, my own cousin. If I want to have a family picnic, all I need is a sandwich."

Mr. Mitchell was the only one to laugh.

"That's my point exactly," Ms. Holt huffed. "She's a close relative, and can't possibly be impartial."

That hiked my hackles. "I can be as impartial as a Supreme Court justice," I snapped. "And for your information, dear, just because I'm related to the woman doesn't mean I like her."

"Ach!" Freni, who was just backing into the room, carrying a large tureen of stew, nearly had conniptions. For a moment I was afraid my hardwood floor was going to get drenched with beef gravy.

"Miss Yoder is explaining why she would make an impartial judge," Mr. Mitchell said quickly.

Freni's face lit up like a jar full of lightning bugs. *"Magdalena?"*

"You rang?" I joked pleasantly.

"Yah, Magdalena is always fair. And who should know better than the woman who has been a second mother to her all these years." Freni looked like the cat that licked the cream, *and* followed it with a mouse chaser.

"You see what I mean?" Ms. Holt cried indignantly.

"She's right," Gladys said.

The twinkle was gone from George Mitchell's eyes. "This is my contest, and I will choose whomever I damn well please to judge it. Anyone who has a problem with that can drop out now."

I forbid swearing on my premises, and usually take any such offenders to task, but that evening I prudently bit my tongue. The guests bit their tongues for other reasons—one hundred thousand reasons, to be exact.

"Then it's settled?" George Mitchell looked at each contestant in turn.

One by one, they nodded mutely.

Freni, however, shamefully continued to gloat. I was going to have to take her aside and tell her that gloating did her cause no good. It might even prejudice me against her.

I try and give credit where credit is due. Ms. Holt, I am obliged to say, was no dummy. She was able to switch sides like a governor who has seen the political light.

"Did I say how charming I find your inn, Miss Yoder?"

"Not to my face, dear."

She smiled, revealing a mouth full of sparkling caps. "Last year, when I took my cooking show on the road, we did a segment from an inn just like this. Only it was in Vermont. You know"—she paused and pretended to be thinking—"this would be a perfect location for one of my shows. Maybe even two or three. What would you say to that?"

"I'd say you have more chutzpah than the man who killed his parents, and then threw himself upon the mercy of the court because he was an orphan."

"I beg your pardon!"

"Chutzpah, dear. It means nerve. Unmitigated gall." Thanks to Babs, I knew almost as much Yiddish as I did Pennsylvania Dutch.

"I know what it means," she hissed, and then catching herself, gave me another glimpse of her caps. "Of course I understand that yours is a very popular inn, and hosting a cooking show might be a trifle inconvenient."

"Pun intended?"

She chuckled and waved a dismissive hand. From that moment on, I knew I had the upper hand.

Susannah slid into her seat, breathless as usual, and mumbled something about a defective alarm clock. I gave her an obligatory frown, and then prayed for the grace to forgive and, above all, forget. My prayer worked, and the rest of the meal would have progressed without incident had not Carlie found something unusual in her stew.

"Hey, everybody!" she shouted, startling us all. "I found a diamond!"

"I don't think so, dear," I said kindly. Her outburst had caused me to drop my fork, and I had gravy splattered on a relatively new dress.

"But I did!" Carlie held up an object the size of a lima bean. Despite the gravy that dripped off it, I could see that it sparkled.

"Pass that down, dear, will you?"

Her fist closed around it. "No way! Finders keepers, losers weepers."

"This is my inn," I said sternly, "whatever you find here belongs to me." Frankly, I didn't really think she'd found a diamond in Freni's stew, but in a Pittsburgh restaurant, I once found a glass eye in a bowl of bouillabaisse.

"I ain't passing nothing," Carlie said.

I glared at the impudent child.

"Pass it," Art said. He was sitting across from his ward.

Carlie glared back at me, but made no move to give up her treasure.

Thanks to Susannah, who was watching the proceedings with some amusement, I knew how to handle Carlie's type. I stood up and put my fists on my hips.

"Pass it, toots, or you're out of here."

Art could tell I meant business. "Carlie, do as Miss Yoder asked, and do it *now*!"

"Ah shit! Why does everyone get to boss me around? It ain't fair, you know. It's my diamond 'cause I found it."

"Maybe Miss Yoder will give you a reward."

Carlie stuck a ring-studded tongue out at me, but dropped the object in Art's extended hand.

He bravely polished it with his napkin. "Why, it isn't a diamond at all. It's just a piece of glass."

"No way! Let me see!" Carlie lunged across the table and snatched the object in question from her mentor's hand.

"Well?" I said, tapping my foot.

"Aw, shit! It is glass! Man, I could have cut myself on this sucker. I could have split my tongue wide open."

"How would you even know the difference?" I demanded.

Ms. Holt condescended to snicker.

I glared at her. Then I pointed a long, bony finger at Carlie.

"Now you go straight to your room, young lady."

Carlie's eyes widened. "You mean *me*?"

"I don't allow swearing in my establishment. It says so clearly on the back of every bedroom door."

"But I'm staying in the f—well, you know—cellar!"

"Just the same, I've made it very clear. So stop arguing and go to your room—I mean, cellar."

"Man, that's not fair. That's discrimination or something. *He* swears and gets away with it." She pointed a black-lacquered nail at the dapper Mr. Mitchell.

George Mitchell's eyes were twinkling like the lights of Philadelphia on a clear summer night. He seemed to be enjoying the show as much as Susannah.

In the interest of fairness, I glared at him.

"Now scoot," I said to Carlie, "and make it fast if you know what's good for you."

In desperation, Carlie turned to my sister. "She ain't serious, is she?"

Susannah nodded solemnly. "She'll tan your hide."

Carlie scooted, but made a point of slamming the kitchen door behind her. She was, after all, just a child.

We had barely gotten back into the buzz of conversation when George Mitchell tapped on his water glass again. "Ladies, gentlemen—the time has come for another announcement. But first, we need Mrs. Hostetler."

That very second the kitchen door swung open and Freni flounced in, wiping her hands on her apron. To the others she may have been the picture of innocence, but I knew without a shadow of a doubt that she had been holding an empty water glass between her ear and the door.

George Mitchell smiled warmly at Freni before clearing his throat. "It is my pleasure to announce the order in which you will be presenting your efforts to the judges."

The CEO of E.C.D. was anything if not a skilled manipulator. During his dramatic pause the national debt was paid off, peace came to the Middle East, and Michael Jackson grew a beard. Of less consequence, but somewhat closer to home, Ms. Holt gasped softly and then dabbed at the corners of her mouth with a napkin, Gladys Dolby's fork hand began to tremble, Art shifted nervously in his seat, Alma Cornwater shoved her glasses up in yet another futile effort to keep them in place, and Freni frowned.

I confess that I hadn't given the contest dynamics much thought. Now it occurred to me that some of the contestants might prefer specific time slots. A very nervous cook might, for instance, prefer to get his or her stint over with the first night. An extremely confident person might wish to wow us all at the last supper with the spectacular finale.

"The contestants, in the order in which they will cook are"—he paused wickedly again—"Mrs. Alma Cornwater, Ms. Gladys Dolby, Mr. Arthur Strump, Ms. Kimberly McManus Holt, and last, but not least, Mrs. Freni Hostetler."

I would have expected Alma Cornwater to sigh with relief, or Freni to flare with frustration, but that was not the case. The five contestants were as inscrutable as the iguana Susannah briefly had as a pet (this was before Shnookums, and the lizard did not take to being carried around in a bra). Not an eye batted, not a lip twitched.

"Well, isn't that nice," I said finally, just to get the ball rolling again.

Freni was the first to crack. "Ach," she said, looking

at me, "the *last* day? Is this some kind of punishment, Magdalena?"

"Of course not, dear." I turned to George Mitchell for confirmation.

"It was a random drawing from an actual hat," he said. "The lovely Miss Benedict selected the names back at headquarters."

Marge Benedict favored us with the thin-lipped smile and a slight rolling of the eyes.

Art sat back and crossed his arms. "Just like I said yesterday, Mrs. Hostetler has an unfair advantage. Y'all tasted her bread pudding first, and it's the last thing you'll taste. If you ask me, she should be disqualified."

"Ach!" Freni squawked. Perhaps the noble Art seemed a little less so.

"Mr. Strump has a good point," Gladys said in her soft little girl voice. "Couldn't Mrs. Hostetler trade with one of us?"

"What if the order was reversed?" Ms. Holt asked. Personally, I thought it was a remarkably sensible suggestion.

Alma Cornwater came alive for the first time that evening. "Y'all are being ridiculous. Where I come from, we treat our elders with respect. So, she inadvertently served us her bread pudding before the contest began. So what?"

Freni nodded vigorously. "Yah!"

But Alma wasn't through. "It could just as easily backfire, you know. Maybe the judges' taste buds will be in the mood for something else."

"Ach! I thought you were my friend."

Alma removed her heavy glasses and massaged the bridge of her nose. "I am. I just want them to know that it doesn't really matter who goes when."

"Ha," Ms. Holt said. "A likely story. Maybe *you* just don't want to go last."

I stood up. "Well, it's a moot point, isn't it? The bottom line is that this is Mr. Mitchell's contest. He sets the rules. And while I plan to be as impartial as Solomon, a cooking contest can never really be fair. It's not like grading a math problem where there's only one right answer. Besides, life isn't fair. At least four of you are just going to have to accept that."

"Well spoken!" George Mitchell's eyes were twinkling like the Milky Way.

Freni and I were wiping down the counters, the dishes dried and put away, when someone knocked on the door. It was past time for Mose to collect Freni, but Mose doesn't knock.

"Who is it?" I called.

"It's me, Jonathan Hostetler."

"Ach!" Freni practically flew to the door.

Jonathan Hostetler is six feet two inches tall, a good foot taller than his mother, but they share the same beaky features. He is an intensely shy man, and has only graced my kitchen on a handful of occasions. Something clearly out of the ordinary had transpired.

"Where's your papa?" Freni demanded.

"At home," Jonathan mumbled, at the same time looking around the kitchen as if it were the inside of a spaceship.

"Why at home?"

"I think Papa has the flu."

"Ach!" Freni's plump little hands flew to her face. She and Mose may not be the most demonstrative of couples, but their affection for each other is genuine. When Freni had an emergency appendectomy five years ago, Mose was beside himself with concern. During her recovery time in the hospital he had a cot placed in her private room, and stayed with her until she was released. The staff at Bedford County Hospital couldn't get over how devoted the tall, bearded Amish man was to his wife.

"He just has stomach problems, Mama. No fever. He sent me over to do the milking and bring you home."

Freni whirled. "Magdalena, are you up to milking?"

What choice did I have? Betsy and Matilda, my two Holstein cows, have to be milked morning and evening without fail. If not, they will experience significant pain. Imagine, if you will, drinking a two-liter bottle of soda in the morning, not voiding during the day, and then having someone punch you in the groin just before bedtime.

"Sure, I'll milk," I said. I don't mind milking, my head resting against their warm bodies—it's the long cold trek to the barn I detest.

"Thank you," Jonathan said. "Don't worry, I'll do it tomorrow morning, if Papa's not better."

Freni, bless her heart, was already out the door.

"You've got your own chores, Jonathan. If your folks aren't here by six-thirty, then I'll just assume your papa's still under the weather, and your mama's stayed home to take care of him. But not to worry. I can manage just fine until he's back on his feet."

Jonathan thanked me profusely, and followed his mother out into the cold.

But milking two cows and cooking for an inn full of guests was easier said than done. And since even saints grumble from time to time, I may have been doing a little of that when Mr. Mitchell popped into the kitchen.

"Any refills on coffee?" he asked.

Why the English consume caffeine just before bedtime is beyond me, but it is not my place to judge.

"The kitchen is closed, dear," I said politely. "You want to mess up the internal clock the good Lord gave you? Fine, then you're going to have to drive all the way into Bedford. Just stay away from Desperate Joe's."

Mr. Mitchell laughed so hard, I looked around to see if Joan Rivers had popped in for a visit. Alas, Joan and her wonder dog, Spike, were nowhere to be seen.

"Well, I fail to see what's so funny. Now, if you'll excuse me, my cows need milking."

"*You* can actually milk a cow?"

"They can't milk themselves, dear." Although I'd recently heard a rumor that the Japanese were breeding a strain of self-milking cows.

"Do you mind if I tag along and watch? I've never seen it done before. Only in the movies and on TV."

"The more the merrier."

Mr. Mitchell cleared his throat. "Well, would it be possible for me to give you a hand?"

"You want to milk?"

He nodded, his eyes dancing up a storm.

"We'll see," I said. "The truth is, Matilda's shy around strangers and doesn't let her milk down, and Betsey is, well, on the ticklish side. She's liable to slap you in the face with her tail."

But Matilda was charmed by the CEO of E.C.D. In fact, she was downright coquettish. As for Betsey, she fell into a relaxed trance and rumbled like a cement truck, which is the cow equivalent of purring. Both bovines gave a record amount of milk.

"Good heavens," I said, "it's like you had them under a spell."

Twinkling George help up his hands. "It's all in the fingers. Before I went into the food business, I was a chiropractor. If you need an adjustment, I'd be happy to oblige."

"Ach!" No doubt I felt as flustered as Freni when she caught Kevin Costner sunbathing in the nude, and there wasn't a wolf in sight. Now here I was, at night, alone in a barn with a handsome man who had twinkling blue eyes and magic fingers—it was a sin just to think about it.

"I mean it. A little manipulation here and there and—"

"Get behind me, Satan!"

I sloshed the milk in the cooler, and all but ran from the barn. In my haste to escape the temptations of the flesh, I tripped on the piece of old barn siding that I use to prop the barn door open. Fortunately I didn't cut myself on the bent-over nail I've been meaning to remove. I don't enjoy telling on myself, but fear I must, in the interest of truth.

According to George Mitchell, I went sailing out into the yard like a Frisbee, before landing facedown in a cow patty. Fortunately it was an old patty, and a dry as Freni's meat loaf. And fortunately I didn't break my bones or chip any teeth. But it was as undignified an exit as I can imagine.

"Gosh, darn it!" That's as bad as I can swear.

George Mitchell nearly died laughing.

Thirteen

I don't watch television. The good Lord created books before he created TV, and that says it all. Okay, so upon occasion I have been known to watch reruns of *Green Acres* on Susannah's little black-and-white set—but nothing else! Until they started airing quality shows like that again, I refuse to patronize the idiot box.

My guests don't get to watch TV either. This seems to matter only the first day or two. After that they settle into the pace of country living and enjoy the simple pleasures. During the day there are scenic drives, peaceful walks, games of horseshoes and badminton, and of course reading. Summer evenings usually find my guests rocking on the front porch, engaged in mindless conversation, while winter evenings will find them crowded around the fireplace, dishing dirt on those few folks who are even more rich and famous than they.

For those who like to run in the fast lane, I keep the parlor stocked with dominoes, jigsaw puzzles, and even a game of Sorry. In the dining room there is a large wooden frame, upon which one will always find an unfinished quilt. My guests are encouraged to add their stitches to this project, although they are never allowed to keep their handiwork. Late at night, after a quilt has been completed, I replace it with another still in progress. I then sell the finished quilts to a tourist shop in Lancaster. It is a perfect setup. My guests get to work their neuroses out with a needle and thread, and I get to pocket the moolah.

At any rate, after I had cleaned up from my post-milking fiasco, I wandered into the dining room to see if anyone was quilting, and much to my surprise found both the Dolbys. I am all for women's lib, mind you—after all, a hunch from a woman is worth two facts from a man—but I can seldom get a man to sit down and try his hand at quilting. Nevertheless, Bruce Willis does a mean slip stitch, Sly has an eye for color, and Tim Allen is great at tying knots.

"Well, good for you," I said with an encouraging smile.

Gordon Dolby didn't even bother to look up. Perhaps he was embarrassed.

"I learned to sew in the air force," he said. "They teach you to be prepared for anything."

"This is very relaxing," Gladys said. "How am I doing?"

I made the mistake of looking at her stitches. Early tomorrow morning, when everyone was asleep, I was going to have to sneak into my own dining room, rip out Gladys's stitches, and redo them.

"A drunken one-eyed hen could leave straighter tracks than that," I said kindly.

Gladys bit her lip. Perhaps I had gone too far.

"Not everyone has the same talent, dear. You're a great cook, or you wouldn't be here. I, on the other hand, couldn't boil water without a detailed recipe."

She let go of her lip, but refused to smile. "I wouldn't call myself a *great* cook, but I'm okay. At least Mr. Anderson thought so."

"Don't be so modest, dear, you're not even a Mennonite. Tell your daughter, she's a great cook," I directed Gordon.

He grunted.

"Daddy's the real cook in the family," she whispered. "In fact, I'm using one of his recipes."

"Is that so? I thought the recipes had to be original."

"Oh, they do. That is—they can't have been published anywhere. But Daddy's recipes are mostly original."

"Where'd you learn to cook, Mr. Dolby? The army."

"The air force!" he barked.

"Daddy does everything well."

"Well, *he's* not the one who entered East Coast Delicacies hundred-thousand-dollar contest," I said.

She glanced at her father and, finding him engrossed in his work, smiled up at me. "Do you think I have a chance to win?"

I shrugged. "How should I know? I haven't had a chance to taste your cooking. But Mr. Anderson seemed to think so."

"I want it more than anything I've ever wanted in my life," she mouthed. "I want it so bad I can taste it."

I know that's what she said, because I can read lips. Grandma Yoder, in her later years, was as deaf as stone. More often than not, she forgot to actually say her words, and just formed them with her mouth. Well, that's what Mama said—although I think the old lady was just being cantankerous. Grandma too. At any rate, I learned to read Grandma like my first-grade primer. It was either that or get whacked on the behind with a wooden carpet beater.

"Then maybe you'll win," I mouthed back.

If only I'd learn to keep my big mouth shut.

*   *   *

There are times when I'd do well to keep my ears shut too. It wasn't my fault that I just happened to be upstairs stocking the linen closet. It was Mr. Mitchell's fault. His precious E.C.D. was too cheap to pay extra for A.L.P.O. That meant that yours truly had to tote clean towels up from the laundry room.

"Couldn't we just share it?" Alma was saying. I couldn't see the woman, but she had an unmistakable southern accent.

"Don't be ridiculous!" The nasal Boston tones weren't that hard to place either.

The linen closet is at the short end of an L at the top of the stairs. The voices were coming from the long end. Since wallboard tends to muffle sounds, I had to listen carefully.

"What's so ridiculous about that? We both need it, don't we?"

"For your information, I don't need anything. I have my own cooking show, remember?"

"That's a laugh. From what I hear, your ratings are in the toilet. Your show could be canceled any day."

"That's my business."

"Well fine, then, have it your way. But half of nothing is still nothing."

"We'll see about that."

A door slammed, and I prudently stepped into the closet and closed the door. From the sound of the footsteps going past me, Alma Cornwater was one unhappy camper.

Trust me on this one, the only fate really worse than death is sharing a bed with Susannah Yoder Entwhistle. It's bad enough that my sister's snores can wake the dead two counties over, but she thrashes like a combine. A sleeping Susannah, tied to the front of a tractor, could harvest a wheat field the size of Montana in one night. I put on two long-sleeved, ankle-length plaid flannel nighties and a red woolen ski mask to keep me from bodily injury. What I completely forgot about was Shnookums's predilection for wandering, once released from the confines of Susannah's bra. In theory, the dog sleeps on the floor at the foot of his mistress's bed and disturbs her only when it is necessary to use the great outdoors. This was real life, however, not theory.

In real life my sister sleeps too soundly to be disturbed by a runt with a peanut-size bladder. But were she a light sleeper, she would not bother to get out of bed. Susannah solves the potty problem by buying Huggies intended for newborns, cutting them in half, and taping these dinky diapers around her dog's derriere. It's no wonder the mutt is always in such a foul mood.

I awoke in the middle of the night to find the tiny terror perched on my chest, his teeth clamped to the bottom edge of the ski mask. He had the audacity to be growling, and each pathetic snarl sent noxious waves of decaying horse flesh straight to my nostrils.

"Susannah!" It is no easy feat to scream through gritted teeth.

Susannah snorted and rolled over. Shnookums, however, growled louder and shook his Lilliputian head in a futile attempt to unmask me.

"Let go, you filthy rat, or I'll feed you to the first cat I find." I knew better than to lay a hand on the beast. I value all ten sets of fingerprints.

"Susannah! Wake up!"

Susannah mumbled something about it having been good for her too. The repugnant pooch was not nearly as complimentary. He snarled one more time, and then with an audible grunt passed gas so foul that it put anything Aaron did to shame.

I sat up, the dog dangling from my chin, his beady little eyes staring up at me definitely. "You beast!" I screamed.

This time it was an openmouthed scream, and Susannah woke up. The second her eyes fluttered open, that minuscule mongrel on my mask let out a yowl intended to break a mother's heart. Fortunately, in doing so, he fell loose from the mask and landed on my lap.

"Magdalena, how could you?" Susannah shrieked. She scooped her cunning canine into her arms and rocked him like a baby.

But I was through being abused by a dog in diapers. "How could I *what*? You're the one who won't let him out to do his number one."

Susannah howled, shocking Shnookums first into whimpers, then silence. "*Number one?* You're forty-six years old, for crying out loud. Can't you even say the word *pee*?"

"I have a right not to be vulgar."

"There's nothing vulgar about the word *pee,* Magdalena."

I turned on my right side, my back toward my sister. "Take that animal outside and let him urinate," I said.

More howls, and a few yowls as well.

"Take him out *now,* dear, or you can spend the rest of the night sleeping on the floor in the parlor." Heeding the wisdom of my grandmothers, I do not have a sofa on the premises.

"Okay, okay, don't get your panties in a bunch."

"Susannah!"

My sister is a slow learner, but stops just short of being incorrigible. Protesting loudly—I'm sure at least some of the guests heard her—she heaved herself out of bed and stomped out of the room, slamming my bedroom door behind her. Believe me, a huge part of me wanted to chase after my sister and force her to repeat her exit, this time without the melodrama. But what was the point? A proper attitude was the water to which my equine sister could be led, but not made to drink.

I pretended to be asleep when she came back in, for all the good it did me.

"Magdalena?"

Silence.

"Magdalena. I know you're still awake. I can tell by the way you're breathing. Your mouth's not open wide enough."

"Thanks."

"Hey, you're not still mad at me, are you?"

"Of course, dear. What makes you think anything has changed?"

"But I'm not still mad at you."

"At *me*? That's because you have no reason—never mind, Susannah. Just go to sleep and leave me alone. Did that ferocious fur ball do his business?"

She giggled. "You're a hoot, Mags, you know that? Mama would have been so proud of you."

I sat up. "Of me? You're the one she doted on."

"Ha, that's a laugh."

"What do you mean? Everyone could tell she liked you best."

"Get real, Mags. I once heard her tell Papa that I was the bane of her existence. Her 'cross to bear,' " she said.

"But that's impossible. She bent over backward for you. Mama let you get away with things that I never, in my wildest dreams, imagined possible."

"Oh, Mags, you don't have a clue, do you?"

"What's that supposed to mean? I'm not blind, for

Pete's sake. I watched you wear pants and paint your nails, and before I could catch my breath, Mama was doing the very same thing."

"Mama never painted her nails, Mags."

"But she wore pants and cut her hair!" To a conservative Mennonite, like Mama, that was akin to a Methodist dancing naked in Times Square in the middle of rush hour.

"You *are* clueless. Mama had to do those things!"

"Mama *had* to dress like a harlot and make a fool of herself in front of the entire community? Who forced her? Papa?"

"No! I did."

"You?"

"Yes, me. It's all about the birth order, Mags, don't you ever read?"

This from a woman who needs help with the hard words on her cereal box? "You're absolutely right, Susannah. I don't have a clue on what goes on in that pumpkin head of yours. Next time I want sense from you, I'll ask for pennies."

"Not even funny, Mags. I do read, you know. I read this book on birth order, and it explained everything. You want to hear what it said, or not?"

"Enlighten me, O wise one."

"I'll ignore that, Mags, because I know you're tired and just being your usual cranky self. Anyway, this book said that firstborn children—that's you, Mags— tend to be like their parents. You know, conservative, concerned about appearances, that sort of thing. While later-born children, especially youngest children— that's me, of course—tend to rebel. Independent thinkers, it called us."

"Are you sure it didn't say 'original thinkers'? Because that's the biggest load of *huafa mischt* I've ever heard."

"You swore!" Susannah sang out gleefully.

"I did not!"

"You said horse—"

"Manure! And anyway, Mama was not the youngest child in her family."

"Urrrgh! Sometimes I think you're denser than Melvin."

"You take that back!"

"What you don't get is that Mama was trying to save me."

"Your soul?"

"That too, I suppose. But Mama knew I was a troublemaker, and she tried to get close to me by acting like me. Not the really bad stuff I did, of course, but the smaller stuff. The stuff that really isn't important—like how you look."

"Did it work?"

Susannah was silent for a minute. "Judge for yourself," she said in a small, strangled voice.

"Aw, Susannah, you're not so bad."

She choked back a sob. "I'm not? Funny you should say that. You think I'm the Whore of Babylon."

"I most certainly do not!"

"Get off it, Mags. You've called me that plenty of times. Anyway, that's not the point"—she blew her nose, presumably on her half of the sheet—"where were we? How did we get started on this? Oh, yeah—you said Mama liked me best. But that's not true at all. You were just like her. She was so proud of the way you turned out that she almost burst. That's what she told all her friends. She said it was a sin how proud she felt."

I was stunned. "*Really?*"

"You better believe it! And Papa too. But not me, of course. I hated you, Mags, you know that?"

"Because Mama and Papa were proud of me?"

"Oh, yeah. When they died, I wished it was you who was in that tunnel, squished to death between a truck full of turkeys and a tanker of maple syrup."

"That was running shoes and milk, dear. Anyway, how do you feel about me now?"

I could sense her eyes rolling in the dark. "Don't expect me to get all mushy, Mags, and say something corny like I love you. But if you must know, I'm kinda glad you're around."

"Ditto."

I slept sounder that night than I had since Aaron left—although actually, since Aaron's amorousness knew no bounds, that wasn't a fair comparison. Let's just say I had one of my best nights ever, but even that was hardly enough to prepare me for what the morning brought.

Fourteen

On the Magdalena Scale of Horrors, waking up to a ringing phone in the middle of the night ranks just below sharing a bed with Susannah. The next step down is to have someone shake you out of a sound sleep.

"Stop it, Aaron! How many times is enough?"

"Miss Yoder!"

"Aaron, you don't need to be so formal. After all—"

"Magdalena! Wake up! Please wake up. I have something important to tell you."

It had all been a bad dream. There was no spouse stashed up in Minnesota. I wasn't an adulteress after all. I could hold my head as high as anyone, and given the fact that I am five feet ten, I could even hold it higher than most folks. I threw my arms joyously around my Pooky Bear.

"Ach!"

I opened my eyes, only to find myself gazing into the terrified eyes of Jonathan Hostetler.

"Jonathan! What on earth are you doing?"

"*Me*?" he croaked.

I released Jonathan's neck and scooted back under my covers. I may have been sleeping in two long-sleeved, ankle-length flannel nightgowns, but—and this is for your ears only—underneath them, I was as naked as a baby jaybird. Besides, the nightgowns I was wearing that morning were a provacative pink.

"Jonathan, what's wrong? Is it Mose? Is your father worse?"

"Papa's feeling better. A little bit. But my Rachel—ach, that can wait. It's the man in the barn."

"What man? And whose barn?"

"There's an Englishman in your barn, Miss Yoder!"

Jonathan is only a year or two younger than I, and we've known each other all our lives, but out of some weird deference to the fact that I employ his parents, he insists on calling me Miss Yoder—unless, of course, he's absolutely desperate to get my attention.

"The barn is not off limits to guests, Jonathan. Well—to smokers, yes, but then again, the whole place is off limits to them."

"Ach! This man isn't smoking. It's much worse than that."

"*That's* off limits too. Who is he, and who is the woman with him?"

"No woman, Miss Yoder. He's by himself."

"That's even worse," I cried, sitting back up, and thereby exposing some of my alluring flannel.

"Magdalena!" Jonathan was waving his long, knobby arms, like a conductor trying to flag down a through train.

"Well, spit it out, Jonathan, I don't have all day."

"I think the man is dead."

"*Dead*?" As familiar as that word was becoming, it never failed to raise the short hairs on the back of my neck, and the down on my cheeks.

Jonathan nodded victoriously, his grim news finally delivered. "Yah, dead. Maybe very dead."

"*Very* dead?" Now that was a new one.

"He was kicked in the head, I think. It is a terrible sight." At the moment Jonathan wasn't a very pretty sight either. His face was the color of an uncooked asparagus stem.

"I'll call 911," I said. "You go in the bathroom and throw up. Remember to lift the lid, dear. Then when you're done, go back and get your mama."

I made the call, and then reluctantly called Melvin Stoltzfus, our chief of police.

I found George Mitchell lying facedown in Matilda's stall, beside an overturned milk bucket. Matilda, bless her shy hide, was pressed against the far side of the enclosure stall, her head turned into the corner. Her long tasseled tail, which she twitches when she's nervous, was thumping regularly against the wooden slats behind her.

"Mr. Mitchell," I called softly.

There was no answer.

"Mr. Mitchell!"

I made the mistake of turning him over. The left side of the man's face was depressed, like an angel food cake upon which a can of peas has been dropped. His left eye was either missing or had been altered to the point that it was no longer recognizable. There had been a great deal of blood, and bits of straw clung to thickening ooze.

There is no point in lying, so I will confess that I too threw up. But I had regained some, if not most, of my composure by the time the paramedics showed. I was perfectly rational and in charge of all my faculties a few minutes later when Melvin arrived on the scene.

The paramedics, God bless them one and all, pronounced George Mitchell dead. Melvin seemed to have no quarrel with that.

"Take him to the county morgue," he directed. "I'll get the necessary information from Miss Yoder here."

Now, I'm not blaming the Bedford County paramedics for heeding an order from Hernia's chief of
police. They're trained to save lives, not investigate
suspicious deaths. It was Melvin who should have
known better.

I couldn't believe it when a pair of paramedics
picked up poor George Mitchell's inert body and
plopped it on the stretcher like a sack of potatoes.
They may as well have been unloading the produce
truck at Pat's I.G.A.

"Melvin, tell them to stop! Stop!" I shouted at the
paramedics.

Perhaps I sound more authoritative than I give myself credit for sounding. At any rate, the men, who
were at that moment reaching down to pick up the
stretcher, seemed to freeze.

Melvin turned. Ironically, it was his left orb that
finally fixed on me. "What the hell was that for,
Yoder?"

There was no time to chide him for swearing. "This
is a crime scene, you idiot. You can't remove the body
until you've made a thorough investigation."

"*Crime scene?*" The aberrant issue of some ancient
ancestor's loins had the audacity to laugh. "You've
been watching too much television, Yoder."

"I don't watch television," I hissed. There were
never any corpses on *Green Acres,* so that didn't
count.

"Then you've been reading too many mystery stories in those girlie magazines of yours. There hasn't
been a crime committed unless"—his right eye fixed
on Matilda—"unless it was your cow's intent to kill
the deceased."

"What?"

"Which, come to think of it, just might be the case.
She looks pretty guilty to me."

The paramedics laughed nervously. But Melvin, I knew from experience, was dead serious.

"Don't be ridiculous, Melvin! Matilda doesn't have a murderous bone in her body."

"Don't be so sure. It's happened before." No doubt he was referring to the time a bull kicked him in the head.

"What are you going to do, Melvin? Throw Matilda in jail."

Unfortunately, the paramedics laughed again. Melvin gave them his famous one-eyed glare.

"This isn't funny, Yoder," he said pointedly to me. "You remember what we had to do to Henry Kurtz's rottweiler when it bit the Brubaker boy?"

I gasped. "You're taking Matilda into the Bedford pound?"

"The pound doesn't take cows. But Mishler's slaughterhouse does."

"*What*? You can't kill an innocent cow!"

"She's dangerous, Yoder. She could do it again."

"*She* didn't do it, you idiot! That's what I've been trying to tell you. Mr. Mitchell here was murdered, all right, but his killer was two-legged."

In a rare moment of cooperation, both eyes settled on me. "Are you saying this man was murdered? I mean, *really* murdered."

"Bingo!"

"And just what would you offer as evidence?"

"I don't know. Melvin. That's your department, isn't it? I'm just saying that if you check Matilda's hooves, you won't find any blood."

I immediately realized my gaffe. "Of course I'd be happy to check for you."

Melvin's silence spoke volumes.

I walked over to my cowering cow and spoke calmly to her. Cows, unlike horses, do not take kindly to having their feet inspected. No doubt it is a matter of balance for them.

"Matilda, dear, that mean little man over there wants to see your feet. Be a good girl now and don't kick me."

Although Matilda swatted me repeatedly with her tail, she didn't kick me. But that's as far as her cooperation went. I had to wrench that splayed foot off the floor. It was like lifting one of Aaron's barbells.

"Nothing, see?"

"Now the other," said Melvin, who was watching from a safe distance.

"He's being unreasonable," I cooed, "but just go along with it."

But no matter how hard I tugged, I couldn't get Matilda's right rear foot off the floor.

"It's no use," I said, huffing and puffing.

"Maybe she's got something to hide."

I don't for the life of me know why I allow that man to get under my skin. "Oh, yeah?"

"Yeah. So, I guess it's Mishler's slaughterhouse after all. Too bad she's such a bag of bones. Otherwise I'd say put me down for ten pounds of hamburger and a couple of nice sirloins."

That really hiked my hackles. "Hold on, dear," I whispered to Matilda. Then in a burst of righteous fury, I hiked her hock halfway up my hip.

The poor cow bellowed in outrage, but remained standing. From her neighboring stall, Betsey bellowed in sympathy.

"You see! No blood!"

Any other lawman would have apologized, both to Matilda and myself. But oh, no, not Melvin Stoltzfus.

"That still doesn't prove she didn't do it. Maybe she wiped her hoof on all this straw."

One of the paramedics, a baby-faced man named

Sean, cleared his throat. "Actually, sir, it's not likely that the cow is responsible."

At least one of Melvin's eyes turned in the direction of the speaker. "What the hell are you talking about, boy?"

"Well, sir, when we were putting him on the stretcher I noticed a gash—or maybe a stab wound—on the back of his neck. I don't think it's likely that the cow kicked him in the face, turned him over, and then cut his neck."

"And you waited until now to say that?" I screamed.

Melvin had to paddle fast to save face. "Okay, so maybe the damned cow didn't do it. But she's a witness. Yoder, you are forbidden to sell or otherwise remove that cow from these premises, until I have completed my investigation."

"Would it be all right to trade her for a handful of beans?"

Someone other than myself giggled. That may have been the straw that broke the camel's back. I have never seen him so mad. He lit into me like a fox in a henhouse. When he was through ripping me to shreds, he turned his fury on the paramedics.

"You incompetent bunch of morons! Why the hell didn't you point out that neck wound earlier? Is this what passes for professionalism these days? My eighty-year-old mother could do your job with blinders on and both hands tied behind her back!"

More words followed, most of which were unfit to repeat. Not all of them were mine, either. By the time he ran out of breath, Melvin had so thoroughly alienated the Bedford paramedics that they threatened to leave without the body, or—in the words of young Sean—"maybe *two* bodies."

Had I not been a good Christian woman, I would

have taken the empty milk bucket, put it over Melvin's head, and drummed a rousing rendition of the "Boogie Woogie Bugle Boy of Company B." Instead I chose to settle for "When the Saints Come Marching In."

Unfortunately, Melvin didn't cooperate with my drum session—in fact, he threatened to call it assault. Matilda, unhappy with all the commotion in her stall, began milling around and accidentally stepped on Melvin's toe. Had it not been for the timely arrival of Freni, I would have ended up in the hoosegow, along with my Holstein.

Fortunately, Freni is not only a distant relative of Melvin's, she is his sainted mother's best friend. In less time than it takes to knead a pound of dough, Freni had the body in the ambulance, and Melvin out of the barn. Of course Melvin had to investigate the crime scene first, but there really was nothing else to see, and Matilda refused to answer direct questions. Before he left, Melvin declared Matilda's stall off-limits to anyone except himself, but thanks to Freni's intervention, he graciously allowed me to move Matilda.

I milked the witness in Betsey's stall while my cousin tried to calm me down.

"Ach, never mind him. He's a silly man. Everyone knows his bite is worse than his teeth."

There was no point in correcting her. "This barn is cursed," I wailed.

Freni flapped her arms, and then folded them across her stomach. For a second I thought she wanted to hug me.

"Ach, there is not such thing as a curse."

"Two murders, Freni! That one with the pitchfork last year, and now this! This barn is over a hundred years old, and before I came to own it, how many murders were there?"

To my surprise, Freni was nodding her head. "It's the English. Always so violent. It's not my place to say so, Magdalena, but maybe you should give up on this inn idea."

I was aghast. "And do what?"

"Become a missionary to Zaire. Or is it the Congo now?"

"And Susannah? Who will take care of her?"

Freni wagged a stubby finger at me. "There you go again, always trying to control other people's lives. Susannah is a grown woman now. She is responsible for herself."

"But aren't I supposed to be my sister's keeper?"

"Yah, but sometimes it is better to keep loved ones at an arm's length."

"But I don't *want* to give up the inn," I wailed. "It's my life. I enjoy meeting all the people that come to stay here. It's only every now and then that I get a really bad apple, and there have only been two murders, after all."

"Three," Freni said. "Remember the woman who was pushed down the stairs?"

"So? Only three, then. Pick up any mystery book— one that's part of a series—the death rate can be far higher than three."

Although I do not watch television on principle, my principles do not prevent me from reading, and Mystery Lovers Bookshop in Oakmont, Pennsylvania, is one of my favorite out-of-town destinations. Freni, however, reads only the Holy Bible, *Reader's Digest,* and *The Budget,* a weekly publication that chronicles Amish and Mennonite news from around the country.

"Maybe, but you would make a good missionary, Magdalena. That skinny head of yours would look good in a helmet, and you wouldn't have to worry about cannibals wanting to eat you."

"Thanks, but I'm not sure they have cannibals these days."

"So? The lions won't want to eat you, either. Or the leopards. Even those big mosquitoes that carry malaria and sleeping sickness will leave you alone. And the snakes—a python will take one look at you, and say, 'Not worth the trouble. Too many bones.' "

"Freni!"

"But skinny is good, Magdalena. You won't get so hot in that tropical sun. Just remember to stay out of the sun as much as possible."

"I know. I don't want to get skin cancer."

"Yah, that too. But Agnes Brontrager from over by Somerset went to Africa for three years as a missionary, and when she came back she looked just like a prune."

"With or without a pit?"

"Ach, make fun, Magdalena. But I'm just trying to help you look on the bright side and give you a few tips."

"Is that it?"

"Yah. Agnes had to shake out her shoes every morning before putting them on."

"Is that a missionary ritual?"

"Ach, no! Scorpions! They crawl in the shoes at night. And never sleep with your mouth open, Magdalena. Agnes almost choked on a cockroach the size of a baby robin."

Suddenly it occurred to me what Freni was doing. "I love you," I cried, and despite four centuries of breeding to the contrary, I threw my bony arms around her, gave her a bear hug, and hoisted her into the air like a sack of potatoes.

"Ach!" Freni squawked, her short arms flailing. "Put me down."

I dropped her. "You're so clever, dear. You know exactly how to put things in perspective. So what's a couple of corpses compared to scorpions in my shoes?"

Freni shook her head. "Ach, you are a strange one."

"*Me*? You're the one who entered a contest so you could get rid of your daughter-in-law."

Freni frowned. "Do you suppose that now the contest will be canceled?"

"My, how you talk! A man died here sometime this morning! But speaking of your daughter-in-law, how is she? Jonathan said she had the flu. And how is Mose?"

My cousin swallowed back her disappointment. "Mose is better, but still a little shaky. Barbara—ach, what do the English say? A woose!"

"You mean a wuss?"

"Yah, a woose. She wants Jonathan to drive her to the doctor in Bedford. For the flu, yet!"

"Just pitiful," I said and burrowed my head into Matilda's warm side. I couldn't help but smile. It was comforting to know that some things never change.

Fifteen

Alma Cornwater's Curried Lamb Loaf with Peach Chutney

◆

Lamb loaf

¾ pound ground lamb
¾ pound ground beef
½ to ¾ cup rolled oats
3 tablespoons tomato ketchup
2 eggs
1 teaspoon salt
1 teaspoon curry powder
½ teaspoon ground cumin
¼ teaspoon pepper

Mix above ingredients thoroughly with hands. Add just enough rolled oats so that meat becomes doughlike and holds its shape. Form into a loaf in center of 9 x 13 glass baking dish. Do not use loaf pan. Loaf will brown nicely on all sides. Bake in 350-degree oven for approximately one hour.
Serves 4–6.

Peach chutney

5 or 6 fresh peaches, peeled and sliced
1 green pepper, finely chopped
¾ cup sugar
¾ cup water
¼ cup vinegar
½ teaspoon curry powder
½ teaspoon ground ginger
¼ teaspoon salt
dash nutmeg
dash cayenne pepper (to taste)

Mix above ingredients and bring to boil in nonstick pot. Reduce heat and simmer for approximately one hour, or until peaches and pepper have become soft and jamlike. Stir occasionally and add water as needed to keep from sticking. When cool, serve as condiment for lamb loaf.

Sixteen

When I got back to the house, Melvin had all my guests rounded up in the parlor, except for Ms. Cornwater. Even Susannah was there, somehow managing to look sleepy, baffled, and alluring all at the same time. Well, she didn't look alluring to me, but you get the picture.

"Has anyone seen Ms. Cornwater?" Melvin has an advantage in that he can scan a room in two directions simultaneously.

No one answered.

Hernia's pitiful excuse for police chief unsnapped a miniature bullhorn from his belt and held it to his invisible lips.

"I repeat, has anyone seen Ms. Alma Cornwater?" Fortunately, the tiny instrument distorted more than it amplified.

"She told me she was going for a walk," Ms. Holt said. "Officer, is there a problem?"

Although it was not yet seven a.m., an hour that, in my experience, finds few Englishwomen out of bed, Ms. Holt was fully dressed and coiffed. I hate to admit this, but she looked elegant in a vanilla-colored cashmere turtleneck dress with matching kidskin boots. The dress was what Susannah refers to as "Episcopal length." That is to say, it came down almost to her ankles, and not for religious reasons either. Ms. Holt's shiny auburn hair was arranged in a flawless French twist, and held in place with a mother-of-pearl comb. A lesser woman might have been tempted to slap Ms. Holt silly.

Melvin was clearly impressed with the woman. Both eyes were stuck on her, like a fly on wallpaper. If he kept it up for long, Susannah was not going to be a happy camper.

"Did she say where she was going?"

"The woods, I think." No doubt she was referring to the woods behind the cow pasture, the one that separated the Hostetler homestead from my place.

"So then, we're all here?"

"Mr. Mitchell isn't here," Mr. Dolby said.

Heads nodded.

"Ah, so he isn't," Melvin said.

"Aw, man," Carlie said, "you don't suppose he went with her? I mean, that wouldn't be fair, would it? Screwing a judge in the woods like that?"

"Stop it!" I snapped.

Although that was no way to speak of the dead, to be truthful, I was more irritated at Mr. Dolby than I was with the child. He had picked up my poker and was jabbing at the log in my fireplace as if it were his own hearth. What's more, I had no recollection of building that fire. True, I do tend to keep the inn on the cool side, but a neat sign, laminated and tacked to the mantel, specifically states that guests must ask permission before building a fire.

"What the hell are we doing here?" Art asked. His swear word aside, it was a reasonable question.

Ms. Holt picked an imaginary piece of lint off her cashmere-clad chest. "Maybe if we are all quiet for a minute, Chief Stoltzfus will tell us."

Melvin graced her with a smile as rare as Cuban frost. "Thank you, Ms. Holt, and you're exactly right.

But now, before we begin, I'm going to lay down some ground rules. First—"

"First, let the rest of us get dressed," I suggested sensibly.

Everyone nodded, except, of course, for Ms. Holt. She was the only one dressed. The others, myself included, were wearing a pathetic collection of nightclothes and bathrobes. Two of our number, Susannah and Carlie, had wrapped themselves in quilts, and frankly, I doubt if either of them had a stitch on under them.

Melvin's smile became a smirk and his left eye abandoned Ms. Holt's comely face and settled on mine.

"Fashion is not an important consideration at a murder scene."

Everyone gasped except for Freni and me. It was such a predictable ploy, I wanted to gag.

"Murder?" my guests said in unison.

Melvin was in seventh heaven. "The victim was a white male, age fifty-seven. George Mitchell was his name."

More gasps.

"So, you see why I gathered you all together, don't you? As soon as Miss Cornwater returns, we're going to have ourselves a nice little roundtable discussion. Because one of you"—he paused for dramatic effect—"is the killer."

"That's preposterous!" Without any makeup, and wearing a hooded white terry robe, Marge Benedict looked like death warmed over. I've seen corpses, George Mitchell's included, that showed more vitality.

Melvin turned to his challenger. "Oh, is it?"

Marge all but disappeared inside her terry shell. "I only meant that it isn't logical. It's not like the inn is part of a gated community. Anyone could have sneaked onto this property and killed George. The killer could be hiding in the barn right now."

Melvin's spindly frame straightened. "Barn? Now, why would you say barn, Miss"—he consulted his notes—"Benedict?"

"Well—I—or the woods," she said.

"Aha! But you said 'barn' first."

"Give her a break," Gladys said, her voice barely audible above the crackling of the flames. She was wearing thin polyester pajamas, no robe, and was shivering.

Melvin wheeled. "Who said that?"

I took a step forward. "Does it matter? You'll have your chance to grill them all like weenies, but first you're going to give them a chance to get dressed."

"Yoder!"

I cannot be cowed by a coward. "This is my inn, and I'll not have anyone catching their death of cold." Of course that was nonsense, since colds are not transmitted by temperature, but Melvin has a hypochondriac streak in him a furlong wide.

"What the hell are you talking about, Yoder? It's hotter than blazes in here."

I pretended to sneeze. Quite frankly I am a very good actress, and if Hollywood were not *the* den of iniquity—believe me, I *know*—I would have accepted Babs's offer for a bit part in her next movie.

"They say that new strain of flu from Japan is spreading a mile a minute." I sneezed again.

"All right. Get dressed—the bunch of you. But I'll be keeping both the front and back doors covered. Anyone who tries to escape will be—"

I snatched the bullhorn from his scaly hand. The darn thing wasn't even turned on. A flip of a switch rectified that. I may be a simple Mennonite woman, striving to shun the ways of the world, but thanks to six weeks spent with a film crew, I knew my way around amplifiers.

"Just get dressed," I boomed. "See you in five."

Fortunately Melvin was too embarrassed by his technical ineptitude to chew me out.

I prefer a long hot shower in the mornings, but there was no time for that. I had to settle for what Mama used to call a spit bath—a couple of licks with a wet washcloth and a fresh swipe of deodorant. At least I didn't use real spit, like Mama sometimes did, and of course I put on clean underwear. Other than that, it was yesterday's outfit.

Much to my surprise, I was the last one back in the parlor. Except for Melvin, that is. If I played by my own rules, not only would I have to miss out on the questioning, but I might have to skip breakfast.

"Where's Hernia's finest?" I asked brightly. My cheery tone and informal reference were intended to set my guests at ease. The last time I saw so many nervous faces in one spot was when I caught a raccoon in the henhouse.

"He's outside," Ms. Holt said. The woman had actually changed her clothes, if you can imagine that. Now she was wearing a red silk dress—also Episcopal length—with a belt that had an enormous buckle, the kind schoolbook illustrations show the Pilgrims wearing. Unlike the Pilgrims, Ms. Holt's buckle was gold, and quite possibly the real thing. Between you and me, however, the red dress clashed with its wearer's auburn hair.

"Guarding the doors, no doubt," I said.

Art shook his head. "No, some woman drove up, and now they're off some place together. I think they went back to the barn."

"Was she a short little thing with broad shoulders, huge bosoms, and no hips?"

"Yeah," Art said.

"A man's haircut, no chin, rabbit teeth, and a nose like Karl Malden's?" Trust me, I was being kind.

"Yes, that's her exactly," Ms. Holt said.

"Does her makeup look like it was applied with a trowel?"

"Yes," they chorused.

"The mystery woman is Zelda Root," I said. "She's a policewoman. Hernia's second in command. She and Melvin used to be a thing." I eyed Susannah.

"*Used* to," my sister said. "Chief Stoltzfus is all mine now."

The front door opened and a few seconds later Melvin and Zelda walked in.

"Speak of the devil," I said. Then I nodded to his companion. "Good morning, Zelda."

"Good morning, Magdalena. Mel—Chief Stoltzfus tells me there's been another incident here."

"You can go ahead and say it, dear. There's been another murder."

"*Another*?" Marge Benedict looked only slightly more alive in the winter white pantsuit in which she'd arrived. What a pity those enormous brown eyes and luxuriant brown-black hair were wasted on a mere twig of a woman. If God had given me assets like those, I would have eaten myself into a fine full figure—either that or bought one.

"Those were a long time ago," I said quickly.

"Maybe in dog years," Melvin said.

Zelda, bless her mannish, but painted little head, has always been a peacemaker. "Well, back to the current incident, are we all present and accounted for now?"

"Alma's still not back," Freni said, and then clapped a hand over her mouth.

"Oh, yes, I am."

We all turned to face Alma, who was standing in the opposite doorway, the one that opens on the back hall. Her blue jeans were muddy at the knees, and she was still wearing her multicolored parka, which had mud streaks along the front. The thick glasses had slid even farther down than usual, and the mound of thick, graying hair had come down on one side and was covering one lens. The other side of her do was barely held aloft by a tortoiseshell comb. I don't mean to be insensitive, given that she's a minority and all, but she looked like a loser. Even I could see that.

"What's up?" she said, between deep gasps. "Did somebody die?"

"You tell us," Melvin snarled.

"Yes, I'm afraid there's been a murder," I said. "Mr. Mitchell is dead."

"Oh, my!" Alma steadied herself against the doorjamb. Unfortunately all the chairs were taken.

"You can cut the act," Melvin said. "We have our proof."

I strode over to Alma, forcibly ejected the saucy Carlie from her chair, and seated the older woman. Kids nowadays have no manners.

"What proof," I demanded.

"This," Melvin said. From the pocket of his trench coat, he extracted a small plastic bag containing a tortoiseshell comb.

"That's a very nice comb, dear," I said, "but first you have to grow your hair a little longer."

"Very funny, Yoder. It's not mine. It's hers." He nodded at Alma.

"Is it?" I whispered.

Alma patted her head. Apparently she wasn't even aware of the missing comb.

"Well, I guess it is—"

"This doesn't prove anything," Freni said, stepping forward in defense of a fellow Native American. "Lots of English wear combs. She"—Freni pointed at Ms. Holt—"has them in her hair."

"Well!" Ms. Holt patted her mother-of-pearl combs. They were both accounted for. "I would never wear that disgusting thing. It's plastic!"

"Let me see the comb." Alma sounded exhausted.

"You don't have to say anything without a lawyer present," I whispered.

"I heard that, Yoder."

Alma looked at me. "It doesn't matter. I have nothing to hide."

Zelda, bless her heart, took the bag containing the comb from Melvin, loped across the room, and showed it to Alma.

"It's mine," Alma said without expression.

Melvin's orbs lit up like twin spotlights. "Aha! I thought so."

"But I didn't kill anyone."

"Oh, no? Officer Root found that thing just outside the barn."

"Ach!" Freni clapped a hand over her mouth.

I patted Alma's shoulder. "Tell us what happened, dear."

Alma shoved her glasses back into place and wedged a hank of the lose hair behind her ear. She crossed, then uncrossed, her chubby legs.

"I'm in the habit of getting up early, you see. Back home I'm a waitress at Cherokee Bob's Wigwam of Pancakes. Breakfast shift. Anyway, I woke up at five o'clock like I usually do, and then I couldn't go back to sleep. Instead of just lying there, I decided to take a walk."

"You headed straight for the barn, didn't you?" Melvin's mandibles were chomping at the bit. He couldn't wait to arrest poor Alma Cornwater.

"No, sir. It was cold down here, so I decided to surprise Mrs. Hostetler and light a fire."

I cleared my throat loudly and nodded at the sign. To my credit, I didn't verbally chide her in front of the others.

Instead of looking at me, Alma turned to Kimberly McManus Holt. "Then I went into the kitchen, and I ran into her."

Ms. Holt fidgeted with the monstrous gold buckle. She did not look up.

"I get up early too," she said. "We start taping *Cooking With Kimberly* at nine, but I have to be there by seven-thirty for hair and makeup. And I don't live right in Boston. Anyway, I was in the kitchen, about to fix myself a cup of coffee, when Ms. Cornwater walked in. We had a brief conversation in which she told me she was going for a walk in the woods."

"And then?" Melvin asked with uncharacteristic gentleness. Susannah and Zelda exchanged worried glances.

"And then I made the coffee and took it up to my room. I brought a lot of work with me. Being the star of a cooking show is much more than slinging hash."

"Ooh," Arthur said. "Low blow."

Melvin focused on Alma again. "So that's it?"

I cleared my throat, and rolled my eyes at Zelda. She's both the brains and brawn of Hernia's fearless duo.

"Please finish your story, Miss Cornwater," she directed.

Alma readjusted hair and glasses. Perhaps she didn't

have the money for contact lenses, but the odds were she had a pair of scissors.

"Just like Ms. Holt said, I told her I was going for a walk in the woods. And I did. I don't know what I was thinking, but I kind of expected it to be like the woods back home. I live right next door to the Great Smoky Mountain National Park, see? It's thousands of acres of forest that—"

"Spare us the travelogue," Melvin snapped.

Poor Alma looked like she'd just been slapped. "Well, there was less than a mile of woods before I hit a fence—y'all sure have a lot of fences around here—anyway, I climbed over that and hadn't gone much farther when I saw the naked man."

Seventeen

I looked at Freni, who was trying to suppress a smile.

"I mean, it's really cold out there, and suddenly there's this guy walking along stark naked—well, except for a hat. He had on one of those three-cornered hats, the kind they wear in Australia."

Melvin smirked. "Yeah, right."

"Dinky Williams," Freni said, shaking her head.

Zelda was nodding. "I've heard of him. He's that back-to-nature freak, right?"

"An urban refugee," I explained for everyone's benefit. "Dinky—I think his real name is Bill—moved here from New York City last year. He's a retired architect. Anyway, he bought a piece of the Mishler farm so he could build his dream house. All glass, I hear. Only thing is, Dinky and his wife are nudists and seem to be very fond of nature walks. In the summertime it's hard *not* to see what the Good Lord intended to be covered."

I turned to Alma. "I didn't realize Dinky was a cold weather buff as well. Did he speak to you?"

Alma flushed and fiddled with her glasses. "Oh, yes. He asked me if I wanted to see his Tinkertoy collection."

"Ach!" Freni clapped her hands to her cheeks.

"What did you say?" Melvin asked, with sudden interest.

"I said 'no,' of course. Then I walked away as quickly as I could, without being too rude. Only I got turned around somehow and—and—well, I got lost."

"There's no shame in that," Freni said loyally.

"But I'm a Native American!" Alma wailed.

"Yah, but so am I, and I get lost all the time."

"Ladies," Melvin said sharply, his patience having waned along with Dinky's Tinkertoys, "can we just get on with the story?"

Alma took a deep, brave breath. "Well, I tried to look for landmarks, but since y'all don't have any mountains—"

"Just a minute," I heard myself say, "we're surrounded by mountains! These are the world-famous Alleghenies."

"I meant mountains that you can see over the tops of the trees." She looked at Melvin before continuing, and he had the audacity to look at me.

"Quit interrupting, Yoder. Continue, Miss Cornwater."

"Anyway, I found a little stream and I was following it when I heard two men talking. At first I couldn't see them, and I didn't want to say anything—just in case they were—well, you know—nudists too. But boy, was that ever a big mistake, because then I heard one of them say, 'It's a big buck. A six-pointer.' The next thing I knew they were shooting at me."

Freni gasped.

Melvin snorted. "That's impossible. Deer-hunting season isn't for another two weeks."

"That's never stopped the Mishler brothers," I said.

Freni nodded vigorously. "And they're both blind as cats."

"You mean bats, dear." I turned to my nemesis. "Well, just don't stand there. You've a job to do."

"What the hell—"

"Maybe we should check it out," Zelda said. "If what she said is true, that doesn't leave a lot of time in which to commit a murder."

"How much time *does* a murder take," Melvin growled. "Besides, that still doesn't explain this." He waved the bag containing the comb.

"Maybe it does," I said angrily. "You never even let her finish her story."

"Finish!" Melvin barked.

Alma looked like a deer caught in headlights. "When they shot, I ran. I kept following the creek, and I slipped in it a couple of times. But they kept coming and shooting. 'Make me a nice trophy,' one of them yelled.

"So I left the creek as soon as I found a thicket. It had a lot of brambles in it, you see, and it tore at my hair. Anyway, after a while I didn't hear them shouting or shooting anymore, and I was a little calmer by then myself, so I started to use my head. I remembered that Miss Yoder's inn was set in a little valley between two hills"—she glanced at me—"I mean, mountains, and that the mountains run north and south. I also remembered that just outside of town there is a bigger creek—"

"Slave Creek," I said helpfully.

"Yeah, that's it. So, I figured the little creek had to run into the big creek, and since I hadn't crossed the little creek—only sort of followed it—that meant Ms. Yoder's place was to the north. By then the sun was up high enough so that I could see it through the trees. It was easy finding my way back then."

"The comb!" Melvin flapped the bag. At that moment, he looked more like a vulture than a mantis.

"Well, it must have come undone in the brambles. I wasn't paying attention to my hair then."

"Of course not, dear." I patted her shoulder.

Melvin gave me a look that could scald milk. "But Officer Root found this just outside the *barn*."

Alma swallowed and looked at me. "I wasn't trying to be a snoop, really. I saw that the barn door was open, but there was yellow tape across it—you know, like the kind the police use on TV to seal off a crime scene. I thought it was odd that the tape would be there. I only wanted a closer look. Anyway, my comb must have fallen off then."

Melvin sneered. "Just like that?"

"Coincidences happen," I said. "Live with it."

Perhaps I had gone too far. Real mantises are capable of flight, and Melvin looked as if he were about to fly across the room, grab my scrawny neck in his front teeth, and bite off my head. Thank God for Zelda Root. She may not be much to look at, and she has the personality of a washing machine, but she's one levelheaded woman.

"Isn't it time to implement departmental procedure number two?" she asked calmly.

"Number two?" It was clear Melvin didn't have a clue as to what she meant.

Zelda turned to me. "Magdalena, do you have a more private room where we could interview the official suspects individually?"

"I'm sure that can be arranged, but just out of curiosity, who are your official suspects?"

"Every last one of you," Melvin snarled.

"Ach!" Freni squawked. "I was at home nursing a sick husband and daughter-in-law. I only thought about murder—I didn't do it."

"Even *me*?" I couldn't believe the chutzpah, asking me to hostess my own interrogation.

Zelda nodded. "As I understand it, the victim was the sponsor of a contest, in which most of you had a stake."

Marge Benedict waved her arm like a schoolgirl who knew the solution to a math problem no one else could answer.

"Not me! I'm just a judge. I didn't care who won or lost, so I certainly didn't have a reason to kill George."

"I guess that leaves me out," Gordon Dolby said, the relief evident in his voice. "I'm not a contestant either."

Susannah yawned. "Count me out too. I just live here. This contest thing is my sister's responsibility."

I glared at her. "Thanks!"

Carlie jumped up. "Hey, don't forget me. I just came along for the ride."

"So what am I, chopped liver?" I asked. "And anyway, like I said before, Mr. Mitchell could just as well have been killed by a total stranger."

"Magdalena," Zelda said through clenched teeth.

"All right. How about the dining room? If you take the quilt off its frame, it makes a nice torture rack, and none of the furniture is upholstered." Well, it was my inn after all, and I would decide where they would set up the bright lights. I surely wasn't going to allow my furniture to fade.

Zelda glanced at Melvin and gave her eyes a quarter turn. Take it easy, she said silently. I can handle the idiot, if you'll just give me a chance.

"It needs to be more private," she said aloud.

"Okay, you can have my bedroom. But I reserve the right to be grilled first."

Take one verifiable idiot, and one heavily painted but otherwise almost normal person, throw in yours truly, and what do you get? A headache, to say the least. Still, it wasn't as bad as it might have been, thanks to Zelda, and a surprise call from Reverend Schrock.

"Babs, is that you?" Hope springs eternal even in the boniest of breasts.

There followed what would have been a moment of silence, were Melvin not breathing so hard. The man had the nerve to be exasperated because I answered my own phone.

"It's Reverend Schrock," the caller finally said. "Did I call at a bad time?"

"Oh, you mean the heavy breathing? No, that's just Melvin Stoltzfus, as usual."

"But isn't this your private line? The one that rings only in your bedroom?"

"Yes."

"I see. Then I did call at a bad time."

"Any time with Melvin is a bad time," I muttered under my breath.

"Who is that?" Melvin demanded. "Are you talking about me?"

"Yes."

"Doesn't he mind that you're on the phone?" the reverend asked.

"Yes."

"Whoever it is, you better make it snappy," Melvin said. "Do you hear me?"

"Yes."

"I didn't *hear* you, Yoder!"

"Yes, yes, yes, yes!" I screamed.

Mercifully, both men were silent for a minute. "Well, well," Reverend Schrock said at last, "I must say, this certainly is a first."

"Oh, don't let it bother you. It happens all the time."

"Magdalena! Isn't this a little soon—I mean, after what happened with Aaron and all."

"As if I had any control over it," I wailed.

The reverend mulled that over. "Confidentially, I know what you mean. There are times when my loins ache so bad I just have to give in to the urges of the flesh. Of course the good Lord in His mercy—"

"*What?* Loins? Flesh? Reverend Schrock, shame on you!"

"Shame on *me*? You're the one who does it all the time!"

"There's been a murder," I shrieked. "Melvin's here to investigate a murder!"

I could hear him swallow, and it was a gulp big enough to suck up Jonah. "Melvin's there investigating a murder?"

"Eureka! Say, how did you get my private number anyway?"

"It's written on the wall of the men's room at church."

"Remind me to kill Susannah—oops, sorry, Reverend."

"No harm really meant, I'm sure. Uh—about what I said before, it was said in confidence, you know."

"I can only hope you were talking about that razor-tongued wife of yours."

"Why, yes, of course! And speaking of whom, that *is* why I called."

"I know, I know, I've been booted out from teaching my Sunday school class."

"Actually, you haven't. That's why I'm calling."

"Come again?"

"Lodema told me about her visit yesterday. She had no right to say what she did."

"You can say that again."

"It's not within her power to drop you from our Sunday school teacher roster. Would you like me to have her apologize?"

It was time for me to schedule a hearing test with a specialist over in Bedford. "I thought I heard you offer"—I chuckled pleasantly—"to make your wife apologize to me."

"That's exactly what I said. She's out right now, but as soon as she comes back, I'll have her give you a call. Better yet, I'll make her come over in person. Would you like me to be along?"

"That won't be necessary," I said graciously. "Since she insulted me one on one, that's how she should apologize."

"Consider it done. Magdalena—this is rather awkward for me, but you do still plan to remain an active member of Beechy Grove Mennonite Church, don't you?"

"Why, yes, my beef has to do with your acid-mouthed spouse, not with God."

"So, you'll continue on as usual?"

"I only missed that one Sunday!"

"What I mean to ask—how should I phrase this delicately—will the offering plate be as happy to see you now as it has been in the past?"

So that was it! Let it be known that I tithe. That is to say, I give to the church one tenth of my considerable income. That makes me Beechy Grove Mennonite Church's largest contributor. But I would never dream of withholding money from God, just because the pastor's wife had a bee in her bonnet.

"Render unto Caesar what is Caesar's, and to God what is God's," I said quoting the King James version of Matthew.

"Does that mean you'll continue to give?"

"If you'll talk some sense into one of your congregants." We Mennonites do not use the term *parishioner*.

"Magdalena, I'm sorry about what Alberta Weaver

said about you at choir practice. Believe me, I chewed her out good."

"That's not who I'm talking about!" I wailed. As if Alberta Weaver had room to talk. Her husband was serving a three-year prison sentence for growing a crop of cannabis along with his corn.

"Oh, you mean that little skit Alice Kauffman put on for the adult Sunday school class last week? The one she titled 'God Loves Harlots Too'?"

"I'm talking about that idiot Melvin Stoltzfus," I screamed.

"Put the idiot on the phone," the good reverend said.

For all intents and purposes, my interrogation was over.

"So how did it go?" I asked Freni.

She had been the second to step into that torture chamber formerly known as my boudoir.

"Melvin, shmelvin," she said. "Just wait until I tell his mama what he said about me. Elvina will put that boy over her knee and give him a good paddling."

"We could save her the trouble and call the Orkin man," I said, not uncharitably. After all, Elvina Stoltzfus was a widow woman in failing health. Bunions were just one of her many burdens. "But, just out of curiosity, what did he say about you?"

"Ach! He said I was as stubborn as a team of mules. Do you think I'm stubborn, Magdalena?"

I turned away, crossed all my fingers, my eyes, and even a few of my toes. "Of course not, dear."

"If that boy had half the sense of a mule, he'd know that the killer couldn't be one of the five contestants."

I turned to face her. "Please elucidate."

"Ach, I am not elucidating! That boy—"

"What I mean is, please explain your theory that the killer is not a contestant."

"Why didn't you say so? You always talk in riddles, Magdalena. You are worse than Samson."

"Humor me," I begged. "Make me a beneficiary of your wisdom."

"No wisdom, Magdalena. Even a dumpling knows not to kill the hen that lays the golden eggs."

I scratched my head. "I believe that's goose, dear. But what you're saying is that the contestants stand nothing to gain by killing Mr. Mitchell, and everything to lose. Therefore the murderer had to be someone from the outside. Right?"

"Yah, that's what I'm saying."

"It is rather obvious, isn't it?"

"Like the nose on your face."

"Freni!" I rubbed my proboscis. It is maybe a tad on the large size, but it's the one God gave me, and I have no plans to change it. Besides, Babs said she would no longer speak to me if I did.

"So, you have the Yoder nose," Freni said. "Me"— she patted her ample bust—"well, I look like a Miller."

"Whatever you say, dear. But you know, a wealthy man like George Mitchell could have had lots of enemies. His killer, or killers, as the case may be, might have followed him to Hernia, waited until he or they got him alone, and then—pow!"

"Ach! Lock the doors, Magdalena."

"Now who's thinking like a dumpling? George Mitchell is dead. You can rest assured that his killer is long gone."

"Back to New York?"

"Not all killers are from New York, dear. Remember, California has its share. Anyway, East Coast Delicacies is headquartered in Philadelphia."

"Pennsylvania?"

"There is only *one* Philadelphia. I wonder if Mr. Anderson might be able to shed some light on the subject."

"Ach, he might even be the killer! And such a nice man he was."

I rolled my eyes, taking care not to roll them in the get-stuck position. "He's in the hospital, for crying out loud. Suffering from food poisoning."

"Yah, but maybe he's just—how do the English say it . . ."

"Faking it?"

"Yah."

"It's not likely, dear, *but* I suppose anything is possible. I'd run out there and pay him a visit, if it weren't for one small problem."

"Magdalena! Did you get in trouble with that Danish doctor again?"

"Susannah did, but I was there."

"And that crabby nurse with the hemorrhoids?"

I hung my head. "The hemorrhoids are just a rumor that I started. But yes, consider me banned from the Bedford County Hospital."

Freni shook her head, but I knew her well enough to know she wasn't really angry. "Where there is a will, there is a way. You find a way to speak to that Englishman, Magdalena."

I thought of a way.

Eighteen

Barbara Hostetler was delighted to see me. Jonathan had yet to take her to the doctor. On his way back from dropping off Freni, he'd noticed a stretch of fence that was down, and had doubled back to fix it. Apparently fifty-eight Holsteins had been stuffing themselves silly on the Mishler brothers' hay.

"Not to worry, dear, I'd be happy to take you. But just so that you don't worry, the flu is really no big deal for someone your age."

Barbara beamed. "Yah, I know, but this isn't the flu, Magdalena."

I tried not to smile. No doubt the woman had some Stoltzfus blood in her. Oh, well, the easiest way to deal with hypochondriacs is to humor them.

"What sort of disease are you hoping for?"

Barbara laughed. "I don't think it's a disease."

"So you're just pretending to be sick?"

"Can you keep a secret, Magdalena?"

"Was Jacob Amman Swiss?" That's the Hernia equivalent of asking if the pope is Catholic.

Barbara glanced needlessly around. Mose was in bed, and Jonathan had several dozen cows to round up.

"I think I'm in the family way," she whispered.

"Nonsense. You're not in Freni's way, and don't you let her make you believe it."

"Ach no, not Freni's way—the family way. You know . . ."

"I'm afraid I don't, dear. Just spit it out."

"I think I might be *pregnant*."

"No way!"

"Oh, yah. My Jonathan and I—"

"I know how it happens, dear, it's just that it's a bit of a surprise."

"For me too!" She giggled.

"How sure are you?"

"Pretty sure. That's why I want to see a doctor. My friend Hilda says that prenaval care is very important."

"Pre*natal*, dear. Well, I guess congratulations are in order."

But that's as far as I could go on the subject. To be honest with you, I had suddenly come down with a severe illness of my own. *Jealousy.* I, Magdalena Portulacca Yoder, would never feel life stirring in my womb. I was doomed forever to be as barren as the Mojave Desert.

Perhaps it was a blessing that Aaron's seed had fallen on stony ground, but that had been my one and only chance at motherhood. Even then, my biological clock had already wound down so far by the time I married that it would have taken more than the Energizer bunny, as Aaron sometimes called *it,* to get my clock running again. I know, these days even the elderly are giving birth, but I will never marry again. The only pitter-patter of little feet I'll hear will be when Shnookums leaves the sanctuary of Susannah's bra.

"Thank you," Barbara said, "but remember you can't tell anyone yet. Especially Freni!"

"My lips are sealed tighter than a clam at low tide."

"So, you'll take me to the doctor?"

"I'd be delighted to, dear, but on one condition."

Her face fell. "What's that?"

"Let me borrow your clothes."

Barbara Hostetler is two inches taller than me, and a good twenty pounds heavier, but I'd rather flop about in someone else's clothes than be strangled by them. Her feet, unfortunately, are a full size smaller than mine, but I made do by curling my toes inside the high-topped brogans. Her apron and bonnet fit perfectly.

"Yah, you look Amish," she said with satisfaction. "Have you ever considered changing churches?"

"Not really." The truth is, I have. Oh, I wouldn't become Amish, mind you, but maybe Methodist. There are times when I get a hankering to watch television (other than *Green Acres*), and I've even toyed with the idea of wearing lipstick—a very pale pink shade, to be sure. Of course I would never be so radical as to become a Presbyterian and paint my nails or—God forbid—drink beer.

Barbara took a step back to further admire her handiwork. Then to my dismay, she shook her head.

"Ach, you look Amish, but you also look so—well, you know."

"No, I don't know. What is it?"

"You still look so much like *you*."

I involuntarily fingered my schnoz. "Lots of Amish have the Yoder nose, dear."

"Yah, but you have the Hostetler eyes too."

"What do you mean by that?"

"Like shiny beads," Barbara said, and then prudently bit her tongue.

"Beady-eyed and beak-nosed," I wailed. "It may as well be the mark of Cain." No wonder Mama wouldn't let me wear blue jeans—all the genes I could handle were already on my face.

"Just a minute," Barbara said, and fished about in a chest at the foot of her bed. "Here, these are my old glasses. Put them on."

I put them on. It was like looking through the bottom of a cola bottle.

"Yah, now you look different."

"You mean my eyes are no longer beady?"

"Ach, no. Now we look like sisters."

I looked at my reflection in Barbara's hand mirror. It was amazing how a bonnet *and* a pair of glasses could change a person's appearance. I did look just like Barbara—well, maybe two Barbaras—apparently her old prescription was making me see double.

"Barbara, dear. Look closely at this mirror. Is that a crack in the glass?

Barbara put her head next to mine and looked. Sure enough, there were four of us. Prudently, I decided not to wear the glasses while driving.

Fortunately, Barbara's doctor was right on our way to the hospital, and by the time I dropped her off, we were almost giddy from laughing so much. Amish folk do accept, and sometimes even solicit, rides to distant places, but you will never catch an adult person of the Amish faith behind a steering wheel. You will most certainly never see them driving a cherry-red BMW. Folks in Bedford are familiar enough with Amish ways to know that, and the startled looks we drew as we approached town were a hoot.

At the stoplight on Penn Street, one old geezer actually lost his dentures. A young woman in a flashy yellow sports car was so astounded by the sight of us that she put on her windshield wipers, instead of shifting. However, we were *not* responsible for the three-car fender-bender on the corner of Thomas and Penn Streets.

Of course I parked the car in the far reaches of the hospital parking lot, and I made sure no one was looking before I got out. The second those automatic doors hissed open, I put on the glasses and became Barbara Kauffman Hostetler.

You can rest assured the real Barbara didn't know I was going to borrow her identity, in addition to her clothes. Many faithful Christians have yet to figure out that the Good Lord doesn't mind a white lie or two, as long as it's for a good cause.

The receptionist didn't suspect a thing, and was therefore quite pleasant. I had forgotten that visiting hours are between two and eight p.m., but much to my relief, I discovered that an Amish outfit is every bit as much of an entree as is a nun's habit or a Roman collar (don't ask me how I know this).

"Ich hahf koom to see Meester Anderson," I said in my best fake Amish accent, which admittedly is not very good. But it was good enough for Lauren Brightwell.

"He's in Room 134," she said brightly. "Just go down that corridor and hang a right." And then thinking perhaps I didn't understand such complicated English, due to my attire, she paraphrased her instructions in loud, torturously slow baby talk.

"Danke!" I screamed back.

I couldn't have timed my arrival any better. It was after breakfast and morning baths, but well enough before lunch to allow for a leisurely chat. What's more, my luck seemed to be on a roll because Mr. Anderson was sitting up in bed, watching television. He looked remarkably perky.

"Good morning, Mr. Anderson."

The poor dear was clueless. I whisked off my bonnet.

"Do I know you, ma'am?"

Off came the Coke-bottle lenses.

"Oh, it's you, Miss Yoder. Good morning. How are things back at the inn? Is the contest in full steam?"

Obviously the man hadn't heard about his employer's unfortunate demise, so I would have to tell him. Much better that he should hear the news from me than from Melvin, but I wasn't going to do it with the TV on. Some talk-show hostess with an alliterative name was interviewing women who first beat their husbands, and then sleep with their husbands' fathers' mistresses' former boyfriends. Apparently it was the first time the topic had ever been discussed on national television.

"Do you mind if we turn this off, dear?" I reached for the remote.

"Actually, I do. Grace there beat her husband with a Teflon spatula, and that same afternoon was cozying down between the sheets with her father-in-law's mistress's ex-boyfriend who, as it turned out, was Grace's seventh-grade math teacher. It's such a small world, isn't it?"

I snatched the remote from his tray table and zapped it off.

"Hey! What's that all about?"

"It's about George Mitchell, dear. The man is dead."

"*Dead*? How? Where?"

"He was found dead early this morning in my barn. He was murdered."

Mr. Anderson turned the color of Freni's best meringue. "He what?"

"Mr. Anderson—may I call you James, dear?"

"Jim will do nicely," he croaked. "Tell me about George."

"Like I said, he was murdered. The police don't know who did it yet. They're not even sure what he was murdered with, but it appears that he was hit in the face with a hard, heavy object. Oh, and stabbed or cut on the neck."

"God," Jim groaned. "I didn't really expect that to happen."

"Well, neither did I, dear, but—what do you mean, you didn't expect that to happen?"

Perhaps my voice was a little too loud, or my tone too strident, but before Jim could answer, Nurse Dudley poked her head in the door.

"Everything all right?"

I slapped on my bonnet and glasses. "Yah."

Nurse Dudley gave me the fish eye.

I nudged Jim. "We're just fine," he called.

"Oh." But Nurse Dudley didn't budge. She was a few watts brighter than Lauren Brightwell, and no doubt she found it odd for an Amish woman to be visiting an out-of-town executive.

"Tell her we're praying," I whispered.

"We're praying," Jim said.

"Praying? How nice—say, you look awfully familiar."

"Ach, we all look alike," I said, trying to sound like Barbara Hostetler.

"Come to think of it, you even sound like someone I know."

"Shush," I said, putting a bony finger to my lips. "The prayer isn't over."

I grabbed Jim's hand, closed my eyes, and cast about for something to say in Pennsylvania Dutch. Alas, I know very little.

Although my parents were Mennonites, Mama's

parents were Amish, as were Papa's grandparents. Both my parents were fluent in Pennsylvania Dutch and sometimes spoke it to each other, but I couldn't be bothered to learn something so quaint. Not when my friends at school were more modern, with-it Mennonites, or in one case, heaven forfend, a Methodist. I don't pretend to think fast on my feet, so at least give me credit for coming up with something.

"Eens, zwee, drei, vier, fimf, sex, siwwe, acht, nein, zehe."

Counting can sound like praying if one varies the cadence and emphasizes every third or fourth word.

"Amen," Jim said loudly.

"Wait a minute," Nurse Dudley said, taking a step inside the door.

My ticker was thumping like a flat tire on asphalt.

"My Brutus could use a prayer or two. I found him dead on his side of the bed this morning, all stiff and cold, and I haven't been able to get that picture out of mind."

"You have my sympathy," Jim said, and extended his hand.

Nurse Dudley ignored the gesture. "It was awful, believe me. Brutus and I had been together almost eighteen years."

Poor Nurse Dudley. It just goes to show you how one shouldn't judge. Who even knew the old battle-ax was married? But Brutus Dudley, what a name!

"But still you came to work," Jim said, shaking his head. "Now that's what I call dedication to one's calling."

"Yes, well, a calling is a calling, but a snake is a snake."

"Ach, that's no way to talk about a husband," I said on Barbara's behalf. Aaron might have deserved that epithet, but Jonathan was the salt of the earth.

"*Husband?* Brutus was not my husband! He was much more than that."

"Ach!" Just because I was an inadvertent adulteress does not mean I believe in unsanctified hanky-panky.

"Your lover?" Apparently Jim played by a different set of rules.

"My lover? Like I said, Brutus was a snake. A Burmese python."

"Ach!" Then my curiosity got the best of me. "What was he doing in your bed? How did he die?"

After all, Nurse Dudley is no small woman. It was quite possible she rolled over on Brutus, and squashed him flat as a pancake. Shnookums is not the first little mutt to hitch a ride in Susannah's bra.

"Who knows how he died? And what does it matter?" Nurse Dudley grabbed my hand. "Now pray for me," she ordered.

I silently prayed for a prayer, and getting no answer, gave her the numbers eleven through twenty. That sounded so convincing, I repeated the numbers in reverse order.

"*Zwansich, neinzeh, achtzeh, siwwezeh, sechzeh, fuffseh, vazeh, dreizeh, zwelf, elf.*"

"Amen!" Jim intoned.

"Amen." Nurse Dudley smiled. "You know, I feel better already."

"*Haufa mischt,*" I said. Horse manure.

"Thank you," Nurse Dudley said, and released my hand. "I know who it is you remind me of now."

I recklessly decided to take the bull by the horns. "Magdalena Yoder? Because she's my cousin, you see—"

"Heavens no, you're much prettier than her. Barbara Kauffman—yes, that's it. Mrs. Kauffman was a patient of mine last year. Do you know her?"

How stupid of me to forget that Barbara had had

an emergency appendectomy. When she came home from the hospital she raved about how kind the nurses were, one in particular.

"Never heard of her," I said.

"Well, if you ever run into her, say 'hello,' " Nurse Dudley said, and strode from the room.

The second the hem of her white skirt disappeared around the door, I turned on Jim. "Out with it, buster! What do you mean you didn't expect that to happen. What is *that*?"

"George's murder, of course. I set it up."

Nineteen

"What do you mean, you 'set it up'? You arranged to have George Mitchell killed?"

Jim squirmed like a worm about to be impaled on a fishhook. "Maybe I should speak to my lawyer first."

"Oh, no, you don't. Out with it. Are you some kind of Mafia hit man?"

For some reason that was worth a laugh. "Nothing like that, Miss Yoder. I'm just plain old Jim Anderson. What you see is what you get."

"You have yet to deny that you arranged to have that nice man killed."

He laughed again. "*Nice?* George? If I was locked in a room with George, Saddam Hussein, and a snake, and had a gun with just two bullets, do you know what I would do?"

"So that's how Brutus died!"

"Huh? No, what I'm trying to say is that I wouldn't hesitate to shoot George Mitchell twice."

"You wouldn't!"

"Not actually, of course. But the man certainly deserved it. I gave that man the best twenty years of my corporate life, and do you know what I have to show for it?"

"A position as a highly paid executive at East Coast Delicacies?"

"That's a laugh and a half. A flunky, is more like it."

I took off my bonnet, which was stifling, and the glasses, which were hurting the bridge of my nose. "But you *are* an executive, and you get to travel around and hold exciting contests—"

"That's a flunky's job, damn it. A kid's job. I should be back at headquarters making executive decisions. Actually running the show. God knows George wasn't qualified."

"Don't speak of the dead that way," I said sternly. "And George Mitchell was qualified. E.D.C. turned a handsome profit last year. I've been following it in the *Wall Street Journal*."

"Ha! Last year was a fluke. George inherited the company from his father, you know. He could have turned it into something really big, like General Foods or Procter and Gamble. But thanks to his leadership, it's gone from a second rate to third rate. How many people in Middle America have ever heard of East Coast Delicacies?"

I shrugged.

"That's my point. It could have been a household name by now."

I took a cautious step back. There was a lot of anger emanating from this man, and over what? Someone else's company? That didn't make a lick of sense. Jim Anderson definitely had a screw or two loose. No, make that a bucket. He should have been admitted to a metal-working shop, not a hospital.

"You don't kill somebody just because they won't turn their business over to you," I said in a soothing voice.

"What about if he takes your wife?"

"Well—"

"And then dumps her—really dumps her—throws

her out on the trash heap. And then that ex-wife of yours—the only woman you've ever really loved—turns to drugs for comfort. Drugs that George gave her. Then before you know it, she's someone you don't even recognize. Is that reason enough to kill somebody?"

"George Mitchell did that? To your wife?"

His eyes fixed on a water spot on the ceiling. "Marcy and I met in high school, for chrissakes. We dated all through college—got married the week after graduation. Had three kids together. Then George took a group of us executives and our spouses on a junket to St. Thomas. A motivational seminar, he called it."

"That sounds pretty generous to me."

"Oh, yeah, real generous. Lots of boring sessions we were forced to attend, only George didn't attend any of them himself, you see. While I was stuck inside some hotel meeting room, George took Marcy out on a catamaran. Somehow George managed to have the mast break, and they were struck overnight on a deserted little island. Just them, the mosquitoes, and enough heroin to keep New York high for a week. Next thing I knew Marcy was filing for a divorce."

He paused, still looking at the spot on the ceiling. There were tears streaming down his cheeks.

"Then what?" I asked gently. "Did she marry George?"

"That was the plan. She moved out—left me and the kids just like that. But three weeks later George had picked up with a new woman. By then my Marcy was hooked. She's been in and out of rehabs since then, but can't seem to shake that monkey off her back. The last time I saw her, she looked like a walking skeleton. Still, she was trying to turn tricks."

I must have given him a blank look.

"She became a prostitute, Miss Yoder. That's how she supports her drug habit."

"I'm so sorry."

He finally looked at me. "So, that's not reason enough to want George dead?"

I should have kept my big mouth shut. "To *want* him dead, yes, but—"

"You're a religious woman, Miss Yoder. Doesn't the Bible say that wanting someone dead is the same as killing them?"

"Words to that affect, yes."

"So, since I was already guilty of wanting him dead, why not go just one teensy step further and grant my own wish?"

"That's not the same," I wailed in frustration. "Just because we feel strongly doesn't mean we have to act on those negative emotions. That Scripture passage does not give us license to commit *actual* murder."

Believe me, I know how hard it is sometimes to keep from doing what one wants. The Good Lord knows I wanted to strangle Aaron after he finally confessed his horrible secret, but I did nothing worse than offer to pack my Pooky Bear's clothes. It was the devil that made me rub poison ivy in all eight pairs of his underpants.

"Well, I did take that teensy step—but then again, I didn't kill the man."

"You make as much sense as Braille instructions on an ATM machine at a drive-through window. Either you did, or you didn't, kill George Mitchell. It wasn't a halfway job. I saw his dead body."

"Ah, those words are music to my ears. I told you I set up his death; however, I didn't do the actual deed."

"But you paid someone to—"

"Now you're jumping to conclusions," he said with a smug smile.

Jumping to conclusions and dodging criticism are the backbone of my exercise program. I spread my hands, palms up.

"Well, ex*cuuuse* me."

"I didn't pay anyone to kill George Mitchell. I simply gathered together a bunch of people who had their own reasons to kill him."

"Come again?"

Jim smiled broadly. "Every single one of those contestants back at your inn had it in for the bastard."

I gasped. "Not Freni Hostetler!"

"You're absolutely right, not her. But I needed a nice quiet, out-of-the-way place where the ingredients of my stew—so to speak—could work their magic."

"Their evil magic! And I still find it hard to believe. Gladys Dolby wouldn't step on an ant if you paid her, and as for Alma Cornwater—"

"Never judge a cookbook by its covers."

I stared at him.

"What?" he said. "Surely you don't still suspect me. Perhaps it's escaped you, but I'm in a hospital. I have more alibis than you can shake a thermometer at."

"Do you know who the killer is?"

He had the temerity to chuckle. "That's the beauty of it. I haven't the slightest idea. It could be anyone of four people, or even a combination of those four. And you know what the best part is? I couldn't even be sure that old George would actually get bumped off. And so soon in the game! I would have settled for major trouble—a lawsuit, or a first-class scandal. Speaking of which, that's another reason I picked the PennDutch Inn."

"What?"

"Thanks to your inn's reputation as a vacation spot

for the rich and famous, you have almost as many reporters sniffing around there as they do down at the White House."

"You are a wicked man."

"Right now I'm a very happy man."

"Let's not forget despicable. If you ask me, what you did is every bit as bad as if you had been the one to bludgeon and stab George Mitchell."

He frowned. "Well, I don't recall asking you."

Perhaps I had gone too far. It was time to turn off the vinegar, and turn on the honey, if I didn't want the fly in the hospital gown to get away.

"Still," I said, shaking my head as if in wonder, "it was ingenious of you to gather a bunch of George Mitchell's enemies together. What *did* Alma Cornwater have against the man?"

"Oh, no you don't, Miss Yoder. You're not getting any more information out of me. Not until I talk to my lawyer."

"Please."

"No."

"Pretty please," I begged. "I love puzzles, you see. Riddles of any kind. Can't you just give me some clues? Sort of a mix and match test. You tell me the motive, and I'll match up the contestant."

I think Jim Anderson was about to crack, but Nurse Dudley burst into the room, her arms flapping like a rooster about to crow. Her face and neck were as red as any wattles.

She pointed at me with a spur. "Aha! Just like I thought! It *is* you!"

"Moi?"

"Barbara Kauffman, indeed!"

"But I am she." Strictly speaking, this was a clever evasion on my part, not a lie.

"How can you be Barbara Kauffman when she's in

the lobby asking for someone else?" She paused to gulp some air. "And that someone else is Magdalena Yoder!"

"Well, I couldn't possibly be her, now could I? I'm much prettier than her, remember?"

Nurse Dudley glared at me. "Where are your glasses? And why aren't you wearing your bonnet?"

I popped on the glasses, nearly jabbing my left eye in the process. As for the bonnet, it had slipped off the foot of Jim Anderson's bed, and I must have inadvertently kicked it under during the heat of our conversation. I had to get down on all fours to retrieve it. When I stood up I experienced a moment of vertigo, and that's why I plopped the bonnet on backward, completely covering my face.

Nurse Dudley was not amused "Security!" she screamed. "There's an Amish impersonator in Room 134."

I flipped the bonnet around. "Calm down, dear. There no need to get your knickers in a knot. I'm sure I can explain everything."

"I bet you can! Dr. Rosenkrantz said to have you, and your sister, thrown out the second I saw you."

"Well, Susannah maybe, but—"

"Do you have any idea how much trouble you caused?"

"Me?"

"Three patients called the Board of Health and complained about that rat you brought in."

"That was a dog! And a very clean dog, I might add." Trust me, I never thought I'd be defending the mangy menace.

"Security!" she screamed again.

The distant thunder of footsteps in the hallway made it clear that Bert, the security guard, was already on his way. No doubt this will come as a surprise to you, but I do not suffer manhandling well. The last time an authority laid a hand on me, I ended up in Hernia's hoosegow. It was not a pleasant experience. I saw no need to give the Bedford County jail an equal opportunity to damage my fragile psyche.

So said, I hiked up my skirts and hightailed it out of there like a bat out of a cave at sundown.

The real Barbara Hostetler was beaming like the searchlight in front of Wal-Mart when they run their Labor Day sale.

"What on earth are you doing here?" I snapped.

"Magdalena!"

I grabbed her by the elbow and did my best to steer her toward the door. The woman must wear suction cups on the bottoms of her shoes.

"Aren't you suppose to be at the doctor's, tinkling in a cup?"

"Ach, how you talk! I'm done at the doctor."

I dragged her through the hissing doors. "So soon?"

"Yah, there was no need to make in a cup. The doctor listened to my stomach and said—well, you know."

"That he heard it growl?"

"No!"

"Let me guess then—you're pregnant?"

"Yah. Very."

I looked at her. Amish aprons cover a multitude of sins. Obviously Barbara was a lot further along than I'd expected. Most probably further along than even she had expected.

"What do you mean by 'very'?"

"Ach, I'm going to have triplets!"

"What? You mean twins?"

"Triplets!" She held up three fingers.

Believe me, I nearly swooned right there on the

sidewalk. Twins are rare enough among my people, but I'd never actually known anyone who'd given birth to triplets. As a staunch Amish woman, Barbara had most certainly not undergone in vitro fertilization. Such matters are always left up to the Creator. But like they say, when it rains it pours, and the once barren Barbara was now harboring a clutch of fertilized eggs. I was so jealous I nearly screamed.

Instead, I smiled graciously. "Three! Wow! And you're entirely sure about this?"

She nodded vigorously. "Yah. He said he heard three heartbeats."

"When are they due?" I wouldn't have been surprised, merely annoyed, if she had gone into labor there and then.

"The end of March."

I did some quick mental arithmetic. "But that means—Barbara, didn't you suspect anything earlier?"

"Yah, of course. That's why I came to see him today."

"No, I mean *earlier*. Didn't your monthly visitor cancel his visits?"

"Ach, *that*!" She had turned the color of old rhubarb. "Magdalena, I'm over forty. I thought the visits had stopped."

"I didn't know women got morning sickness into their fifth month," I said. It's possible that there was envy to be heard in my voice. Imagine that! Here I was, a successful businesswoman—friend and confidante of the stars, and I was jealous because a distant cousin's wife was puking into the john every morning.

"The doctor said each person is different." Barbara giggled. "He said except for that, I have the construction of a horse."

"You mean constitution, dear." Suddenly it hit me

like a dozen of Mama's pound cakes. "Freni is going to be a grandmother!"

"Yah! And my Jonathan a papa!"

"Let's not forget Mose. He'll love being a grand-father. He loves children."

We were halfway to the car by then, but Barbara suddenly stopped. "Do you think she'll like me better now?"

"Who, dear?"

"Freni."

I thought guiltily of my complicity in Freni's scheme to oust the barren daughter-in-law from the family, even though she stood no chance of installing a new, more fertile one. Freni didn't want anything or anyone to come between her and her beloved son, but if someone did, and that someone was actually three someones—weighing in at less than five pounds each—and her own flesh and blood, would she change her tune? In a heartbeat.

"She'll worship the ground you walk on, dear."

Barbara beamed, brighter than that Wal-Mart searchlight. "I told the doctor I don't want to know the sex of my babies—until they're born, I mean. But if one of them is a girl, I'll name her Lily after my mama."

"And if there's a boy?"

"Jonathan."

"What if there are two boys?"

"That's easy. Mose. My father's name is Mose too, you know."

"How fortunate."

"Yah. Otherwise it would be hard to choose. Jonathan's father has been like a father to me. Maybe all three babies will be boys." She giggled.

I decided to take the old bull by the horns again. What did I have to lose, except my pride?

"What if more than one is a girl? What other names are you considering?"

Barbara grinned from ear to ear. The Kansas Mose had been unwilling, or unable, to pay for braces.

"Well, Freni of course. But if there are three girls—" She paused dramatically.

"Yes?"

"I was thinking Magdalena."

I threw four hundred years of inbred standoffishness to the wind and gave her a big hug.

"But promise me you won't tell Freni."

"Oh." That was like asking a child not to open her Christmas presents until the day *after* Christmas.

"Promise?"

I crossed my fingers behind my back, but really meant it when I told her that wild horses wouldn't be able to drag the secret out of me. It seemed like a safe thing to say at the time, since feral equines are few and far between in Pennsylvania.

"I can't wait to see the look on her face when I tell her," she said. "All these years of feeling like I don't belong—ach, that will all change now, won't it?"

"You can be sure of that, dear." I hugged her again.

A wiser Magdalena would have turned around and rushed right back to the hospital—Nurse Dudley or no—and demanded to have her lips sewn shut.

Twenty

Arthur Strump's Seafood Crepes

✦

Crepes

1 cup flour
3 eggs, well beaten
1½ cups milk
½ teaspoon salt
1 tablespoon melted butter
oil for frying

Sift together flour and salt. Add beaten eggs, milk, and melted butter. Beat thoroughly. Coat preheated skillet bottom with thin layer of cooking oil. Pour small amount of batter into pan, tilting the pan in all directions so batter will spread thin. Cook for approximately two minutes or until brown. Turn and cook reverse side.

Seafood filling

10 medium or five large shrimp, cooked, shelled
½ cup cooked monkfish, flaked

2 hard-boiled eggs, coarsely chopped
3 tablespoons butter
3 tablespoons flour
3 tablespoons freshly grated Parmesan cheese
2 tablespoons dry cooking sherry
½ teaspoon salt
¼ teaspoon ground nutmeg
dash cayenne pepper

Melt butter in sauce pan over medium heat. Stir in flour, salt, nutmeg, and pepper. Stir until bubbly. Gradually add milk and stir constantly until mixture is thick and smooth. Stir in sherry. Fold in shrimp, monkfish, and eggs. Remove from heat. Spoon filling (approximately 2 tablespoons) on to each crepe. Roll and fold edges under as with tortillas. Place crepes fold-side down in greased baking dish. Cover with remaining sauce and sprinkle with Parmesan cheese. Bake at 350 for 15 minutes or until cheese melts or place briefly under broiler.

Serves 5.

Twenty-one

I found Freni in the kitchen, along with Alma. They were the only two souls about.

I sidled up to Freni. "Where is everybody?"

"Ach, that Melvin changed his mind and had everyone go to the station. He said he wanted the jail cells handy when the murderer confessed."

"Even Susannah?"

"Yah, but she should be back soon. She was the next one on his list, after Alma."

I looked around my normally tidy kitchen. There seemed to be an unusually large number of pots, pans, and utensils scattered about. There was definitely more going on than just lunch preparations.

"What's all this?" I asked. "Cooking for the wake?"

"Shhh," Freni said, pressing a stubby finger to her colorless lips. "Alma's trying to concentrate. It's her cooking day, and she thinks she might be able to submit her sample after just one try."

"*What?* Don't be ridiculous! There isn't any more contest. Mr. Mitchell is dead, remember?"

Freni thrust her ample chest forward and drew back her head, in what is her classic confrontational stance. History has shown me that this is not the time to have a reasonable conversation with her. Unfortunately I am a slow learner.

"We have contracts," she said through pursed lips.

"Contracts? What contracts?"

"We all signed contracts when we entered the contest. The contracts say that the contest will be held no matter what."

"Even if the contest's organizer is murdered?"

"Yah, even then."

"Show me your contract, Freni."

"Ach!"

But much to my surprise, she reached down in her apron and from the depths of that ample bosom pulled a wrinkled sheet of yellow paper.

"Here. Read it!

I smoothed the paper on a small patch of unclaimed counter. The contact was written in standard legal gobbledygook, but sure enough, near the bottom of the page it read, *"In the event that I, James Boyd Anderson, am in any way incapacitated, and/or in the event that George Grayson Mitchell, CEO of East Coast Delicacies, is in any way incapacitated, the contest will continue as scheduled."*

"So this means nothing," I said. "You can't have a contest with just two judges. It has to be an odd number, in case they disagree."

"Gut Himmel!" Freni cried. "Read the rest. It says that if Mr. Anderson is decapitated, the two judges left will appoint a third."

"But that's ridiculous. Who could we possibly appoint, and what if Ms. Benedict and I can't even agree on that?"

"You'll find someone," Freni said firmly.

"But—"

Freni grabbed my wrist and pulled me to the far corner of the kitchen.

"You want there should be more trouble, Magdalena?" Freni grunted. To her credit, the woman was doing her best to whisper.

"Of course not."

"Melvin wants everyone to stay for more questioning. A bunch of English with nothing for them to do, now that's trouble."

"Agreed. But I can't just snap my fingers"—I snapped them—"and expect a third judge to show up."

As if on cue, my saucy sibling sallied into the room. "Has anyone seen Shnookums's binky?"

"Ach! That's it."

Susannah wheeled. "Where?"

I nabbed a bit of what passed for Susannah's sleeve. "You, dear. You've just been appointed a judge in the East Coast Delicacies one-hundred-thousand-dollar cook-off—that is, unless Marge Benedict has any strenuous objections."

"Me? A judge?"

Normally, one needs to court my sister's cooperation with a series of small bribes, and if that fails, I have an armory of threats into which I am not above delving. But there was no time for either tactic.

"Isn't that great, dear?" I said, my voice dripping with manufactured enthusiasm.

Susannah shrugged. "Depends. What's in it for me?"

"You'll *do* it," I snapped. I was prepared to head straight to the threats if I had to.

She shrugged again. "Fine. Whatever you say. Just help me to find the binky. My poor little Shnookums is pouting. He thinks his mommykins is just being mean."

"That pitiful pooch is pouting over a misplaced pacifier?"

She peered down into the myriad folds of her outfit. "We're just as upset as we can be, aren't we,

Shnookums Wookums? Yes, we are, yes we are," she cooed.

No doubt Alma, who was watching us from across the room, thought Susannah was certifiably nuts. She would be right, of course. But then again, who isn't just a little bit off their rocker, at least from another person's perspective?

There was only one thing to do at the moment, and that was help Susannah find the lost binky. God forbid the mangy mongrel should try to satisfy his oral cravings elsewhere. Allow me to clarify quickly that this was not a nipple-shaped pacifier, like the kind babies use. This is a tiny rubber bone that has been in Shnookums's possession since he was a pup.

I found the tooth-marked toy under Susannah's dining-room chair. It was the logical place to look, since Susannah feeds Shnookums table scraps, even though she is forbidden to do so under pain of expulsion. Many a guest has watched, intrigued and perplexed, as my sister drops bits of her meager meals down her front to feed the mongrel menace. Most folks are quiet unaware that next to my sister's heart beats another one as small as a thimble. This often comes as a rude surprise to suitors, and has been more effective in running them off than I have been with my broom.

With the pacifier returned, and the hairy hound happy once more, it was time to turn my attention to more urgent matters. The first thing I did was to retreat to my room, where I prayed for patience and for the Good Lord to curb my tongue. The second thing I did was to call Mr. Anderson at the hospital. He answered after the first ring.

"Just how valid is this stupid contract?"

"Ah, Miss Yoder! I was hoping that would be you."

"Who else could it be? I can't imagine that a lowlife

like you could have a friend in the world." I was going to have to pray harder next time.

"So tell me, have you made any headway in this investigation of yours? Who's the culprit? Not that mild-mannered little Gladys, is it? That's often the case, you know—the one you suspect the least."

"I don't know who it is, and if I did, I wouldn't give you the pleasure of finding out."

"Well, it wasn't the butler, I can tell you that"—he laughed—"because there isn't a butler in the bunch. Although Art Strump worked as a headwaiter before he made the decision to go to cooking school."

"Stop it! I didn't call to gossip about my guests. I want to know if that silly piece of paper they all signed is valid."

"Isn't that what your attorney is for?"

He was right, of course. Unfortunately, I don't have a regular attorney. Bill Zigler, who probated my parents' estate, and subsequently drew up my will, died six years ago of a heart attack suffered on a golf course. Sure, I've gotten into some scrapes since then, but somehow I've always managed to get myself out. With Bill's passing there is only one attorney left in Hernia, a corpulent, mealymouthed man who once served as mayor. Stereotypes aside, one can actually smell the chum on Ervin Stackrumple's breath.

Sometimes it is necessary to call one's bluff, which I'm sure you'll agree is not the same as lying. "My attorney says that this so-called contract isn't worth making into a paper airplane."

"Then your attorney's a jackass." What he really said was much worse than that.

I hung up, prayed some more, and dialed again.

"Oh, it's you," I said. "I was trying to dial the police. I thought they might be interested in interviewing the mastermind behind George Mitchell's murder."

The truth is, I would have to tell Melvin sooner or later. But since Melvin couldn't find his way out of a paper bag with the directions printed on the inside with phosphorescent orange crayon, I was planning on later. Let Melvin get all the credit for catching the killer, what did I care? My reward, as every good Mennonite knows, will come in heaven.

I thought I heard Mr. Anderson gasp. Although given hospital food and his recovering digestive system, it could have been something a whole lot more earthy.

"But while I have you on the line," I said, toying with my mouse, "I'll give you another chance to tell me all about this contract. Every miserable, rotten little detail."

"Well, it's valid, I can tell you that. As a licensed attorney—"

"You're a *lawyer*?" What a stupid oversight. I'd forgotten to smell his breath for fish.

"All corporations need to have good lawyers on board, and I'm one of the best."

"And no doubt one of the most modest. Look, buster, why would George Mitchell want the contest to proceed if he was dead?"

"I suppose he wouldn't."

"But that's what is says, 'In the event that . . .' "

"Ah, the incapacitation clauses. Clever, eh?"

"So clever, I haven't a clue."

"Incapacitation does not always equate with death, Miss Yoder, although a case might be made for the other way around."

"Come again?"

"It has broad legal definition. Suppose old Georgie Boy had merely burned his tongue so bad on the first entry that he was unable to sample the second. In that case, a stand-in judge would have to be found."

"Why not just cancel?"

"So as not to disappoint the contestants, of course."

"Not to mention you."

"Now you're catching on."

"Oh, yes, I get it now. If George Mitchell had somehow survived that blow to the head, or any other attempt at his life, the contest would go on in order to provide his would-be killer another opportunity."

"Exactly. What a smart student."

"But George Mitchell is dead. What do you gain by having it play through? Thanks to your tender tum-tum, you're no longer even one of the judges."

"Quite right. However, you now have a seasoned killer on your hands, and a tidy little enticement for he or she to kill again."

"The hundred thousand dollars?"

"Bingo. Aren't you the least bit curious, Miss Yoder? Don't you want to see if, and when, the killer will strike again? My God, woman, it's more interesting than a soap opera, and you don't have to watch any damn commercials."

"You're despicable," I hissed, spraying my receiver with spittle. "You make me ashamed to be a human being."

"You're a real hoot, Miss Yoder, anyone ever tell you that? Hey, keep the progress reports coming. Like I said, it's better than anything on television."

I slammed the phone down so hard that I cracked the mouthpiece. This did little, if anything, to improve my mood. You could have fed the lions to this Christian when, a few seconds later, someone knocked timidly at my door.

"Come in!" I roared.

The door opened slowly and Alma Cornwater stuck her graying, unruly head in the widening space. "Is this a bad time, Miss Yoder?"

Aaron once said that I had an antilock temper that I could stop and turn on a dime, if there was something in it for me. I never quite understood his motorcar metaphor, but I am capable of a quick recovery, if I say so myself.

I waved at Alma. "Come on in, dear. I was just about to come get you. I'd like to chat with you, if I may."

Alma doggedly shoved the glasses back into place. "I already went over all that with the police chief. No offense, Miss Yoder, but y'all's chief makes Barney Fife look like Scotland Yard."

Although I had no idea who Barney Fife was, I got the gist of what she meant by the look on her face.

"Melvin Stoltzfus is socially challenged." I pointed to a straightback chair on which I habitually lay out my clothes for the following day. "Have a seat, dear, and tell me how it went."

She sat and crossed her pudgy, jeans-clad legs, ankle over knee. "He doesn't seem to grasp the concept of taking a morning walk."

"The man rides his lawnmower when he goes out in the yard to pick up his morning paper. That's why he and my sister get along so well."

"And he doesn't just ask questions. He accuses."

"Makes you want to put your hands around his scrawny neck and throttle him, doesn't it?"

She uncrossed her legs. "Please don't put words in my mouth. Miss Yoder. I did *not* kill Mr. Mitchell, and I have no intention of killing Chief Stoltzfus."

"Of course not, dear! That was just a figure of speech. I was just trying to let you know I understand how frustrating he can be. Mr. Mitchell, on the other hand, was a kind, sweet, considerate man."

You can be sure I was watching her eyes as closely

as those thick lenses permitted. Alas, she seemed unaffected by my goading.

"In fact, I don't believe I've ever met a nicer man. Have you?"

She was as still as Lot's wife.

"I was thinking of writing to East Coast Delicacies' Board of Directors and suggesting they set up a scholarship fund in George Mitchell's name. If they don't, I might consider doing it myself. It would be a scholarship for cooks, of course. I hear those cooking schools in Paris cost a lot of money. So, what do you think of that idea?"

"I think it stinks," she said calmly. "Mr. Mitchell was a scum-sucking son of a bitch who deserved to die."

Twenty-two

Now we were getting somewhere. I have long maintained that there is nothing quite as irritating as praise for one's enemies. Apparently Alma Cornwater was in agreement.

"Do tell, dear! Only please, don't swear again."

"Look, Miss Yoder, like I said, I didn't kill Mr. Mitchell, but I sure the heck don't mind seeing him dead. The man was a thief."

"A thief? What kind of thief?"

"The kind who steals," she said flatly.

"You mean, like a car thief, or someone who breaks into homes. Really, dear, that's going a little far, don't you think? Mr. Mitchell held the controlling stock in a thriving company. I'm sure he was a wealthy man."

She pressed a finger to the bridge of her nose and nodded. "And that's why he's wealthy—he steals."

I sighed. There is not a whole lot a layperson can do about paranoia. Audrey Schlabach was convinced that a blue pickup followed her from Hernia all the way to Peoria, Illinois, when she went to visit her cousin last April. When she got there, her cousin, a much more sensible woman, discovered that Audrey's teenage son, Tom, had glued a picture of a blue pickup to Audrey's rearview mirror. It was supposed to be an April Fool's joke. You'll be glad to know that Audrey Schlabach now wears glasses.

"Well, stealing is a sin, dear, and I'm sure the Good Lord will make him account for that in the hereafter."

"I could have hired someone to stay with the children and gone back to school a long time ago," Alma said sadly. "Lot of things might have been different."

I didn't say anything. What was the point? She obviously believed George Mitchell was at the root of her troubles, and now that he was dead, she couldn't do him any harm. And I didn't think for a minute that Alma had killed George Mitchell. I have a gut instinct about these things. Although my gut won't necessarily tell me who is guilty, it invariably tells me who is *not*.

"And they were my best recipes too."

"What?" Even Reverend Schrock doesn't digress that much in his sermons.

"The recipes I sent Mr. Mitchell. The ones he turned into low-fat TV dinners and marketed as Smoky Mountain Memories."

"Those are *your* recipes?" With Freni to cook for me, I don't have much occasion to sample that plethora of frozen entrees now out on the market. I know, the woman quits her job as often as Elizabeth Taylor bails out on marriage, but she always leaves enough food behind to last until she's cooled off. However, last year when Freni slipped on some ice and was out of commission for over a week, Smoky Mountain Memories saved my life.

My guests couldn't compliment the chef enough, although they had a hard time understanding why she couldn't spare even a minute to come in and take a bow. I had to tell them it was that old Amish thing about pride, which was at least a half-truth. Even Julia, who was a guest at the time, raved about the food.

Of course one has to remove the dinners from their plastic trays and arrange them on real plates, and don't forget to dress them up with a sprig of parsley or two. A bit of garnish does for a plate what a bit of makeup does for a woman—that's what Julia said at any rate. Never having worn the latter (the garnish was accidental), I have to take her word for it.

Alma Cornwater removed her glasses and rubbed her eyes with the back of her hand. I suspected she might be crying.

"Those recipes were going to be my way out."

"Out of the mountains?"

"No, out of a trailer with eight kids and a husband who beat me—but only when he was sober, so I guess I shouldn't be complaining about that."

"Good heavens!"

"I was only sixteen when I married Ed. He was twenty-two, fresh back from the army."

"Viet Nam?"

"Nah, that was over by then. Germany. A place called Bamburg, although Ed called it Beerburg. I didn't realize it at the time—I guess I didn't want to see it—but all Ed did, when he wasn't with me, was drink."

"I see."

"I drank too in the beginning. Just to keep him company. But then I got pregnant, and stopped. Ed never could hold down a job, so after Gary was born, I found a job waitressing at Grandma Mae's diner, and Ed stayed home to take care of the baby. After a while Grandma Mae—her real name was Lucinda—brought me back into the kitchen and taught me how to cook. Lucinda said that it was next to impossible to find someone who could do really good home cooking."

"Is that a fact?" Personally, I've never understood the concept of leaving home to sample home cooking.

When I go out, it is specifically to sample something that tastes "store bought."

Alma nodded. "After a while I guess I got kinda good at it, because I started fooling around with the recipes, and if the customers really liked something, then Lucinda would make it a standard. Anyway, one day this woman comes in, and after she's eaten and everything, she asks to speak to me.

"So I talk to the woman, and it turns out she's some kind of a food critic. She said that my gooseberry meat loaf was food for the gods."

"No kidding." That was not one of the selections offered by Smoky Mountain Memories, and frankly it didn't sound very appetizing.

"That's exactly what she said. And she said I should start writing down my recipes and send them off somewhere."

"So you jotted them down and sent them off to East Coast Delicacies and—"

Alma was shaking her head. "I didn't send them anywhere. I had another baby. And then another."

I wanted to ask her if she had ever heard of birth control, but of course it wasn't my business. Maybe large families was a cultural thing for her. The Amish have huge families. Grandma Yoder, who was born Amish, and later became a Mennonite, was one of sixteen children. According to one Amish historian, the Amish population doubles every twenty years.

"So how did East Coast Delicacies get a hold of your recipes?"

"That's the funny thing. About a year later the same woman came into Grandma's, only this time she really liked my lemon walnut chicken."

"So do I!"

"This time she gave me an address, and that's how I sent them to E.C.D. But then nothing happened.

After about a year I wrote to the company and asked for my recipes back, but they didn't answer. I wrote a couple of more times, but still nothing. Then about eight years ago, just a month before my little Lucinda—she's my youngest child—was born, I went into this big supermarket in Asheville, North Carolina, and there was my lemon walnut chicken *and* my cream cheese spinach soufflé."

"Get out of town! I love that soufflé."

"Twelve recipes in all, Miss Yoder. And every one but the gooseberry meat loaf and candied cauliflower made it into the Smoky Mountains Memories line. And do you know how much I got paid for those recipes, Miss Yoder?"

I opened my mouth, but that's as far as I got.

"Not one dime! Nada. Then last year I read an article in *Homestyle Cooking* that called the Smoky Mountains Memories meals 'the most appetizing sensation to hit the human palate since the discovery of sugar.'" She gasped for air. "They've probably made millions off me. Millions! And there's not a damn thing I can do about it."

I gently wagged a finger at her. "No swearing in my boudoir, remember? Now have you tried suing them?"

Alma put her glasses back on, all the better to see what kind of fool she was talking to. "I saw a lawyer, if that's what you mean. But it's almost impossible to enforce copyrights on recipes."

"How do you mean?"

"Well, take my gooseberry meat loaf—you and I might both have invented the dish."

"Not hardly, dear. Although once I saw one of my mama's recipes in a book that the author claimed were her mama's recipes."

"Exactly. Recipes get handed down through generations and spread around like a cold in kindergarten.

Sure, there may be minor changes, but you can't prove you were the first one to come up with it. People have been eating for millions of years."

"Well—" I prudently closed my mouth. There was no point in telling her that I believe—Reverend Schrock does, at any rate—that the world was created in six days and was nowhere near a million years old. Forget millions.

"Anyway, the lawyer said I had as much chance of winning a suit as I did being elected president."

That was indeed a shame, but probably quite true. Perhaps someday we women will wise up and realize that we comprise over half the population, and that it's about time we get a chance to officially wear the pants in the White House. What's the worst we can do? Plunge the country into war? Allow the country to slip into an economic depression? Been there, done that, as Susannah says.

"So how did that make you feel, dear?"

"Angry, of course—hey, I know what you're doing! You're trying to get me to spill my guts. You want me to say that I was so mad I killed Mr. Mitchell to get even."

"Well, did you?" I'm sure I said it in a gentle, coaxing sort of way.

Alma was a tougher nut to crack than I thought. She was on her feet in righteous indignation, her glasses literally steaming up.

"I already told you I didn't mind seeing him dead. Unlike you, I don't lie, Miss Yoder—"

"I beg your pardon!"

"Yes, I hated the man's guts, but I also hate Miss Benedict's guts. You don't see her dead, do you?"

"Our Marge Benedict? Skinny, practically anorexic, roving judge and columnist for *American Appetite* magazine?"

"She's the one."

"I must admit she's not a particularly friendly woman, but she's not nearly as unpleasant as Miss Holt. Why on earth would you want to kill her?"

"I don't want to kill her," Alma practically screamed, "I just hate her guts. She's the woman who came into Grandma Mae's all those years ago and got my hopes up."

"Good heavens! Marge Benedict? You don't suppose the two of them—no, on second thought, I don't think so. She wasn't too fond of George Mitchell either."

Alma's glasses had slipped again and she was squinting at me over the rims. The woman might consider trying Krazy Glue.

"What do you know about Miss Benedict and Mr. Mitchell?"

"Nothing," I said, for her protection. "It's just a hunch. Have you spoken to her about this?"

"Oh, yeah. The day before yesterday, just after she arrived. But she claims she doesn't even remember me."

"You're kidding."

"No, she said she used to travel all around the country reviewing restaurants, but that she doesn't remember even meeting me. She said she thought it was *possible,* because she's been to North Carolina. Of course I had to be careful not to accuse her of anything, since she is one of the judges."

"Hmm," I said. "Maybe if we could get our hands on some back issues of that magazine, we could find a review of Grandma Mae's. If her name's on the review, that would prove she was there."

Alma traced an imaginary something on my floor with a mud-covered sneaker. "I don't remember ever seeing a review from *American Appetite* magazine.

That's the kind of thing Lucinda would have posted by the front door."

I pointed to the phone. "Why don't you call her?"

"Can't. Lucinda died in May. Breast cancer. Her son sold the restaurant to a chain called Applebee's. They tore down the old place, and built their own. You'd never recognize it now."

"Tell you what, I'll talk to Marge. Just sort of generally beat around the bush. Maybe I'll ask her if she knows of a market for some of Freni's recipes. It couldn't hurt, could it?"

Alma shrugged. I think she was writing my name with her shoe. Either that or a very long swear word.

"So, dear, you wanted to see me about something?" I nudged pleasantly.

"Speaking of Mrs. Hostetler, do you think it's fair to have your sister be the third judge? I mean, y'all are some kind of cousins to Mrs. Hostetler, aren't you?"

"Is that all? Don't you worry about Susannah, dear. She and Freni might be cousins, but they're not the kissing kind. They're as different as night and day, and those differences drive them both crazy. Anyway, just between you and me, Susannah despises Freni's bread pudding. It's Freni who should be worried."

"Oh." She didn't look up. "Miss Yoder, there's something else."

"Spit it out, dear," I said patiently.

"Uh, it's about Freni—I mean, Mrs. Hostetler."

"What about her?"

"She means well, I know, but she kind of—you know."

"Gets in the way?"

"Yeah, and she's sort of—"

"Bossy?"

"Well, yeah."

"I'll speak to her too, but if you want my advice, just get used to it. Live with it, as young people say these days."

She mumbled a salutation, started to shuffle out, and then turned. "Did you like the lamb burgers with lemon sauce?"

"I beg your pardon?"

"Smoky Mountain Memories sixth entree."

"Oh, yes, of course," I said out of kindness. The truth is, I'm not terribly fond of lamb, and that is the only one of their frozen entrees I didn't sample. And it has nothing to do with the fact that Mama let me bottle-feed little Mary when her mother refused to nurse her, and then served her to the family as Easter dinner three months later.

Alma smiled, and for the first time I saw that she had teeth. "My entry in the contest is curried lamb loaf with peach chutney."

I willed the contents of my stomach to stay put.

Freni poked her head in the door a few minutes later. "Yah?"

I motioned her in. "Shut the door, dear."

"Ach, I have things to do."

"This will take only a minute."

She shut the door. "God gave you long monkey arms, Magdalena. You should zip your own dresses up."

"It isn't that, dear. I wanted to talk to you about our kitchen policy."

Freni's chin edged forward. "I don't have a policy. As long as it's my kitchen, I do whatever I want."

"Yes, dear, but technically it's not your kitchen."

"Ach!" Freni squawked. A stranger might have thought she'd been struck by an assassin's bullet.

"Why don't you sit, dear?" I pointed to the chair.

She waved a stubby hand rapidly in front of her chest. "I knew it would come to this someday, Magdalena. Like Daniel in the Bible, I saw the handwriting on the wall."

"If any of these guests have been marking on my walls, East Coast Delicacies is going to pay for it!" I was as steamed as a bowl of Chinese rice. You'd be shocked at what the rich and famous can do to a room—no telling what the hoi polloi are capable of doing.

"Ach!" Freni gasped, both hands flapping now. "I'm not really talking about your walls, it's just a metamorphosis."

I scratched my head until it hit me like one of Mama's angel food cakes—with a thud. "Ah, a metaphor! What did you see coming, Freni?"

"Don't you play dumb with me, Magdalena. When you were a little girl, I used to baby-sit for you. I've diapered you. I know everything there is to know about you. You can't fool me. I know you're going to hire one of these English cooks. Well, I may be an old horse, but you're not going to be the one to put me out to pasture. I quit!"

"Freni! Stop—"

Arms still flailing, she barged for the door. I practically had to tackle her to stop her. In the process, more of my body—clothed, mind you—came into contact with hers than it has with anyone except for Aaron. And possibly Mama.

"I'm not firing you," I puffed, "and I'm certainly not hiring an English cook. This is the *PennDutch* Inn, for crying out loud. My guests expect hearty Pennsylvania Dutch cooking, not decorative little snippets to tempt the appetite."

Freni's eyes bored into mine. "Really?"

"Yes, really."

"Then what is this policy business?"

"I just—well—you see, some of the contestants might prefer it if you left them alone when they're cooking their entries."

"Then why didn't you just say so?" Freni said, gave me a pitying look, and strode from the room, head held high.

Twenty-three

I prudently decided to talk to Art Strump before I talked to Marge. Perhaps Art, as another southern cook, had had his recipes pilfered as well. Fortunately, Art was the third of Melvin's victims to be interviewed and released, so I didn't have to wait.

We literally bumped heads, he going in the front door, I going out.

Since I do not swear, I had to content myself with a gaggle of grunts, groans, and gasps. Art, on the other hand, said a few things that would have made a sailor blush. Since he was technically outside my house, I decided to go easy on the man. And anyway, my head is undoubtedly harder than his.

"Well, it was your fault, dear," I said as kindly as I could. "After all, I opened the door. You should have known someone was coming out. This isn't one of those automatic jobs like at Pat's I.G.A."

Art made a reference to copulating feces.

"Hold it right there, buster. Either you can the toilet talk, or it's back into the cold with you."

"Sorry, ma'am," he mumbled. He was holding his head with both hands. "It hurts like the dickens. Your chin's like a rock."

"That was my nose, dear, and it's more like a needle. But don't just stand there, unless you want to pay to heat the great outdoors."

He staggered in and I steered him by his coat sleeve to a warm spot by the fire.

"I thought we might have a little chat," I said pleasantly.

He had taken off his gloves and was gingerly fingering his forehead. He is, after all, a good three inches shorter than I.

"What do you want to talk about?"

I smiled. "Well, for starters, how did the interrogation go?"

"No offense, ma'am, but y'all's police chief is—uh—"

"Nuttier than an oak in October?"

"Yes, ma'am. As my mama would say, that boy is two eggs shy of an omelet."

"Well, at least he didn't arrest you. He has been known to arrest innocent people before."

"Ma'am?"

"Oh, yes. It's happened a couple of times. Of course each time I had to step in and get the accused off the hook. I'm getting pretty good at it now. Some people say I have a sixth sense. I wouldn't know about that, but if someone looks me straight in the eye, I can usually tell if they're lying or not." I leaned forward and stared into his dark brown eyes. "You didn't have anything against George Mitchell, did you?"

To my relief, he didn't squirm. "No, ma'am, I never met the man before this contest started. He seemed like a nice enough man though, if you ask me."

It was time to bait him. "Nice? He was always laughing at people behind their backs."

He said nothing.

"In fact, he snickered so much, I think they named a candy bar after him."

He regarded me calmly, as mute as a turnip.

I shook my head. "It's awful what happened to him,

but frankly, I wasn't surprised. Some of the things he did were unconscionable."

Zip, zero, zilch, nada. Even a Mennonite woman in bed is more responsive than Art Strump.

"Know when to hold them, and know when to fold them," a country-western signer said to me on his last visit to the PennDutch. Clearly, it was time to fold.

"Well, enough about George Mitchell. I really wanted to talk about Marge Benedict. Did you know that one of her jobs is to collect original recipes for East Coast Delicacies?"

"Isn't that what this contest is all about?"

"No, I don't mean just one recipe for some big new campaign. I mean lots of recipes, over the years. Like the ones they used for the Smoky Mountains Memories line of frozen dinners."

His broad nose wrinkled. "Ugh. I don't eat frozen dinners."

"Still, that's pretty exciting, right?"

"If you say so, ma'am."

Another dead end. It was time to turn this chassis on a dime.

"Where's that sweet little Carlie?" I asked brightly.

"She's still in town, ma'am."

I shook my head in sympathy. "Poor child. Melvin will grill her like a cheese sandwich. Maybe I should go down there and run interference."

Something in him flickered.

"What's the matter, dear? Is there any way I can help?" You'll have to trust me on this one, but I've been told before that I have a voice that could calm the Bosporus Straits.

Art glanced around the room, his eyes lingering on the two doorways. "Carlie is seeing a lawyer."

"Did you say 'a lawyer'?"

"Yes, ma'am. You know, an attorney."

"Who?"

He grinned. "A Mr. Stackrumple."

I clapped my hands against the sides of my head. "Ach!"

"Pretty funny name, isn't it?"

"Funny name, maybe, but the man's a shark. He'll eat Carlie for lunch. If she wanted to confess, she should come to see me. Now—"

He waved his hands in a desperate attempt to stop me. "She's not confessing to anything, ma'am, except that Mr. Mitchell was her father."

"He *what*?"

At that very instant Freni came flapping into the room, as silently as a barn owl.

"I need to see you *now*," she screeched for the second time.

"Tough turkeys, dear," I said, exercising commendable patience. "I'm in the middle of a very important conversation."

"Magdalena Portulacca Yoder! You come with me this very minute or I'll—" She raised a hand hip-high, as if to give me a swat on the behind. Although pacifists, Amish, like we Mennonites, do not consider a swat on the bottom to be violent. That is, most of us don't. As the unfortunate recipient of a good number of those nonviolent acts (most of which Susannah deserved, if anyone) I beg to differ. Hitting—especially when done out of anger—is no way to teach peaceful coexistence. On the other hand, we two pacifist denominations have one of the lowest, if not the lowest, murder rates in the country.

"Hey, y'all, I'm out of here." Art stood up, and holding his hands up, as if he were taken hostage, backed out of the room.

"Now see what you did," I hissed at Freni. "That man just dropped a bombshell on me."

"Ach!" she squawked, her beady eyes darting around the room.

"Not a real bomb! It's an English figure of speech. It means—never mind. What is so all-fired important that you have to barge in here and interrupt our conversation? Do you realize just how rude that must seem?"

"Rude shmude," she snapped. "What's the matter with Barbara?"

"Barbara?"

"Ach, is there an echo in here?" Freni has picked up one too many of Susannah's annoying phrases.

"That does it. If you're going to be rude too . . ."

I meant to stride righteously from the room, but Freni's nails dug into my arm. They were every bit as sharp as claws, and reminded me of the time Rahab the cat climbed up my skirt.

"Let go!"

"Not until you tell me what the doctor said."

"What doctor?" Honestly, I had already put Barbara's good news out of my mind. Besides, since Freni does not have a telephone in her house, there was no way she could have called her daughter-in-law. The last Freni heard, Jonathan was going to use the family buggy to drive his wife to Bedford.

"You told me to back off the supervising," she said accusingly, "so I went out front to gather black walnuts. You said I could take as many as I wanted."

"Yes, so?" I tapped my right clodhopper. Unless Freni got right to the point, she could add me to her bucket of nuts.

"So, Elizabeth Mast drove by, and said she'd stopped in to see how Mose and Barbara were doing."

"And?" Tap, tap, tap.

"Mose is up and moving around, but that Barbara!"

My pulse put the Indy 500 to shame. "Is something wrong with Barbara?"

"Ach, isn't there always. Elizabeth said the silly girl was jumping around—*dancing,* she said—and singing!"

"Good for her!"

"But she's supposed to be sick. What kind of sick is that?"

I shrugged.

"Ach, you should know, Magdalena. Elizabeth said Barbara told her you took her to the doctor. That's all Barbara would tell Elizabeth. Nothing else. Is that true?"

"I suppose it is, dear. I don't think Elizabeth lies."

Although she keeps them short, Freni's nails are capable of drawing blood. "You know what I mean, Magdalena. Did you take Barbara to the doctor?"

"Suppose I did?"

"Well, what is it? Is it that mad cow disease Mose was reading about in *The Budget*?"

I stifled a laugh. "I hardly think so."

Then the most extraordinary thing happened. For only the second time in my life I saw tears well up in Freni's eyes. The first time that happened was at my parents' funeral. Even that had surprised me. But to cry because of a little good-natured verbal sparring? Surely not the same Freni Hostetler who could wring a chicken's neck and gut it, all without flinching.

"Freni! What is it?"

"Ach, as if you don't know! You have always taken Barbara's side against me, Magdalena. And you, my own flesh and blood!"

"I have not," I cried indignantly. For me justice is not only blind, she is often deaf. She is seldom, however, mute.

"Yah, you have," Freni wailed, and then shocked me with a full-blown sob.

"What? When?"

"That very first day Barbara stepped off the train in Pittsburgh, you said she was beautiful."

"I did not. I simply said how nice it was for Jonathan that his new wife wasn't vertically challenged. But what if I did say she was beautiful, how does that hurt you?"

"Ach, there you go again, pretending you don't know. Everything is Barbara this, Barbara that—only you don't know what that woman has done to me!"

I grabbed Freni. I wanted to shake her by those sloped shoulders until her eyes fell out. This was all about Jonathan, of course. The apron strings that attached Freni to her son were forged out of steel. No, make that industrial diamonds. Weren't they supposed to be the hardest substance in the world? Well, there was only one thing in the world that could cut, or at least loosen, those unnatural bonds.

"I'll tell you what she's done! She's gotten herself pregnant. She's about to make you a grandma!"

Freni fainted.

I screamed.

"You didn't need to give her mouth-to-mouth," I said crossly to Art.

It was sweet of him to come running back into the room when I screamed, but not every woman in a prone position needs a man's breath to get her on her feet again. When poor Freni, who was out only for a few seconds, realized what was happening, she fainted again. This time I had to run to the refrigerator and retrieve that lump of Limburger cheese I save just for that purpose.

"Ach!" Freni sat up abruptly, her face greener than the cheese.

"Feeling better, dear?" I moved to help her up, but she slapped my hand away.

"Say it again."

"Feeling better, dear?"

"Ach, not that! What you said before!"

I took a deep breath. When the cat is out of the bag already, you have only two choices as far as I can see: pretend you let the cat out on purpose, or put the bag over your head and suffocate. Since Art was there, ready to resuscitate me with a lip-lock, I had no choice but to go with the former.

"I said she's pregnant. She wanted to tell you herself, of course, but the smell of Limburger cheese makes her sick, so I thought it best that I break the news. Now when she tells you, remember to act surprised."

Freni wasn't listening. "With a *baby*?"

"That's usually how it goes, dear, unless your Melvin Stoltzfus's mother."

Freni was on her feet in a nanosecond. Before I could resist, she had my face between her worn hands, and was pulling my head down.

"Magdalena, look me straight in the eye."

I did.

"Is this true? Is my daughter-in-law pregnant?"

"Yes, but, Freni, remember to act surprised."

"Yah, yah," Freni said, hopping about like a frog on hot pavement. She was literally beside herself with joy.

"Freni, you have to promise!"

"Yah, yah, I promise."

Alma appeared out of nowhere. "What's going on? I would have come sooner but—"

Freni grabbed Alma in what can best be described as a clumsy embrace, and then kissed the top of her graying head. "I'm going to have a baby, I'm going to have a baby!"

Alma struggled free of Freni's grip. Clearly she was in the presence of a madwoman.

"Miss Yoder," she said sternly, "aren't you going to do something for her?"

"Like what?"

"Give her whatever medication she's normally on."

"She's just happy about the baby, dear."

Alma's brown eyes widened. "It isn't true, is it? I mean, it *couldn't* be true."

Art winked at me and grinned. "You never know these days. Mothers keep getting older and older."

"Yes, but"—she paused, and I could sense the light clicking on in her head—"I get it! Congratulations, Mrs. Hostetler. Is this going to be your first grandbaby?"

"Yah, yah, my first grandbaby!"

Alma smiled broadly. I should have guessed she was up to something.

"I hate to spoil the moment, Mrs. Hostetler, but I broke that big glass bowl you set out for me. I'm terribly sorry."

Freni didn't as much as frown. "Ach, what's a bowl, when there's a baby?"

"When there's three babies," I almost said, but wisely *didn't*. Barbara wasn't going to accuse me of telling her entire secret.

"Okay," I said to Art Strump, "Ms. Cornwater's back in the kitchen, and Mrs. Hostetler is somewhere off on cloud nine. It's time for you to spill the beans."

"Ma'am?"

"Sit"—I pointed to a chair—"you and I have a lot to talk about."

"Ma'am?"

"Ma'am me all you want, but you're not getting out of this one. What did you mean when you said George Mitchell was Carlie's father?"

He swallowed. "Well, I suppose it's all going to come out anyway, so I may as well tell you everything now."

I nodded vigorously. "Leave out one word, dear, and you'll end up on my compost pile."

Art spilled enough beans to fuel a gas-powered engine from coast to coast.

Twenty-four

"**S**o, what you're saying is that George Mitchell abandoned Carlie when she was a baby?"

"No, he never even knew about Carlie. Not at first. It was Carlie's mama George Mitchell skipped out on."

"What was she in the pecking order?"

Art's eyebrows fused. "Ma'am?"

"I mean, was she his first wife, second wife, whatever?" Not that it mattered, but rumor had it that George Mitchell had been married a handful of times. I have a theory that oft-married men, if given enough time, will eventually gravitate back to their first wives. Perhaps not for their physical needs, mind you, but for emotional security. First wives are, after all, the ones who really raise men.

"She never was his wife. She was a lounge singer in Charleston. A itty-bitty woman by the name of Gardenia. Well, that was her stage name, the one Mr. Mitchell knew her by."

"You don't say. Did he hook her on heroin too?"

"Ma'am?"

"Never mind. Do you know this woman?"

"No, ma'am. She died—killed herself—when Carlie was just a baby. But I've seen a picture. She was beautiful. Imagine Carlie without all the rings and stuff."

I tried to imagine the girl without apertures in inappropriate places. It was like imagining Swiss cheese without holes.

"I'll take your word for it, dear. Did Gardenia kill herself because of George?"

"No, ma'am, she was already over him. She killed herself over some other dude. Women, go figure!"

"Indeed! So, if Gardenia, uh—dated—more than one dude, as you so elegantly put it, how does Carlie know George Mitchell is really her father?"

"Gardenia left a letter in a safety deposit box. Mr. Mitchell wasn't quite the hot stuff then that he was up until yesterday—he was just a salesman—but Carlie's mama had a feeling he was going somewhere. She had the name of the company written down. East Coast Delicacies—only then it was East Coast Treats. Something like that."

I vaguely remembered East Coast Treats. All I remembered was that their products were not such treats—gelatinous meat loaf and dry mashed potatoes accompanied by cardboard vegetables. When I discovered E.C.D. several years ago, I never even associated the two.

"That doesn't prove much, dear. Anyone can make a paternity claim."

"Yes, ma'am, but Carlie's mama was no fool. She wrote down a couple of Mr. Mitchell's—uh—most distinguishing features as proof that she really knew him."

I willed away thoughts of poultry. "That still isn't enough proof. Carlie is going to need DNA tests to back up her claims."

"Exactly. That's why she had to see Stackrumple right away. We're going to need tissue samples from Mr. Mitchell."

"What if his next of kin won't allow that? I can't imagine allowing some stranger to scrape cells from my sister. Then again, since my sister is not a man, it's not likely to be an issue to raise its ugly head."

Art gingerly fingered the spot where my proboscis had almost probed his cranium. At least there didn't seem to be a dent.

"Mr. Mitchell has only one living relative, an elderly aunt living in a nursing home out near Phoenix. According to the staff there she is in advanced stages of Alzheimer's disease. I don't think she'll object."

I chewed on that. "Well then, is her approval necessary?"

"Not if Carlie can show reasonable proof that her claim is true."

"Carlie certainly seems to have done her research, I'll grant you that. It might even appear as if she was waiting and ready."

"Ma'am?" My statement so startled him, he almost fell off his chair.

"Of course this is just an amateur's opinion. Who knows what a professional would think."

"Ma'am, are you implying that Carlie killed Mr. Mitchell?"

"Well, let's see if we have the three basic ingredients . . . first, motive. I'd say being the sole heir to a wealthy man is enough motive, wouldn't you? Throw in a jilted mother, and a difficult childhood that no doubt could have been made easier by money and—well, gobs of people have killed for far less."

"I don't know about any gobs, ma'am, but Carlie didn't kill anyone."

I ignored his feeble protest. "Next we consider means. Carlie might be a scrawny little thing, not much bigger than a bantam rooster, but she's young. That counts for a lot. I have no doubt that she was capable of bludgeoning George Mitchell with a heavy object."

"Yes, ma'am, but—"

I waved a hand impatiently. "Don't you 'but' me until I'm done, dear. Then I'll give you an opportunity to speak—which brings me to my third point. Opportunity. What better opportunity to kill someone than to spend a week with them sequestered on some isolated Pennsylvania farm? Agatha Christie couldn't have come up with a better location."

He looked positively stricken. His mouth opened and shut a couple of times, like a baby bird begging to be fed.

"If the shoe fits," I said smugly.

He was on his feet. "No, ma'am, not this shoe. Carlie would never do such a thing. Anyway, entering this contest was my idea."

"How fortuitous for her. Also, a bit of a coincidence, don't you think?"

He licked his lips. "Excuse me?"

I stood up as well. As a woman of stature, I often prefer to be seated in the presence of men, particularly short men with fragile egos. But I was trying to prove a point, and felt at a definite disadvantage seated in my chair.

"I mean, what are the odds that her benefactor would enter a contest sponsored by her absentee father? Hmm, this smacks of collusion, if you ask me."

His eyes flashed. "Okay, okay, just don't put the blame on Carlie. It was all my idea."

"Keep right on spilling, dear."

"Ma'am?"

"The beans, Art. And get to the point. *Tempus fugit*, and I don't have all day."

"Yes, Carlie knew that her father would be here, but she only wanted to confront him, not to kill him. It was while doing the research on her father that Carlie came across the announcement about the contest. You'd be surprised what you can find on the Internet."

"So I've heard." Alas, as a technologically challenged person, I would never know this firsthand. I find an electric can opener daunting.

"Anyway, it seemed like a perfect opportunity. I stood to win one hundred thousand dollars—I really am a good cook, Miss Yoder—and Carlie could check out her father."

"And if you didn't win the contest, you could always bump him off. How much do you think he's worth dead? Two hundred thousand? Maybe even a million?"

The muscles along the left side of his jaw twitched. "No offense, ma'am, but you're really pissing me off."

"I beg your pardon!"

"Carlie did not kill her father," he said through clenched teeth. Then, without as much as a by-your-leave, he turned and strode from the room.

I went for a walk. I love the woods at any season, but particularly in the late fall, when a few colorful leaves still cling to the trees, but there are enough already on the ground to give crunch to my footsteps. Thanks to Alma's unfortunate experience, I knew to avoid the Mishler brothers, and of course I always stay well away from Dinky Williams and his Lady Godiva wife. But just between you and me, a woman whose adipose deposits have drooped to the point she could stand while nursing a child lying on the floor should seriously reconsider nudity as a way of life.

At any rate, directly across the road from my house is the old Miller farm, which was just recently bought by a conglomerate, but just down the road, toward Hernia, is a lovely stretch of woods that has somehow managed to escape development. This bit of woods is my favorite, because it contains many large boulders, some almost as big as a house. Many was the time when I humored Susannah and played hide-and-seek with her among the rocks.

Because there are a lot of brambles growing between the woods and the highway, the best way to get to this idyllic spot is to follow the road about a quarter of a mile and enter where some trees overhanging the road have shaded the brambles back into submission. Susannah always had a hard time with this; walking along a highway was a "geeky" thing to do. I rather enjoy it. Hertlzer Lane sees very little motorized traffic, and as for the Amish buggies, the clip-clop of the horses and the grating of metal wheels against asphalt is music to my ears. Besides, I know virtually all of the occupants of those buggies, and with the exception of Annie Zook, we are all on good terms.

I had just waved to the Stutzmans when I noticed the lone figure of a woman walking toward me from town. This naturally came as somewhat of a surprise, since not many women are as confident about walking alone as I am. I was even more surprised when I discovered that the lone figure was none other than Gladys Dolby.

I paced myself so that we met where the trees overhung the highway. Gladys must have been deep in thought, because she seemed surprised to see me.

"Ah! Miss Yoder."

"Fancy meeting you here," I said pleasantly.

Gladys shook her head. Frankly, her bob did nothing to enhance her looks, although I must say it did fall neatly back to place.

"When I got done being grilled by that awful man, I needed to clear my head."

"I know exactly what you mean, although with me it's my stomach."

"He's even worse than Daddy," she mumbled.

"What?"

"He didn't take me seriously at all. He barely asked me any questions."

"Count your blessings, dear. The man is a certified twit, and I mean that charitably. You could be on your way to Sing-Sing as we speak."

"Stereotypes. I hate it when people stereotype me." She mumbled something unintelligible. "Do I look like a killer to you?"

"Yes."

"I do? You really think so?"

"Well, not you specifically, of course. But everyone looks like a killer to me. You wouldn't believe the unassuming types who—"

"So that's how I come across—unassuming?"

It would have been unkind to tell her the unadulterated truth. "You look innocent, dear. There's no crime in that."

I, on the other hand, have a face the Good Lord must have copied from the wanted pamphlets at the post office. Aaron called it a face that would make the devil drop his drawers—and that was when we were courting. No telling what this face is capable of doing now.

Gladys took a step back and stared up at my face. "I'm full of surprises, you know."

"I wouldn't doubt it, dear."

"You're just saying that to be nice."

"Random words of kindness are not my forte, dear. The truth is, nothing on God's green earth would surprise me anymore—not after what my pseudo-ex-husband sprung on me. Go ahead, tell me that Arnold Schwarzenegger and Michael Jackson are one and the same person, or that Bill and Hillary were both virgins when they married. See, I didn't even blink."

"You're patronizing me, aren't you, Miss Yoder? I can't stand it when people patronize me."

"Honestly, I'm not—"

I had spoken too soon. I was genuinely astonished when Gladys Dolby threw back her head and burst into song.

"Gladys Dolby took an ax and gave her daddy forty whacks. When she saw what she had done, she gave him fifty just for fun."

I closed my mouth before my tongue had a chance to freeze. "That's all but been disproved, dear. Lizzie Borden was probably as innocent as—well, as me."

"Maybe. Maybe not. I told that police chief I thought Mr. Mitchell was revolting. He pinched my bottom once. Can you believe that?"

"Melvin Stoltzfus?" Just wait until Susannah heard about this.

"No, Mr. Mitchell pinched me! I was going up that—uh—impossibly steep stairs of yours—and he was right behind. Suddenly I feel this sharp pain, and when I looked around back at him, he winked! Isn't that disgusting?"

"That's hardly grounds for murder, dear."

Her face fell. "You can't prove that there weren't other times when he harassed me."

Gladys was not a woman I needed to talk to, she was a woman who needed to talk to me. Since I have never been one to sacrifice in silence, I'll tell you now that I did the Christian thing and invited her on my walk. Perhaps that will help make up for the fish I mailed to Aaron by parcel post on the hottest day of the year. By the time I scooped it out of the pond, it had no doubt been dead for several days.

I'll say this for Gladys, she was every bit as nimble as a mountain goat. Despite the fact that she was wearing a tweed skirt suit, topped with a heavy knee-length jacket, she scrambled to the top of the highest rock in a matter of seconds.

"Are you sure you're not part bighorn?" I puffed when I joined her some minutes later.

"I'm nothing like my daddy. He climbed Everest, you know."

That did not impress me. Why anyone would want to risk their life climbing to the roof of the world is beyond me. Most folks can't breathe up there without oxygen tanks, and I hear it's colder even than Hernia. Why not wait until you die, and get the very same view on your way up to heaven?

"I have no doubt, dear, that you could climb Everest if you wanted."

"I'd like to. Without oxygen. Daddy climbed with."

We settled ourselves on the crest of a boulder I call Baldy. The others are covered with lichens and moss, but Baldy occupies a position in the sun and its surface is smooth, gray granite. I would guess it to be about fifteen feet high.

"Now, dear, tell me more about your father. He sounds like such a fascinating man."

"Oh, he's that all right. You name it, Daddy's done it."

"Served as president of the United States," I said.

She rolled her eyes. "*Served* the president. Daddy is a four-star general."

"Get out of town!"

"I made him swear he wouldn't tell anyone. I didn't want special treatment, and I certainly didn't want *him* getting special treatment."

"Land o' Goshen!"

"Do you know what his middle name is?"

"I haven't a clue, dear."

"Good, because I also made him swear not to put it down when he registered at the inn."

I gave her a moment. "Well?"

She looked away. "It's Oliver."

"Oh."

"That's right. Daddy's initials spell G.O.D. That's one thing he never lets you forget. Once, when I was about eight years old, I left my bike out in the rain. It was a brand-new bike, and I didn't want it to get all rusty, but I was afraid to go out and get it because there was a lot of lightning. Well, Daddy went out and got it for me, but when he got back he made me say, 'Thank you, God.' "

"One should always remember to thank God," I said, not understanding her point.

"The real God yes, but Daddy was talking about himself."

"That's blasphemy!"

"That's Daddy for you. He thinks he's invincible. But you know what?"

"What, dear?"

"He's afraid of spiders!"

"You're kidding."

"No, I'm not. Even those little tiny brown house spiders make him crazy. One crawled onto his sleeve once, and Daddy about had a fit. He jumped around, screaming and hollering, until I brushed it off."

"Get out of town, girl!" An eclectic stream of guests has vastly improved my vocabulary.

She clamped a hand over her mouth to stifle a laugh. Then she shook her head.

"No, I've just got to tell somebody."

"I'm all ears."

"The thing is, Miss Yoder, I didn't brush it off right away. I let him dance around for a few minutes before coming to the rescue. I know that sounds awful—but

I enjoyed watching G.O.D., the four-star general, be afraid like that."

It's hard to say who laughed the loudest. We both laughed until our throats were raw and our collars soaked with tears. The curator at the Pittsburgh zoo told the *Post-Gazette* that, for some strange reason, their pair of spotted hyenas started laughing for no apparent reason around noon that same day, and laughed for twenty minutes straight. He thought it might be some kind of world record. Little did he know.

Twenty-five

Kimberly McManus Holt's
Boston Baked Beans

✦

2 cups navy beans
½ pound bacon
1 large onion, sliced
¼ cup brown sugar
3 tablespoons molasses
1 teaspoon dry mustard
¼ teaspoon ground ginger
2 apples, peeled, cored, sliced

Soak dried beans in water overnight. Drain. Line bean pot or deep baking dish with bacon strips. Mix brown sugar, molasses, and spices with beans. Spread layer of bean mixture on top of bacon strips. Add a layer of bacon strips and onion slices. Repeat with layer of beans. Spread apple slices evenly across top layer. Cover with water. Bake covered at 300 degrees for five hours. Add water as necessary to keep from drying out.

Serves 6.

Twenty-six

We got back to the inn just in time for lunch. Theoretically. The table had not been set, and when I entered the kitchen, I found Freni with her arms around Alma.

"Ach," I heard her say, "you still have this afternoon."

"Ahem," I said. Don't get me wrong, I didn't for a second suspect Freni of anything untoward. It's just that the last time I saw Freni with her arms around a woman was almost ten years ago, and my cousin was trying to drag the poor soul, an Avon dealer, out into a snowdrift. I know, I am not the most nurturing person on the planet, but compared to Freni, I'm a master gardener. I hug Susannah on an annual basis, and once hugged a toddler at church just because she was crying.

Alma looked slowly up at me. Even through the Coke-bottle lenses I could tell she'd been crying.

"Somebody swiped my paring knife."

"They did?" Years of experience have taught me not to take customer accusations at face value. The English are a confusing lot. Take for example the pair of white women who checked in last year. Halfway through their stay I discovered they had smuggled in a baby. Then at checkout time the one in the surgical mask and high-pitched voice had the audacity to accuse me of stealing her glove. Just *one* glove, for Pete's sake!

A tear squeezed out beneath the rim of one lens. "Yeah. Mrs. Hostetler was real nice. She gave us each a drawer and three cupboard shelves to store our things in."

"She *did*? And I thought I was going to have to call in the National Guard."

"Ach, very funny, Magdalena. Now we have an English girl living in the cellar with my pots and pans. Don't say I didn't warn you if some of those grow feet."

"Legs, dear." I turned to Alma. "I'll ask around about your knife. You know, it doesn't smell half bad in here. Are you ready for the judges?"

"Oh. Miss Yoder—well, uh—the lamb turned out fine, but—but—" She turned away to blubber privately.

"She burnt the jam," Freni whispered in a voice loud enough to wake the dead.

"You mean chutney, dear. It's an Indian condiment." Freni colored.

"Like a sweet relish," I explained quickly.

"It's Indian from India," Alma said, "not Native American."

"Yah, not one of *our* recipes," Freni said, and somehow managed to wrinkle her beak of a nose.

I glanced around a surprisingly disorderly kitchen. "Speaking of food, how's lunch coming along?"

"Ach," Freni said, "I completely forget."

"You *forgot*?"

Freni shrugged. "I'm only human, after all."

"My kingdom for a tape recorder," I moaned. "Freni, in case you've forgotten it as well, this is an inn that serves food to its guests."

"I'll throw something together in a minute."

"Make that a New York minute, dear. Melvin has

graciously interrupted the inquisition until after lunch."

"Yah, yah, like I said, in a minute." She turned to Alma. "After lunch, I'll help you figure out what went wrong. Maybe it was the saucepan. Magdalena is as tight as last year's dress when it comes to money, so the quality isn't the best. But"—she glanced at me, and then back at Alma—"we must try not to be too hard on her. She's an orphan, you know."

I stared at my cousin. Same beady eyes, same beaky nose, same monstrous bosom so unfairly straining at the pleated bodice of her dress. It was indeed the outer shell of my kinswoman. What had happened to the Freni inside was anyone's guess.

"Freni!" I snapped.

Freni gently patted Alma's arm before turning to me. "So what's more important, Magdalena, English stomachs or this child's heart?"

"Well, this child's heart, of course, but—"

"I am not a child," Alma mumbled and ambled from the room.

At last I could turn my full wrath upon Freni. "Why, Freni Hostetler, you should be ashamed of yourself! You have never been late with a meal since the inn opened—not counting those times you quit."

Freni nodded. "Yah, I have always been on time."

"So, what do you have to say for yourself now?"

Freni yawned. "I'm sorry."

My mouth opened wide enough to bob for apples, and might have fossilized in that position if Susannah hadn't floated into the kitchen, trailing yards of tulle.

"Everyone's gathered in the den," she announced. "Even that horrible Ms. Holt. They want to know when lunch is. I told them I'd be happy to drive into Bedford and bring back pizza, or we can call the order in." She gave me a meaningful look that I ignored.

I see no sense to pay the extra ten-dollar delivery charge to get stone-cold pizza delivered from Bedford. Someday, if Hernia ever got a pizzeria, then maybe. In the meantime I have a perfectly able cook—well, you know what I mean.

"Is that Carlie back too?" I asked pleasantly.

Susannah shuddered. "Ugh, that horrible Ervin Stackrumple brought her back from Hernia. What's that all about?"

"Later, dear. In the meantime, tell them lunch will be ready in the shake of a lamb's—" I remembered Alma's contest entry and shuddered. "Just tell them to relax and make themselves comfortable. We'll have it on the table as soon as we can."

I did my best to get lunch on the table within the hour, but the once frenzied Freni was now unfazed. She poked along like a turtle in molasses, all the while telling me what she planned to sew or knit for the baby.

"Maybe I should just quit," she suggested at one point. "Just think of all the cute little outfits I could make for the sweet little pumpkin."

I shuddered. "You're Amish, dear. Everyone dresses the same. How many identical little outfits does a baby need? Anyway, if you quit now, I'll tell Barbara all about the contest—how you schemed to get rid of her."

"Ach!" Unflappable Freni flapped just that once.

"On the other hand, if you keep working, you can buy the little darlings their own farms. I'm sure they'd like that much better."

"*They*! Did you say *they*?"

My heart pounded. "I said no such thing."

"Yes, you did. I just heard you. Is my precious Barbara going to have twins?"

"Ha! Don't be ridiculous."

Freni flapped again. "Ach, then why did you say 'they'?"

"It was just a slip of the tongue, dear."

"Slip, shmip! That dear girl is having twins, and you want me to make lunch for the English? I should be home right now—"

"Barbara's not having twins," I screamed, and then before I could say more, I shoved my fist in my mouth.

Lunch, when we finally got it on the table, was the worst fare the PennDutch has ever served. The chicken was chewy, the dumplings doughy, and the sherbet had to be sucked through a straw. It was definitely not typical Pennsylvania Dutch cooking. I've eaten in Presbyterian homes with better food. A bigger woman would have taken down her shingle or, at the very least, openly converted to another denomination.

Time and tide waits for no man, and many is the time I've wished the tide would come inland as far as Hernia and wash Melvin Stoltzfus out to sea. When the phone rang during our delayed lunch, I knew without a doubt it had to be him.

"Aren't you going to get the phone?" Susannah asked, treating us all to a glimpse of masticated chicken.

"Susannah, dear," I said, furrowing my brow in a meaningful way. That's all I needed to say, but it was two words too much. One would think that after almost a lifetime—she was married less than a year—spent in a Yoder household, she would be wise to the fact that we do not let that plastic box with bells pull our strings. *Not during meals.*

The front desk phone rang until the machine picked up, then it immediately rang again.

"It could be important," Susannah said, risking my wrath. Either she was expecting a call, or the six pairs of guests fixed on me were making her nervous. Freni, incidentally, does not eat with us, and never answers the phone anyway.

I would have unplugged the blasted thing, had it rung again, but immediately after the desk machine picked up for the second time, the phone in my bedroom rang. That's when I sprinted. That is an entirely different matter, mind you. My bedroom number is given out to only a select few. Besides Freni and Susannah, the only folks who have officially been given the number are the crème de la crème of celebrityhood. If it wasn't Babs this time, I knew it had to be Brad. His recent split was the pits, and although it may be bony, mine is a broad shoulder to cry on.

"Babs?" I asked breathlessly.

"Uh"—a phone rang in the background—"hold on a minute please," a male voice said.

I foolishly held on.

"Uh—okay, I'm back. Sorry about that."

"Brad?" It didn't sound like him, but crying will do that to you.

"Uh—this is Stuart. May I please speak to Magdalena Yoder."

My stomach did a sudden flip-flop, which had nothing to do with Freni's flop of a meal. The caller had pronounced my surname to rhyme with "otter." There were only two possibilities that came to mind; either one of my celebrity friends could not be trusted and had shared my number with a friend, *or* one of my celebrity friends couldn't be trusted and had sold me out to the paparazzi. Whichever the case, you can be sure that some high-ranking politician or Hollywood personality was going to pay dearly for his or her judgment in error. I know, vengeance is God's call, not mine, but there is nothing in Scripture that says the Good Lord doesn't use common folks like me to mete out his divine judgment. A well-placed rumor, *early* morning phone calls, a five-pound sack of dandelion seeds—the possibilities were endless.

"I have no comment," I screeched. "You, on the other hand, have a lot to say for yourself. Who are you, and how did you get this number?"

During the ensuing silence, the tobacco lobby down in Washington saw the error of their ways, and Joan Collins won the Nobel prize for literature.

"Uh—like I said, this is Stuart. I'm calling on behalf of Tight As A Drum Basement Enterprises."

"What?"

"This is a courtesy call. We've had—"

"How can this be a courtesy call when you just interrupted my lunch?"

"Uh—ma'am, we've had a lot of reports lately from homeowners on your street who say their basements have been flooded. Have you noticed any dampness in yours?"

"I don't live on a street, dear, I live on a country lane."

"Maybe so, ma'am, but many of your neighbors have reported leaky and flooded basements. Uh—when would be a good time for one of our representatives to come out and look your situation over? Let's see, I can squeeze you in tomorrow at—"

It was time to have a little fun. "I don't think that's possible for my neighbors' basements to flood, dear. We live on the peak of a high mountain—you might even say that our homes cling to the crags. If my neighbors' basements are flooded, then the town of Bedford is under water, along with New York City and the entire Eastern Seaboard—in which case, don't you have bigger fish to catch?"

"Miss Yotter, I'm just doing my job."

"You job is to intrude into people's homes and lie about their neighbors' basements?"

"I'm not lying," Stuart snapped. "That's what my information says."

"Well then, dear, who are some of these homeowners with leaky basements?"

"I'm not at liberty to say, ma'am."

"Why not? If my neighbors' basements are being flooded, I need to know so I can help out. You know, like go ark-shopping for them. Round up animals two by two."

Stuart sighed. "Miss Yotter, are you mocking me?"

"Of course, dear."

"I thought so. Well, let me tell you something, lady. You can't have it both ways."

"I beg your pardon?"

"You can't bitch about my generation being lazy, but then when we get jobs, yell at us, or worse yet, mock us like you were just doing."

I swallowed back my irritation at the *B* word. "Surely there are other jobs out there besides telephone sales."

"Hey, if I don't do this job, somebody else will. So what difference does it make?"

"I'm sure there were a few Nazis who said the same thing."

"Nazis? Are you crazy, lady? I don't have to take this, you know."

"Neither do I, dear. Now before I hang up, how did you get my telephone number?"

"That's privileged information, ma'am."

"You're darn tooting," I said. That's as close as I ever come to swearing. "My telephone number *is* privileged information. Now, if you don't want to tell me, put your supervisor on the phone."

In the silence that followed, Dennis Rodman

learned manners, Jerry Springer acquired good taste, and Tamar Myers's latest book was nominated for an Agatha Christie award.

"Uh—well, my supervisor just stepped out."

"Tell you what, dear. You give me your telephone number and I'll call you back in ten minutes. Maybe your supervisor will have stepped back in by then."

Stuart hung up.

I hadn't gotten as far as my bedroom door when the phone rang a third time. Stuart was persistent, I'd grant him that. It would be a shame to let such an admirable quality go unrewarded.

I snatched up the still warm receiver. "You were absolutely right, dear! Help! The water's getting higher. It's up to my knees now. Oh, no, it's up to my waist—no, make that my throat! Glug. Glug."

"Pull the plug."

"What?"

"Pull the plug," Melvin Stoltzfus said. "That's what I did, the time I almost drowned. Had to figure the damned thing out myself though. Mama refused to tell me."

"Melvin! What are you doing on my private line?"

"Susannah gave it to me, remember? Look, Yoder, I don't have time for idle chitchat. Are you still drowning, or can we talk now? This is official police business."

"Babble away, dear." While he lectured and hectored I would think of all the possible ways to pull Melvin's plug. Such thoughts were a sin, of course, but I'd been nursing some major grudges lately—most having to do with my slime-sucking, pseudo-ex-husband Aaron. As long as I was going to take the Good Lord's time confessing my sins, I may as well make it worth His while.

"The coroner just called, Yoder. I tried to call you on the other line. Where were you?"

"Eating lunch." One way to pull Melvin's plug was to put bug poison in his food. As a mantis, he would be especially susceptible.

"Still eating? I told everyone they had to be back here by one. It's quarter after right now."

"Freni got into one of her funks." It was close enough. Anyway, I'm sure lots of Freni's funks have gone by unrecorded. And please note, I did *not* blab to Melvin about Barbara's delicate condition.

"Yeah, well, see that you get them here A.S.A.P."

"I am not your flunky, dear," I said with remarkable restraint.

My Christian charity was wasted on Melvin. "Aren't you even going to ask what the coroner had to say?"

I was stunned. Melvin was itching to share, which wasn't like him. Whatever the coroner had to say must really be good.

"So, dear, what did the coroner say?"

"The coroner declared Mr. Mitchell officially dead."

"Permanently?" Tit for tat for the twit.

"Very funny, Yoder. Do you want to hear the rest or not?"

"Absolutely."

"Like I was about to say, he removed wood fragments from the deceased's forehead."

"Hmm."

"He said one of them was red."

"No kidding, you—"

"Red *paint,* Yoder. What do you think I am, a twit?"

I sat down heavily. What did happen to my barn door prop? Could that possibly be the murder weapon, and if so, where was it now?

"It wouldn't make me liable, would it?" I asked, thinking aloud.

"Yoder, are you there? I mean *all* there?"

"Look who's calling the kettle black. So, did the coroner have anything else to say?"

"Hold onto your hat, Yoder. This is the good part." He was positively gleeful. "Are you sitting down, Yoder?"

"Yes," I said quietly. I had a hunch this was going to be bad, and I had long since learned that a hunch from a woman is worth two facts from a man.

He took a deep, dramatic breath. "The knife blade was still embedded in the back of his neck."

"Get out of town!"

"No kidding. It had broken off, of course. It was stuck in his vertebrae."

"How gruesome." A vision of George Mitchell's dancing eyes played across my mind's screen, and I blinked to dislodge it.

"Wait," Melvin said, "it gets even better. Doc said it looked like some kind of kitchen knife. But one with a short blade. Mama has one of those—what does she call it—oh, yeah, a paring knife."

Twenty-seven

"**D**id you say *paring* knife?"

"You got a hearing problem, Yoder? Boy, wait until Mama hears this. Freni Hostetler—her best friend—my number one suspect."

"What?"

"She didn't fool me for a second, Magdalena. You're the one who insisted that I leave her off my list of suspects. What do you have to say about that now?"

"You're an idiot, that's what! Think for once, Melvin. You *know* Freni. You know her almost as well as you know your own mother. Could your mother kill a man?"

"You're damned straight she could. Only Mama is smarter than Freni. She would have used a rolling pin instead of barn siding. Much less likely to leave splinters with a rolling pin."

"Melvin! I'm telling!"

I distinctly heard him gulp. "I was just kidding, of course. But I'm not about Freni. Have her come in with the rest."

"I most certainly will not. You're a sandwich short of a picnic, dear, if you think a seventy-five-year-old Amish woman stabbed George Mitchell with her paring knife."

"Oh, yeah? You can't argue with evidence, Yoder. Doc said it was definitely a paring knife."

"There are four other cooks staying at the inn, for crying out loud. That knife could have belonged to any of them."

The mantis mulled that for a minute. "Did any of the others bring paring knifes with them?"

It was perhaps the most reasonable question Melvin had ever asked, and as such, it deserved a straight answer.

"Yes."

"Yes?" Melvin sounded as shocked and pathetic as Susannah did when I told her that Santa Clause wasn't real. Susannah, however, was married at the time and at least had a spouse to turn to for comfort.

"So you see, it could have been someone other than Freni."

"Did they all bring knives?"

"How should I know? I didn't make them fill out inventory lists."

"But you know of at least one who brought a knife, right?"

"Uh—right."

I could hear the malevolent mandibles mashing against the mouthpiece. "So who was it, Yoder?"

"I'm not at liberty to say."

"What the hell do you—"

"Don't swear, Melvin, or I'll never tell."

"You tell me, Yoder, or I'll arrest you."

"On what grounds?"

"Obstructing justice."

I cast about for something soothing to say. Unfortunately my brain isn't nearly as sharp as my tongue.

"Look, if you arrest the wrong person on insufficient evidence, you could be sued. We go back a long way, Melvin—I've known you since you were in diapers. We might not always get along, but I care what happens to you." There was truth of a sort in that last statement.

"What are you proposing, Yoder?"

"Give me two hours, Melvin, and I'll tell you who brought a knife and who didn't. I might even tell you more."

"What do you mean by 'more'? You know something, don't you, Yoder?"

"Maybe, maybe not. Is it a deal?"

"One hour, Yoder. That's all you get, and that includes driving time. I want you down here in person, at my office, at two-thirty sharp."

"But that's not enough—"

The phone buzzed in my ear. Melvin, the miserable mantis, had hung up.

The fire in the den had burned itself out. There were still clumps of smoldering ashes, and I jabbed them viciously with my poker. I didn't expect to find anything, certainly not a piece of wood still bearing flecks of red paint.

A faint "ping" sent my heart racing. Could it be a nail? *The* bent nail from the strip of barn siding I once used as a doorjamb? I poked again. Nothing. Perhaps the nail had fallen through the grate. Well, it was certainly too hot to remove the grate, and I was not about to lie on my belly and get a snoot full of ashes.

I put the poker away and hurried back to the dining room. No telling what the mice will do when the cat is away. Especially English mice. I had a hunch this pack of rodents was up to no good.

My hunch was half right. I couldn't believe my eyes when I flung open the door. There, in the dining room, was Freni, frolicking with the guests—like they were equals for crying out loud! She was laughing loudly and hopping about like a toad on hot sand. It was unseemly behavior for a ten-year-old Methodist girl, much less an Amish woman in her seventies. I stood silently in the doorway for a minute watching these shameless antics.

"Twins," Ms. Holt said, as if it were a dirty word.

"Have they picked out any names yet?" Gladys asked.

"Yah," Freni said, without a second's hesitation. "Freni for the girl and Mose for the boy."

"Very interesting," I said, stepping forward. "So they know the babies' sex already?"

"Ach!" Freni blushed from her prayer cap to tips of her brogans, but she recovered as quickly as Aaron did after you-know-what. "Shame on you, Magdalena, for scaring an old woman like that."

I smiled smugly. "This morning when I talked to Barbara she didn't know the sex. And what's this I hear about twins? Barbara didn't say anything about twins."

Freni's face fell like a soufflé when the oven door is slammed. "You were telling the truth? No twins?"

"It is not twins," I said. My fingers were crossed of course, since triplets often include a set of twins.

"That's too bad," Gladys said kindly. "But maybe it will be a girl and they can name it Freni anyway."

"Maybe there'll be a girl," I said, "but if they named her after Freni, they might well call her Veronica. Freni is the Pennsylvania Dutch diminutive of that name."

"What is Mose short for?" Art asked. "Moses?"

"Exactly. But Mose isn't short, only Freni is," I said wickedly.

"Ach!" Freni fled to the kitchen, her apron strings flapping behind her.

I followed. Freni heard me coming and scurried to

the far corner and pretended to be searching for something in a cupboard.

"Looking for something, dear?"

"Just leave me along, Magdalena."

I tugged on her apron until she turned. "Melvin just called. The coroner just called him. It seems he found the blade of a paring knife still in George Mitchell's neck."

"Ach! I didn't do it, Magdalena. Do you want to count my paring knives? I have two. Three, if you count the one Mose's mother gave me when we got married, but it wouldn't cut butter on a summer day."

I patted her arm reassuringly. "I believe you do, dear. But it's Alma I'm not so sure about."

"Alma? But she's family."

"Her family scalped our family, dear, when all our family did was buy land that someone else had stolen from her family. But that's beside the point. She claims to have lost her paring knife, remember?"

"Yah, but anyone could have taken it. There aren't any locks on these drawers."

"You're right, anyone could have taken it. Now we just need to convince Melvin of that."

Freni pulled her arm away. "You told Melvin about Alma losing her knife?"

"Please, dear, do I look that stupid?"

Freni graciously bit her lip.

"He's given me one hour to come up with a suspect. If I don't have a sacrificial victim for him by two-thirty, then he's going to pick the person who looks to him like the most obvious suspect."

Freni's eyes grew behind her rimless glasses. "Who?"

"You, dear."

"Ach!" Freni clutched the bib of her apron. "I can't

go to jail now, Magdalena. Not with little Freni on the way."

"You're not going to jail, dear. You're his mama's best friend, remember? But he will give you a hard time, that's for sure. Freni, when you were spending time with Alma this morning, did she seem at all—well, nervous?"

My stout cook and cousin stamped her right foot. "That woman is the salt of the earth. She did not kill Mr. Mitchell. You're barking up the wrong post, Magdalena."

"That's tree, dear."

"Try barking up the tree with red leaves, Magdalena."

"Excuse me?"

"The one with the fancy shmancy clothes."

"Ms. Holt?"

"Yah, that's the one. She keeps her knives in her room."

"Really?"

Freni nodded and bade me step closer by wagging a crooked finger. "You should see the things she brought with her. Pots and pans made out of glass! Who ever heard of such a thing? I gave her a drawer for utensils, but she didn't put a single knife in it. She said keeping knives in drawers made them dull."

"So where does she keep her knives?"

"In a box. It's in her room, on the dresser next to her bed."

"Did you get a peek inside the box?"

"Ach," Freni said indignantly. "What do you think I am, a snoop?"

"Certainly not, dear. Well, I guess it's time for me to grill Ms. Holt. By the time I'm through with her, she'll be like the weenie that fell off the stick and landed in the coals."

"Be careful not to burn your fingers," Freni said wisely.

Kimberly McManus Holt was daintily sucking sherbet through a straw when I returned to the dining room. I tried to beckon her discreetly away from the table, but she was not a cooperative weenie. I had no choice but to be straightforward.

"Ms. Holt, may I have a word with you?"

She slurped a final time and patted the corners of her mouth with her napkin. "Certainly."

"Alone, dear."

She glanced around at others and smiled stiffly. "Is that really necessary?"

I simply had no more time to waste. "Not if you don't mind being grilled like a weenie."

"I beg your pardon?"

"Let's just say that I'm doing a little legwork for Police Chief Stoltzfus. I have some questions to ask you. Some of the questions might not be to your liking. Now, I can ask you them here, in front of the others, or we can retire to the parlor where we can have some privacy."

She trotted after me like a well-trained poodle. Before we sat, I stoked the fire and threw on another log. If you're going to roast a hotdog, do it right.

"Ms. Holt, did you bring a paring knife with you to the PennDutch?"

She arched a perfectly shaped eyebrow. "*This* is your question? The one we needed privacy for?"

"Just answer the question, please," I said.

I wasn't sure she had heard me at first over the sound of grinding teeth. But after a minute she cocked her head and smiled.

"Of course I brought a paring knife with me."

"Just one?"

"Of course not. Every cook worth her salt has a wide inventory of knives, several of which can be loosely termed paring knives. Although, as we all know, not all knives are created equally."

"Excuse me?"

"There are knives, and then there are *knives*."

"I've always hated riddles, dear."

She rolled her eyes, a shocking gesture in a woman whose mascara probably cost as much as the dress on my back. "Never skimp on quality. When it comes to knives, there is only one brand to buy—Ridgeworth."

Well, la-de-da. Imagine being proud of some stupid old knives. Mama had only one paring knife, one butcher knife, and a bread knife. Yet humble little Freni owned three paring knives, and at least a handful of others. Although, to be honest, if you compared their cooking, Mama would only rank as a three-knife cook. Freni was definitely an eight, present lunch excepted.

"Ah, yes of course, Ridgeworth," I said. "Now, dear, Freni tells me that you prefer not to keep your knives in the kitchen."

A perfectly plucked brow arched ever so slightly. "Is there a rule that says I have to?"

"Absolutely not. It's just that I'd like to have a look at what you brought, if you don't mind."

"Whatever for?"

I had two options: lie, and tell her I wanted to buy a set of replacement knives for Freni for Christmas; or I could tell her the truth, make her really angry, and maybe never get to see an honest-to-goodness Ridgeworth knife. If pressed, I will admit to lying, but only because I'd already racked up so many spiritual demerits for the day, I didn't think it would make much difference. I really did intend to make it right with the Lord, just as soon as I could catch my breath.

If tortured, I might go so far as to say that my lie was worth any consequences a lie of that caliber might exact. In words that Susannah might use, Ms. Holt's knife set was *totally awesome*. The mahogany and brass box, lined with blue velvet, no doubt cost more than Mama's and Papa's coffins combined. Boy did that make me feel guilty. Anyway, tearing my eyes away from the knife box was hard enough, but those knives! Who knew that just looking at steel could give so much pleasure? And those handles—could they possibly be ivory?

Ms. Holt read my meager mind. "Sanded bone," she said. "Less slippery than wood. A dull knife is much more dangerous to its user than a sharp knife, and every one of these could slice a hair lengthwise, but slippage is always a problem. My predecessor— the show used to be called *Cooking With Connie*— rolled a knife when she was deboning a particularly stubborn chicken. Left her little finger lying on the cutting board."

I shuddered. "Which ones are the paring knives?"

Ms. Holt brushed her own well-groomed pinkie across the row of handles. "There are twelve in all, but these five are what most people would call paring knives, although they each have their own function."

It was as clear as Hernia water that Ms. Holt did not take her knives lightly. If I were a betting woman, I would have been willing to wager the farm that the knife lodged in George Mitchell's spine was not a Ridgeworth. As for the possibility that Ms. Holt might have used someone else's knife, well, there was as much chance of that as there was that I would wear someone else's underwear. In other words, Susannah would become a nun first.

I glanced at her bedside clock—I do not wear a watch—a third of my precious hour was already gone.

I got straight to the point in my own inimitable, indirect way.

"It was a horrible way for Mr. Mitchell to die. He was such a dear, sweet man."

"He was a louse. People step on bugs all the time. Why not stab them if they are large enough?"

I disguised my gasp by adding a "choo." Hopefully it passed as a sneeze.

"Do tell, dear. No one loves a juicy story more than yours truly."

Ms. Holt lovingly closed the mahogany and brass box. "It was a fitting way for him to die. A backstabber stabbed in the back of the neck. Frankly, it didn't surprise me at all. I'm just surprised it didn't happen sooner."

"I take it there are others who shared your sentiments."

She looked me straight in the eye. "I know what you're doing, Miss Yoder, but there is no need to play psychological games. I didn't kill George Mitchell. I don't have that kind of nerve. But you don't need to waste my time, or yours, beating around the bush. Yes, I did very much want him dead."

Twenty-eight

I sneezed again. "Why?"

"Because he ruined my life, that's why. You see, the son of a bitch came on to me, and when I refused to sleep with him, that was the end of my show."

"You mean—"

"That's right. *Cooking With Kimberly* has been terminated, effective December first. It was owned by East Coast Delicacies, you know. Oh, sure, there other companies out there with cooking shows, but do you have any idea what the competition is like?"

"Vaguely," I said. I have author friends who tell me that the odds of getting published are staggering. Only one out of every one thousand writers will ever see their words turned into a book.

"Well, I'll tell you what the competition is like. It's a twenty-something woman with breasts like cantaloupes, gay men with razor-sharp wits, or someone decidedly ethnic. Thai cooking is big this year again. Upscale white women pitching haute cuisine are not in vogue anymore."

"What about Julia Child?" She seemed as white as Sunbeam bread, and I had yet to hear any rumors that she was gay. As for her cantaloupes—well, that is a subject I prefer to leave alone, being that I am a victim of crop failure myself.

"Exactly my point! There can be only *one* Julia

Child, and I would have been her someday. Now someone else has already moved into my space—some dimwitted housewife named Janet from Rhode Island. Now I ask you, does *Cooking With Janet* have that certain *je ne sais quoi*?"

"*Mais non,*" I said in my best high school French.

"There you have it. I'm thirty-eight years old, and my career has been flushed down the toilet, and all because George Mitchell wanted to put another notch on his belt."

"I beg your pardon?" It seemed to me that an extra notch would have helped George Mitchell keep his pants on, not take them off.

"I mean that George just wanted to add me to his list of conquests. I know for a fact that he slept with this Janet person. Albert—he was my producer—said that on Janet's first day on the set, George took her into the stockroom and—"

"Whoa there!" I had no interest in learning the particulars of George Mitchell's sex life. My own were horrific enough.

"Anyway, like I said, I didn't kill George. I just wished him dead. But wishes don't kill, do they?"

"If they did, there would be no one left on this planet. Still, someone here did more than wish him dead. Sorry, but I don't buy the theory of a hit-and-run killer. Certainly not a professional—they would have used something more lethal than a paring knife." I clamped a large, bony hand over my big, blabby mouth, but it was too late.

"So that's what this is all about? You had no intention of buying Mrs. Hostetler a set of Ridgeworth knives! You wanted to see if one of my knives was missing."

"Guilty as charged."

Her brow furrowed slightly as the highbrow eyebrows strained to meet. Plastic surgery can be murder on a good glare.

"If you're looking for a suspect, try Marge Benedict. It's no secret that she despised George Mitchell."

"I know all about it, dear. She was demoted at *American Appetite* magazine."

"That's only the half of it. Marge Benedict is the only woman George *wouldn't* sleep with. I daresay that you can't blame him—she's nothing but skin and bones. That didn't stop the little wretch from throwing herself all over him. She's been the laughingstock of the industry for years."

"Is that so?"

"*Everybody* knows about it. But to hear Marge talk, they were the love story of the century. If you ask me, that's why George demoted her. He couldn't stand the woman, but then to have her claim she's conquered his kingdom—so to speak—well, that was simply too much."

I focused my beady eyes on the bridge of her sculpted nose. "You aren't too fond of the woman yourself, are you?"

"Me?" She laughed dryly. "I don't know what you're talking about."

"That's a shame then. I thought we were connecting there for a second."

Her sculpted eyes focused on the bridge of my beaky nose. "Okay. The truth is, I despise that woman as much as George. Maybe more. Even though we worked for the same boss, she trashed my show in her column. Chi-chi cooking, she called it. Cream puffs for the masses."

"And George Mitchell let her get away with it? I mean, it was essentially his show she was trashing."

"George thought it was cute. He thought a little in-house tiff would spike ratings."

"So, who did you hate more, George Mitchell or Marge Benedict?"

"Oh, George," she said unequivocally. "But I didn't kill him."

I opened my mouth to ask what surely was a profound question—but is now lost to me forever—when Susannah burst into the room. Fifteen feet of filmy fabric floated in after her.

"Magdalena, come quick! The front porch!"

"What is it? Another murder?"

"No, but there might be, if you don't put a stop to things now."

"Susannah, can't you see—"

"It's that creep from the *National Intruder*," she rasped.

That's all I needed to know. I hiked up my hem and sprinted for the front porch. Carl Lewis, eat your heart out.

My sister was right. It was a murder in the making. In fact, it was a potential double homicide, with me as the killer. Not only was Derrick Simms from the *National Intruder* seated comfortably in one of my rocking chairs, but he was engaged in a tête-à-tête with Lodema Shrock, my pastor's wife.

"Get off my porch!" I bellowed. One eyewitness reports that I even brandished a broom.

Simms snickered, and Lodema laughed.

"I don't understand what all the fuss is about," she said. "I just came over to apologize."

"Is that so? To whom do you plan to apologize, him or me?"

"Well!"

"Your husband—I mean, the reverend—said he was sending you over to apologize to me, not to some slimy snake in a stained overcoat and scuffed wing tip shoes."

She turned to Derrick Simms, who was busily jotting things down in a notebook. "You see what I mean? That woman's tongue could cut through marble."

"It could not!"

Lodema ignored me. "She's a polygamist, you know."

"Is that so?" Simms hissed.

"I am not!"

"Don't lie, Magdalena. You know that lying is a sin. Everyone in Hernia knows you're a polygamist."

"I'm an adulteress," I wailed. "I slept with only one married man."

"You see? She admits it. And I'm telling you, all that stuff about the murder is true too."

Simms smiled smugly and scribbled.

"What murder?" I said, trying my best to sound innocent.

"Ha! As if you don't know. That big shot food executive with the knife in his neck, of course." She turned back to Simms. "There have been other murders here, you know."

"He knows all about them. He's distorted every event in my life since the first celebrity walked through these doors. I wouldn't be surprised if Derrick Simms was the one who murdered George Mitchell, just so he could lie about that too."

Derrick Simms glanced up from his notepad. "Is that Mitchell with two Ls' or one?"

"Two L's I think," Lodema said, "but you can get those kind of details later. It's the important stuff you need to write down."

"Fire away."

"Well, for one thing, Barbara Yutzy said Elvina

Stoltzfus said Freni Hostetler said that the dead man was making goo-goo eyes at Magdalena."

I gasped. "He most certainly was not!"

"Well, not after he died, of course. Anyway, she also said he made goo-goo eyes at just about everyone, but that Magdelena was the only one who made them back. So, you see, it might well have been a crime of passion. Maybe this Mitchell guy—"

I waved the broom at my preacher's wife. "Get off my porch!"

Simms smirked while Lodema lingered.

"Get off this minute!" I shrieked.

"Tut, tut," she said, "how can I be expected to apologize if you insist on carrying on like that?"

I'm pretty sure that the weather was to blame for what happened next. My poor bony fingers were simply too cold to grasp the broom handle any longer. At any rate, the tips of the bristles barely touched her.

"Assault!" she screamed. "Did you see that? Magdalena Yoder assaulted and battered me."

"That's Magdalena with one L," I said to Derrick Simms. "Lodema has only one L as well, but the woman herself has two faces."

She was off her rocker. "What is that supposed to mean?"

I showed Simms a smug mug of my own. "Her husband is the pastor at Beechy Grove Mennonite church. She is, in fact, the organist. While she's at church, she is the sweetest, most gentle Christian soul you could hope to find. The minute she leaves the building she turns into a back-stabbing gossip. It's just like Dr. Jekyll and Mr. Hyde."

"That's not true." I have heard chain smokers swear off cigarettes with more fervor than that.

"But of course she doesn't know everything. She

doesn't know that Lou Ann Stretcher—" I bit my tongue lightly.

"I do so! I know all about Lou Anne's baby. That's not a Stretcher or a Troyer, I said. Just ask Catherine Blough. If you ask me, Lou Anne went and got herself pregnant in Mexico. Or Colombia. Yes, that's it. Little Ernest Stretcher is the spitting image of Juan Valdez."

"Who?"

"You know, that coffee man on TV. The one with the horse who pops up in the aisles—"

I gasped. "You watch television?"

My pastor's wife turned the color of communion wine—although in our church it's grape juice. "Ed-ed-educational television," she sputtered.

"Isn't it all, dear?"

Lodema's eyes were darting back and forth between Derrick Simms and I, like Ping-Pong balls in the China Cup. "Okay, so I watch *E.R.* and *N.Y.P.D. Blue.*"

The initials meant nothing to me, but they obviously meant something to Derrick Simms. His writing hand was a blur.

"All right, all right," she wailed, "I watched one episode of *Seinfeld,* but I didn't understand a thing. It was all about being master of one's domain, or something like that. Isn't that supposed to be Jesus?"

I shrugged. Papa was the official master of our domain and wore the pants, but Mama was always the seat of power.

Lodema clutched my elbow with icy fingers. "You won't tell anyone, will you?"

I shrugged again.

She clutched Derrick. "You're not writing this down, are you?"

"Hmm," Derrick said scribbling faster. " 'Mennonite Matriarch Confesses to Worldly Vice' . . . too tame, you think?"

"Definitely back page, dear. How about 'Pastor's Wife Falls Into Fish Pond and Gives Birth to Frog Child,'" I said. Years of experience have taught me that tabloid titles and content need not be at all related.

Susannah, who had been standing quietly by, cleared her throat. "Once I saw her eating in a French restaurant in Pittsburgh. I didn't pay that much attention, but it could have been frog legs. Maybe you could throw in something about cannibalism."

Lodema's eyes rolled back in hysteria. "Magdalena, help me," she begged.

I smiled beneficently. "Perhaps we could start with an apology."

"I'm sorry!" she wailed.

"Like I said, that's a start. Now—" Someone was tapping me on the shoulder. I whirled.

"Melvin!"

"And Zelda," a high-pitched female voice said.

I stooped and peered behind my nemesis. Sure enough, Melvin had brought his half-pint, painted sidekick with him. Something big was about to go down. Perhaps they were here to arrest Lodema for slander. Derrick too, come to think of it.

"I'd be happy to testify in court," I said.

Melvin arranged his mandibles in a close approximation of a smile. "I'll keep that in mind. Do you know what time it is, Yoder?"

Watchless as usual, I grabbed Lodema's wrist. "Oh, my gracious! It's two thirty-seven!"

"Two-thirty on the dot, I said. Had you forgotten that?"

"No—well, I wouldn't have, but Lodema here fell into a fish pond and gave birth to a tadpole."

"No kidding?" Melvin, who had long since left the fold, looked at the pastor's wife with new respect.

"Yes, kidding, you—"

"Ah, ah, ah, no name calling, Yoder. Not when I'm about to make an arrest. Who knows, the cuffs might accidentally end up on you."

"Arrest?"

"They give free hearing tests at the high school, Yoder."

"I mean"—I desperately rolled my eyes to indicate the despicable Derrick Simms—"you're going to arrest someone *now*?"

"Yes, now. Read the warrant, Zelda."

Dutifully, she began to read. When she came to the name of the arrestee, I clapped my hands over Derrick Simms's ears.

Twenty-nine

"—one Alma Louise Cornwater for the premeditated murder of George Reagan Mitchell."

Derrick was stronger than I hoped, and was able to force my hands away, but not until after Alma's name was read.

"He's a tabloid reporter!" I screamed.

"Is that so? Well, you win some, and you lose some. It looks like Miss—"

Derrick's ears, which were rather large, were easy targets. Unfortunately the man has the reflexes of a fly, and once warned, was able to duck.

"Alma Louise Cornwater," he said gleefully. "Any relation to Barry Cornwater of Arizona?"

"That's Goldwater, dear. You wouldn't, per chance, be related to Melvin?"

"Ah, Alma Goldwater. Is that with two D's, or one?"

"Three," I said. "She's Lithuanian. Lodema, be a dear and tell Mr. Simms all about the mole they removed from Anna Lichty."

Lodema's face lit up like Three Rivers Stadium in Pittsburgh when the Pirates are in town. Next to me, Anna Lichty is Hernia's favorite subject. Imagine carrying a six-pound mole around for twenty years. Not the animal, of course, but the skin condition. Boggles the mind, doesn't it? Then when the mole is finally removed, one of the surgeons faints because the mole, when seen from the reverse side, bears the exact likeness of the Virgin Mary. I know it's hard to believe, but Anna kept it in a huge pickle jar, so I saw it for myself. Hearsay has it that when Harriet Hammond saw the heavenly hunk, her herpes was healed. Rumor even has it that the Vatican has made inquiries into buying the disgusting thing, along with Ripley's Believe It Or Not.

"I don't want to hear about some damn growth," Derrick Simms growled. "I want to hear about the Goldwater murder."

"Oh, you'll want to hear about this," Lodema said, her voice rising with excitement.

She was right. Next week's edition of the *National Intruder* read: "Holy Moley: Vatican Vies for Virginal Visage." There was nothing in it about Lodema, or the murder of George Mitchell. Much to my relief, there was nothing about me either.

Alma had class, I'll say that for the gal. She remained absolutely calm while the maniacal Melvin manacled her. It was only when she was being led away to the squad car that I saw her lips quiver.

"Freni," she said, avoiding eye contact with me, "I hope it's not against your religion or anything, but would you please do me a big favor and call home."

"Yah," Freni said, choking back a sob. Tears streamed down her faintly fuzzy cheeks.

I practically leaped in front of Alma and Melvin. Had the mud puddles not been frozen, I would have lain across them and let her walk on my back. Melvin and Zelda, however, were out of luck.

"I can call."

"You've done enough," Alma said flatly.

"It wasn't my fault that the coroner called Melvin a second time and reported your thumbprint on the knife blade."

Police Chief Melvin Stoltzfus produced one of his more smarmy smiles. "You see, Yoder, my little plan worked."

"That wasn't a plan! That was a pack of lies. You said you knew everything about Alma and the knife. I just assumed that somehow you'd heard that she'd lost her paring knife."

"And then," Melvin said, mandibles barely moving, "you volunteered the information that East Coast Delicacies, presided over by the deceased, stole her recipes. That was the clincher, Yoder. Since we already knew Miss Cornwater was up at the time of the murder, we have everything we need to make a case: motive, method, and opportunity."

"You still haven't proved that the knife is hers," I wailed. "And even if it was, somebody else could have stolen it from her drawer."

To her credit, Zelda at least shrugged her broad shoulders and glanced at Melvin.

It was a small opening, but I can squeeze through a wormhole, if I have to. "You see? Zelda thinks it's possible. I mean, what about Marge Benedict?"

"What about her?"

"Not only did she hate George Mitchell, but she obviously doesn't have any scruples. She stole Alma's recipes to impress George."

Melvin sneered. "I suppose you're going to tell me that the human dartboard has a motive as well?"

"Carlie? As a matter of fact—"

"Can it, Yoder. I don't tell you how to do your job, so you don't tell me. Got it? I'm going to prove that Miss Cornwater killed George Mitchell. In the mean-

time, Zelda here will make her very comfortable at
the Hernia Hotel. Won't you, Zelda?"

The poor woman gave me a pained look. She might
be in love with Melvin, but she has got to recognize
that he is a doofus. Even Melvin's mama can't help
but see the truth. It broke my heart the day poor
Elvina Stoltzfus confessed in church that she had not
given birth to her son, but found him under a cabbage.
What saddened me so was that less than half of the
congregation believed the desperate woman.

"You feed her three squares a day," I admonished,
"and no stripsearching."

"Ach!" Freni was the color of bleached flour, and
poor Susannah looked like she was about to jump out
of her skin, leaving a pile of polyester behind.

"He'll be good," Zelda said firmly. "Besides, I
search the female prisoners."

Susannah and Freni sighed in unison.

Melvin stretched and yawned, quite obviously satisfied with a job well done. If he'd been a rooster, instead of an insect, he would have crowed.

"Thanks for everything, Yoder. I couldn't have
done it if you hadn't sung like a canary."

Freni shook a plump finger at me. "Yah, a canary.
Well, Miss Big Bird, I quit!"

"I'm sorry," I wailed. "I was tricked."

"It's all right, Miss Yoder," Alma said softly. "I
shouldn't have come down so hard on you."

I gave Alma a quick hug. "I'll do anything I can to
help. You need bail money? I'm loaded. Whatever
you need, I'm there for you."

"Thanks."

Susannah grabbed the sleeve of Melvin's coat. For
a second I thought she was going to try and talk some
sense into him.

"You going to call me, Lamb Pie?"

"Not now," Melvin muttered, and rudely shoved her aside.

"Bye," Alma said bravely as she climbed into the back seat of Hernia's only official squad car.

"Don't worry!" I called to her. "I'll find the killer!" I turned to Freni and Susannah. "I mean it. I won't leave one stone unturned until I find the person who really killed George Mitchell."

Susannah touched my shoulder in a rare display of affection, and then went back inside.

"Yah, just like a sparrow," Freni hissed, and trotted after her.

"That's canary!" I yelled, and then burst into tears.

Perhaps there are a few who would disagree, but I see myself as essentially a cheerful person. Jovial might be taking it too far, although surely good-natured would be an appropriate term to describe yours truly. There certainly isn't a lick of truth to the rumor that I am a cantankerous and mean-spirited woman. Grandma Yoder maybe, but not me.

Therefore, it surprised even me when I couldn't shake the cloud generated by Alma's arrest. For example, an hour after it happened, one of the guests— Ms. Holt, I think—spilled coffee on the seat of Papa's favorite chair in the den. The old Magdalena would have been upset, maybe even demanded that Ms. Holt get married, have a child, and subsequently hand over her firstborn in payment of the blotched fabric. The depressed me hardly noticed.

"Mags, darling," Susannah said, doing her best to cheer me up, "I've decided to run away, get a million tattoos, and join the circus. What do you think of that?"

"Peachy keen," I mumbled.

"But that's not all, Mags. Melvin Stoltzfus is coming with me. He's going to join as The Mantis Man."

"Whoop-tee-doo," I said, twirling my index finger.

Even Shnookums got into the act, nipping me playfully through the folds of Susannah's flowing fabric.

"Nice dog," I said, and scratched him obligingly behind the ears.

The next thing I knew Freni was plying me with cake and hot chocolate. "Ach, so I don't quit, already."

"Suit yourself, dear."

"So, I'll never quit. Will that make you feel better, Magdalena?"

I shrugged, too worn-out and dispirited to say anything more. My life was at the bottom of the outhouse, so to speak. My parents were dead, my pseudo-husband was living with his real wife, and now this? An innocent woman was on her way to the hoosegow, and all because I'd had the weakness of character to give in to Freni's request. I should never have agreed to that silly contest. Allowing a bunch of disparate and desperate strangers into my establishment was one of the stupidest things I'd ever done. It isn't even the love of money that is the root of all evil, it's competition.

"Ach!" Freni fluttered around me pretending to plump pillows, but since I keep only two in the den, she soon ran out of things to do. After a while she gave up and, more true to her character, clomped sullenly back to the kitchen. The dear woman does not handle rejection well.

Who knows how long I sat there in my stupor—maybe two hours all told—when I became aware that I was once again not alone. Perhaps it was the pheromones he exuded, but I could sense General Gordon

Oliver Dolby's presence, even with my eyes closed. And I hadn't heard him enter the room either. I'm telling you, that man could walk like a cat.

"Miss Yoder?"

I attempted to will him away.

"Miss Yoder, I need to fly to Pittsburgh this afternoon. Would you care to come along?"

I opened one eye.

"Of course it's only a little Cessna 182, but you might find it fun."

I opened the other eye. "You have your own plane? I mean, you flew it here from Baltimore?"

"Yes, ma'am. I never go anywhere without my wings."

"But—but—you drove up in a car."

"Yes, ma'am, with Pennsylvania plates. I rented it at the Bedford County airport."

That's what I get for not requiring my guests to record their license plate information. They are, after all, an upscale crowd. In recent years most of my guests have flown into Pittsburgh, where they rent cars, or else they drive in from the East Coast. Except for Bill and Hillary, of course, who—never mind, I'm not at liberty to discuss that.

"Your own plane, huh? And you're inviting me along."

"Yes, ma'am. Gladys hates to fly—won't do it more than she has to—anyway, I thought you might like to get away from things for an hour or two."

Would I! Besides, I had never had the privilege of flying. For years I've had to listen to my guests moan about the declining service on airplanes, the shrinking seats, and the insipid food. All the while I wanted to tell them to just shut up and count their blessings. You see, at first I couldn't afford to fly anywhere, but then when my business grew and I could afford to go just about anywhere I wanted, I no longer had the time.

But now, at my weakest point ever, when I couldn't care less about schedules and responsibilities, the good Lord in His mercy had sent an angel to fly me above my troubles. "Those who hope in the Lord will renew their strength. They will soar on wings like eagles," the Book of Isaiah says. Okay, so an airplane wasn't the same as an eagle, but I for one don't think we are required to take *everything* in the Bible literally.

"You bet your bippy, I'd like to fly with you," I cried. We Mennonites eschew betting, and shame on me for using the word, but that's what I said. "How soon can we leave?"

"How about now?"

I could feel life ebbing back into my veins. God had sent me an eagle, and G.O.D. was going to fly me on it to Pittsburgh and back. I couldn't wait.

"Now it is!"

People *do* look the size of ants from that high up. Houses are as small as matchboxes, cars even tinier, and trees are no bigger than broccoli tops. Only now that it was November, the trees looked more like miniature gray lace doilies than vegetables.

"Do you think we can see the PennDutch Inn?" I shouted.

I never imagined that a plane could be so loud. Gordon—or Gordy, as he asked me to call him—had given me a set of spongy earplugs, but they did little to muffle the roar of the engine. It was Gordy's voice I could no longer hear.

I cupped my hands to my mouth. "What did you say?"

He banked the plane and pointed vigorously.

Frankly, at that angle I was afraid to look down, but by leaning away from the door and stretching my neck to giraffish proportions I got a glimpse of two matchboxes, one larger than the other, and several doilies that might have been the PennDutch and surrounds.

Then the plane abruptly straightened and we flew higher and higher until we actually pushed up through the clouds. I was astounded. They were far more wispy than I thought. It didn't seem possible for an angel to sit on one, certainly not one holding a heavy metal harp. I was going to have to do some theological revamping, once I was safely back on terra firma.

Despite the racket, it was so peaceful up there. Just a sea of cottony clouds, and an autumn sun hanging low in the sky. There were, of course, no roads, no cars, and most important, no people. I might not be able to sit or lie on a cloud, but that withstanding, I could live up there indefinitely.

"Where's Magdalena?" folks would ask of Freni or Susannah, and they would point to the sky, where I lounged, floating above a bed of white, dining on white seedless grapes and ladyfingers, or whatever else it is they serve in heaven.

My reverie was short-lived when Gordy banked the plane again, this time steeper than the first.

"Pittsburgh?" I asked in surprise. We couldn't have been in the air for more than twenty minutes.

Gordy shouted something that sounded like "out."

"What?"

He pantomimed removing my earplugs, which I gratefully did. The silly things tickled.

"What did you say?" I shouted. "It sounded like out."

Finally I could hear him. His voice cut through the engine noise like a knife through one of Freni's gelatin molds.

"That's exactly what I said. Out!"

Thirty

Gladys Dolby's
Tomato Brunch Cake

✦

2 cups cake flour
1 cup brown sugar
1 teaspoon baking soda
1 teaspoon cinnamon
½ teaspoon salt
¼ teaspoon ground nutmeg
¼ teaspoon ground cloves
¼ teaspoon ground ginger
1 cup tomato juice
½ cup chopped golden raisins
½ cup chopped dried apricots
½ cup chopped dates

Cream shortening and sugar. Sift flower with salt, spices, and soda. Slowly add tomato juice, then beat into smooth batter. Dust dried fruits with flour and stir into batter. Pour into greased, no-stick loaf pan. Bake at 325 degrees for one hour. Slice when cool and serve with a dollop of whipped cream.

Approximately 8 slices.

Thirty-one

Removing the earplugs seemed to have improved my vision as well. Retired General Gordon Oliver Dolby was waving a gun at me.

"But—"

"Open the damn door."

"Don't be silly, dear, we're hundreds of feet up into the air."

"Five thousand two hundred and eighty, to be exact. I thought you might like to join the Mile High Club." He laughed coarsely.

"I've never parachuted before," I said, glancing wildly around for one. I had no idea what a parachute looked like when folded. Perhaps it resembled a knapsack.

"There aren't any parachutes in this plane, Miss Yoder. You get to do the ultimate in free fall."

I gulped. "No thanks, dear. I think I'll pass."

He brought the gun up and pressed it against my left temple. If I live to be as old as Zsa Zsa Gabor, I will never forget the feel of that cold metal against my bare skin.

"You don't get a choice, ma'am. You see, you have far too big a mouth."

I pursed my lips and rolled my eyes down as far as they could go. All I could see was a blur. Funny, but it was usually the Yoder nose that drew comments.

"Anybody ever tell you that you ask too many damn questions?"

"Oh, that kind of mouth. Well, actually, my husband Aaron used to say that all the time. Susannah and Freni do their fair share of complaining as well. But who are they to talk? I mean, Susannah says words all the time that I would never dream of saying, and Freni is constantly yabbering away to herself in Pennsylvania Dutch. As for Aaron, well—he wasn't really my husband, you know? No, I think—"

"Shut up."

Normally I might have, given that he had a gun. But I suddenly realized that the plane had rolled out of its bank and we were flying level again. Despite what he said, talking seemed to help.

"All right, dear, if you say so. But first, can you at least tell me what I asked you that was so offensive? I mean, no has ever wanted to throw me out of a plane before just because I'm inquisitive. Of course I've never been in a plane until now, but had I—"

"I said, shut up! You know damn well why I got you up here. Well, whoever finds you is going to have a lot harder puzzle to solve than the one involving poor George Mitchell. Hell, I made that one almost too easy."

Although I recoiled in shock, the gun barrel remained snug against my temple. Gordy had quick reflexes, I'll grant him that.

"*You*? You killed George Mitchell?"

"Yes, ma'am. I could have done a far neater job of it, but I wanted it to look like an amateur—a civilian—did the job. It worked too, didn't it?"

"Sure, if that's what you call sending an innocent mother to prison for the rest of her life."

"Someone had to die, didn't they?"

"Did they?"

"You're damn right, they did. Food poisoning obviously didn't put a stop to that damn contest."

"*You* poisoned Freni's bread pudding?"

"*Veratrum alba*—commonly known as false hellebore. Did I mention that I'm a Master Gardener of the state of Maryland?"

"You're a real Renaissance man," I said with just as much sarcasm that shouting and a gun to one's head permit.

"Yes, ma'am, I guess I am. I grew the flowers myself, you know. Dried them, and mashed them up in a stone pestle, just like the Indians might have done. Had a hell of a time sneaking it in that pan of bread pudding, though."

"There were two pans, dear."

"Which explains why only one person got sick."

"Actually *two*. A very innocent and dear Amish man suffered terribly because of you."

He shrugged, and the gun traveled a fraction of an inch along my scalp. "You would think they would call the damn thing off because of that. But hell no, I had to dig into my bag of tricks further and pull out that shard of glass."

"That was you *too*?"

"An air force investigator would have been on top of that in a minute. It should have been clear that someone was trying to sabotage the contest."

"Well, this isn't the military, dear. This is Hernia, Pennsylvania, and all we have is a nincompoop police chief and one deputy, who is so in love with the chief, she doesn't know whether she's coming or going."

"And then there's you."

"Me?"

"The air force could use a woman like you, Miss Yoder. The marines claim they have the best men, but they sure the hell don't have anyone like you."

"Thanks," I said dryly. "And I'm sure the funny farm could use a man like you. Your daughter is a contestant, for crying out loud. Why on earth would you want to stop the contest?"

To my surprise, he smiled. "You've got moxie, Miss Yoder. Too bad I didn't meet you earlier. Maybe things would have been different."

I entertained the briefest of fantasies. "I don't *even* think so, dear."

"You ever been alone, Miss Yoder?"

I noticed for the first time that neither of his hands were on the controls. "Shouldn't you be steering, or something?"

"What?"

"You're not even touching the steering wheel. You don't want to die too, do you?"

"This is a yoke, ma'am, not a steering wheel. I've got her set on automatic pilot. How about you answer my question."

"Of course I've been alone. What a silly question."

"I mean *all* alone. With no one left you can count on."

Well, maybe not *all* alone. Freni and Mose were there for me when my parents died, and Susannah flits in and out of my emotional life like a hummingbird in a flower garden. And of course I've always had God. That's one of the advantages of being sure of one's faith.

"Is this about Gladys wanting to move to Albuquerque?" I asked, no doubt hastening my death.

"You see, ma'am, Glady is the only person I have left. My wife died when Gladys was only three. I raised her myself, you know."

"You did a good job. But surely you have someone else."

"No, ma'am. My parents have both been dead for

years. Last month my only brother died. I don't have anyone else, but my daughter."

"What about your air force pals?"

"I'm retired, ma'am. I see some of the guys now and then, but they're not family."

"Let me get this straight. You killed a man just to keep your grown daughter at home. Those are some apron strings, if you ask me. Apron strings of steel."

The gun barrel pushed against my skull. "No one asked you, ma'am. But now I'm going to ask you to unbuckle your shoulder belt and kindly open that door."

"You won't get away with this, you know. Chief Stoltzfus might be terminally stupid, but someone else will put two and two together."

"Begging your pardon, ma'am, but there won't be anything left of you to put together. You won't amount to much more than a pound or two of hamburger. Besides, that's the Moshannon State Forest down there. It's one of the largest wilderness tracts east of the Mississippi."

"It's almost hunting season!" I screamed. "Some hunter will find what's left of me."

He smiled. It was a sick, not a cruel smile. Believe me, there is a difference.

"The raccoons and coyotes will find you first. Did you know that there is a resurgence of coyotes in this part of the country? Some people even claim to see panthers."

"You don't say!" So that's how it was going to all end. I was never to know *true* love, never to experience the birth of a child—even Barbara's by proxy—but I did get the rare opportunity to end up as dinner for some yipping cousins of Shnookums. Well, Mama, what do you think of that? If you had let me go steady with Jimmy Kurtz in high school, things might have turned out a lot different. I might have married a farmer, raised eight kids, and never had the need to open a bed and breakfast. Well, Mama, think about this—falling from an airplane is every bit as dramatic a way of dying as being squished between a milk tanker and shoe truck. In fact, I think I've got you beat.

The barrel prodded again and I cocked my head farther to the right. "Time to say good-bye, Miss Yoder."

I prayed. If it was my time to die, so be it. But couldn't I at least skip the falling stage and proceed straight to my assigned cloud? I was already up there, after all.

"Unbuckle your shoulder belt. *Now,* Miss Yoder."

Believe me, the good Lord does indeed answer prayer in mysterious ways. My mouth, which had always gotten me in trouble, was the instrument He used to get me out of trouble.

"Look, a spider," I screamed and pointed to the opposite side of the cockpit.

The second Gordy's head whipped around, I bit the gun-wielding hand. I don't mean just a timid nibble either, but a Mike Tyson, flesh-tearing chomp. That sucker—the gun, not the hand—fell right into my lap. The rest is history.

Thirty-two

Freni cut another slice of Gladys's tomato brunch cake. I reached for it, but she waved the knife menacingly at me.

"Ach! This is for my Barbara."

Barbara blushed. An attentive mother-in-law was going to take some getting used to.

"What about me," Susannah whined. "I only had one slice."

"Barbara is eating for three."

"Yeah, well, maybe I'm eating for two."

I kicked Susannah under the table. She had better *not* be eating for two, not unless she was referring to the mangy menace, and if that was the case, she had no business feeding him something as tasty as Gladys's tomato brunch cake.

"So," Barbara said, anxious to move the conversation along, "everything okay now at the PennDutch?"

"Things are peachy-keen," I said. "They all went home yesterday, two days ahead of schedule, which finally gives me some time off."

"And me." Freni was staring at her daughter-in-law, no doubt willing the child within to grow faster.

"A watched pot never boils," I said.

"Ach!"

"Not that anyone cares," Susannah said, still whining, "but I've finally made a decision about Melvin."

I whirled, and then catching myself, smiled slowly. "Really? Do tell."

"He jumps to conclusions more than even you, Mags."

"Yah." Freni nodded vigorously, although her eyes had to still to leave Barbara. "Like with my cousin Alma."

"She isn't your cousin, dear," I said calmly. "You don't have a drop of Native American blood in you. You just happen to be a native of America."

"Yah, whatever. The important thing is that Alma is free now, and that awful Mr. Dolby is behind bars."

"Retired four-star General Gordon Oliver Dolby, and that's thanks to me, not Melvin."

"Imagine him being that scared of a spider!"

"Melvin Stoltzfus is afraid of spiders?" Barbara asked. I'm sure she'd heard the whole thing before, and was just being polite. Either that, or she didn't want the subject to return to her pregnancy. She had yet to tell anyone else she was expecting triplets, because she wanted to tell her own mother first, and had been unable to reach her.

Whatever the reason, one should always humor a pregnant woman, so I repeated the story for the millionth time. I'm not complaining, mind you. It isn't every day I single-handedly apprehend a cold-blooded murderer. And with a gun, yet!

"I still don't see why they couldn't go ahead with the contest," Freni said. She seemed to be blaming me.

"How about plain old common decency? I would have kicked the whole bunch out the morning George Mitchell was murdered, but Melvin asked me to keep the group together as long as possible for the purposes of the investigation."

"Ach, but all that money." No doubt visions of what

that much moolah could buy for her grandchild were dancing through her bonneted head.

"Well, it looks like at least one of that group stands to profit."

"Ach, so that child really is Mr. Mitchell's daughter?"

"Erv Stackrumple seems to think so. It remains to be seen, however, if there will be anything left for her to inherit. Apparently George played fast and loose with his assets and the company's."

"Can we get this conversation back to me?" Susannah wailed. "I'm trying to tell you guys that I've got Melvin out of my system for good."

"What?" If true, those words were worth more than one hundred thousand dollars to me.

"Well, I've been married, so I know what that's all about, and I don't want to be tied down, so what's the point?"

"Exactly, dear, what *is* your point?"

"Well—promise me you won't get mad, Mags?"

"No can do, dear."

"I don't care, I'm going to tell you anyway. I've decided to move to California."

"You *what*?"

"Well, I met this nice guy from Los Angeles who says—"

"Over my dead body!" I roared. Susannah might be more pain than a toe with an elephant standing on it, but I was going to need her company in the months ahead. Freni was obviously going to be too involved with the babies to pay much attention to me. In a very small way, I could almost understand Mr. Dolby. Not the murder part, I don't mean that.

"I knew you were going to get mad!"

"I'm not mad, dear," I said calmly, albeit through gritted teeth.

"Yes, you are. You sound just like Shnookums when he growls with his binky in his mouth."

"Don't you ever compare me to that pitiful pooch! The truth is, the family needs you. What with Barbara having triplets—oops."

"Triplets?" Freni squawked, and fainted into what was left of the tomato brunch cake.